The Shadow Conspiracy

R.D. Shah spent his formative years in the north west of England before attending Rugby School in Warwickshire. At seventeen he attained his private pilot's licence in Florida and shortly after attended the University of Miami where he studied motion picture & psychology before returning to the UK to work in television & leisure. He has travelled extensively throughout Europe, Russia and the Americas. R.D. holds a scuba diving licence, which he gained along the shores of the Hawaiian island of Kauai. All this experience has prepared him for a career in writing. He lives in Wiltshire with his wife and young daughter.

Also by R.D. Shah

The Harker Chronicles

THE SHADOW CONSPIRACY

R. D. SHAH

1☉ CANELO

First published in the the United Kingdom in 2020 by Canelo

This edition published in the United Kingdom in 2020 by Canelo

Canelo Digital Publishing Limited
31 Helen Road
Oxford OX2 0DF
United Kingdom

A CIP catalogue record for this book is available from the British Library.

Print ISBN 978 1 80032 032 1
Ebook ISBN 978 1 78863 324 6

Look for more great books at www.canelo.co

Printed and bound in Great Britain by Clays Ltd, Elcograf S.p.A.

Chapter 1

Audrey Banford sank to her knees beneath the dense foliage and fought for breath as a sound of rustling filled the air. Her lungs felt ready to burst but she knew there was no time to lose.

Should have taken Miguel's advice and never gone back a second time. So damn foolish as you already had what you came for... you idiot!

She was still berating herself when the rustling stopped just metres away. A sensation of terror gnawed at her stomach, and she fought to conceal her heavy breathing as something zipped past her shoulder and lodged itself deeply into the thick base of a tree trunk off to her right. The glinting of a long metal blade had her jumping to her feet, and without looking back she leapt manically forward through the dense shrubs, her matted and mud-drenched black hair slapping against her face to leave layers of grime with each lash. *Don't look back... you know what's there... please, God.*

The edge of the forest was less than twenty metres away and the boat ready to go at a moment's notice, and even with her pursuers so close behind, the sight of dim moonlight ahead offered her a spur of encouragement. With a high-pitched grunt she began bounding over the thick vegetation, like a long-jumper approaching the board, and as she closed the distance her fists clenched ever tighter.

She had already gone through too much to give up now. But as she reached the last tree and caught a clear glimpse of the welcoming expanse of water and the waiting boat, her heart sank. The limp body of Miguel lay slumped across the port railing and the small vessel was already being swept away by the current, with no one at its helm.

'No—' was all she managed, as something heavy slammed against the back of her head and sent her tumbling face first into the nearest shrub. Dazed and with her ears ringing from the crippling blow, she shakily clambered to her feet, just as another vicious blow descended on the exact same spot as the first, and she collapsed back onto the ground with a yelp.

The rustling of leaves being swept aside could be heard from all directions, and as she felt the sensation of warm blood trickling down her cheek, something drew close to the back of her head and began sniffing at the wound.

As Audrey Banford fought against impending unconsciousness she felt a long moist tongue drag itself across the back of her neck and then move further down her cheek. After a single lap, the tongue retreated, and a cacophony of clicking sounds filled the air as the fallen woman was roughly rolled onto her back. What she could now see caused her to expel a shaky breath and her entire body began to tremble. She knew what this creature was, but the knowledge did nothing to calm her as her gaze moved upwards to the thick tendrils protruding from its head, and then she stared directly into those unnaturally large eyes. The sounds of sniffing continued, although a flap of dry skin hung down where its nose should have been, and below that was a mouth with scarred lips and chipped teeth, worn down almost to their roots yet sharp and pointed, grimacing at her menacingly.

'I'm sorry. I can give it back,' she pleaded, as a hand with a bird's talons for fingernails clasped itself around her throat briefly, before releasing its grip and silently moving backwards away from her.

A number of dark silhouettes now appeared amidst the thick vegetation all around, and Audrey dragged herself to her feet and stood shakily before the gathering figures, her knees struggling to support her.

'Please forgive me,' she began, stretching out her palms in submission. 'I meant no harm.'

The beast cocked its head to one side, as if considering her request, but then it straightened up and ominously shook its head slowly, as that sound of clicking began to break out afresh amongst the surrounding silhouettes.

The woman's breathing grew ever quicker as a new wave of fear swept over her. She had opened her mouth to plead further when something whizzed past her with such speed that it appeared nothing more than a blur. She felt herself tumble back down to the ground again and was sent rolling into the undergrowth. She tried to expel a scream but nothing emerged except silence. She began to choke, every neuron in her brain screaming out in panic as she finally realised what had happened. Her tongue stiffened like a rod as it went into spasm, and the strange figure shuffled slowly back into the forest, followed by the silhouettes, disappearing one by one from her line of sight.

As her vision descended into a dark fog and her mind began to fade, Audrey managed to catch one last glimpse before everything went black. Of her own decapitated body spread out beside her head.

Chapter 2

'Alex, this is a bad idea. We should wait until tonight when everyone's together,' Dean Thomas Lercher whispered. He stared through the narrow gap in the door once again, then shook his head. 'I don't even know which ones they are.'

Alex Harker pushed his friend firmly to one side and placed his eye up against the gap, shifting his gaze left and right in an effort to get a proper look. 'I think it's the two of them on the left,' he replied in a hushed voice. 'Yep, that's definitely them.'

Harker glanced back at the dean to find the man playing anxiously with his fingers. 'You're not nervous are you, Doggie?'

The dean ceased his fiddling immediately and placed both hands on his hips defiantly. 'These kind of people are not to be trifled with, Alex – believe me, I know. And I keep telling you to stop calling me Doggie.'

'And I keep telling you no, I won't stop,' Harker shot back with a dry smile, 'so at least I'm consistent. Anyway these kind of people are only as dangerous as you let them be… It'll be fine.'

Doggie looked unconvinced and he flicked his hand dismissively as Harker returned his attention to the gap in the door.

'We'll take them by surprise, then get in and make our escape as quickly as possible.' Harker turned back towards the dean and made an OK sign with his fingers. 'It's a piece of cake.'

Harker's optimistic manner was totally lost on Doggie, and the man's eyes dulled. 'You always say that, but it never really works out that way, does it?'

Harker couldn't help but smile. With everything they had been through over the last few years, there was never a time that Doggie had not veered on the side of caution. Without a doubt he always offered sage counsel, and Harker relied on it, but there was also a hidden, steely resolve to the man when one dug deep enough, and it was this version of Doggie that he needed now. 'Come on, Tom, man up. I need you with me on this.'

Doggie emitted a disconcerted sigh as his shoulders sagged, then with a nod he began to roll his neck in an attempt to limber up for action, much as a boxer would do. 'Fine, I'll back you up, but for the record, I still think we should have waited until tonight... Strength in numbers and all that.'

'Noted,' Harker replied before placing his hand on the polished door, as Doggie moved to his side, clenching his fists apprehensively. 'OK, on the count of three. One, two, thr—' His muscles were already tensing in preparation when the hefty wooden door flung itself inwards and the pair found themselves staring into the face of a woman with long silky black hair, who was wearing jeans and a black T-shirt with the slogan 'Simply the best'.

'I thought I recognised your voice. What are you doing here?'

Dr Chloe Stanton glared at them both with a combination of surprise and anger, as Harker leant forward and gave her a warm kiss on the lips.

'Well, I was passing nearby and I thought why not get it over and done with. So,' he raised his hands upwards placatingly, 'here I am.'

Chloe glared at him disapprovingly, then her expression began soften, and with a slow blink of her eyes she finally began to smile. 'Well, I'm sorry that meeting my parents is such a chore for you, Professor Harker.'

'It really is, Dr Stanton.' Harker was now smiling himself. 'But that shows how much I love you.'

Chloe's smile faded and she inserted two fingers inside her mouth, pretending to make herself sick.

'Yeah, maybe that was a bit over the top,' Harker replied, as Chloe turned her attention to Doggie.

'Thank you, Thomas,' Chloe said, as the dean gave her an apologetic look.

'Sorry, Chloe, but he insisted we come by.'

Harker's eyebrows dipped at the realisation he had been kept out of the loop, and he was about to berate his friend when a voice behind Chloe called out, 'Is everything all right?'

As Chloe turned her head, Harker seized upon this chance to make an introduction and slipped past her, even as she shook her head and tried to tug him back. He raised his hand at her in a confident gesture and began to make his way over towards the short man wearing a pair of round John Lennon glasses, a long-sleeved white shirt and dark brown slacks, who was standing directly in the centre of the aisle, clearly determined to make a good impression. The stained glass windows of St Peter's Church glowed magnificently in the evening light and bathed the stone-built aisle with a spectrum of colours. Even though Harker had visited here once before, this small country church located in one of Wiltshire's sleepy villages still captivated him. With its stone walls and dark oak beams overhead, it was without doubt the perfect place for himself and Chloe to get married.

Harker's initial proposal of the registry office in Cambridge had not gone down well with her, and when Chloe had suggested her family's local church, he had agreed without even seeing it. Luckily he was not disappointed and now he couldn't imagine anywhere more perfect than this hidden gem, tucked away within the leafy village community of Kington Langley. Of course, it helped that the local pub was just minutes away, as he and Doggie had discovered while enjoying a well-earned pint earlier that day.

'Mr Stanton,' Harker began, grasping the man's hand and shaking it enthusiastically, 'it's such a pleasure to finally meet you. And before we get started, I just want to say I consider myself the luckiest man in the world to be marrying your daughter, and rest assured I intend to take care of Chloe for the rest of our days.' Before Mr Stanton could reply, Harker quickly turned his attention to the small, frumpy woman in a flowery dress standing next to him. 'And Mrs Stanton,' he continued, delivering a peck to her chubby cheek, 'you look lovely. I can see where Chloe inherits her looks from. Quite the resemblance indeed.'

Of course Harker knew damn well he was overdoing the pleasantries, but what the hell, you only have one chance to make a good first impression.

'It's a pleasure to meet you too, and my congratulations,' the man replied, with a look of surprise, 'but I'm afraid I'm not Mr Stanton. I'm the priest, and the name's David.'

'What?' Harker stepped back before glancing over towards the diminutive woman who was now smiling at him broadly. 'Then who's this?'

'That's Mrs Penhaligan. She's the organist.'

As Harker stared at them blankly, David gestured over to an older couple standing by one of the pews at the far side of the church. 'I think that's the couple you're looking for.'

Harker craned his head towards the real Mr and Mrs Stanton, who stood staring at him with a look of bemusement.

'Married?' Mr Stanton suddenly blurted out in a thick Yorkshire accent, looking over at Chloe with a deep frown on his forehead. 'You're getting married!'

'*Shit*,' Harker muttered, much to the amusement of Mrs Penhaligan. Chloe now joined him, with Doggie close behind her.

'I hadn't told them yet, Alex,' she hissed from the corner of her mouth, and then strode over to join her parents whilst Doggie approached and slapped his palm on Harker's shoulder.

'Very smooth, Alex. Is that a natural ability or something you've cultivated over the years?'

Harker offered only a wince, then with gritted teeth he crossed the aisle to join Chloe, who was now in the midst of explaining herself.

'I'm sorry, but I was planning to surprise you both tonight at dinner.'

Mr Stanton was looking mightily unimpressed, but Mrs Stanton, although clearly shocked, moved over and gave Chloe a lung-crushing hug. 'Congratulations, darling, we're so happy for you. I just wish we had known about it sooner.' Now she turned towards Harker with cautiously open arms. 'And welcome to the family… Alex, is it?'

'Alex Harker, and it's a pleasure, Mrs Stanton,' he replied with a warm smile and embraced her lightly.

'Call me Sheila, please – and this is Frank.'

Sheila Stanton took a step back as Chloe's father now looked Harker up and down. For a moment it felt like a Mexican stand-off, with both men staring at each other intently – the younger one maintaining a courteous smile and the other looking suspicious.

'Pleasure to meet you, Frank,' Harker began, thrusting his hand out in front of him. 'Alex Harker, your future son-in-law.'

Mr Stanton stared down at Harker's hand for a few seconds, before finally grasping it firmly. 'Frank Stanton… unhappy father.'

Harker let out an uncomfortable laugh and continued smiling until he realised from the man's expression that this wasn't meant to be a joke. 'Well, hopefully I can lighten your mood over the next few days.'

'You can try,' Frank replied, still without any hint of a smile.

'Now, Dad, I'm sure you and Alex will get along fine once you get to know each other. In fact, I'm sure you'll get on famously.'

Jesus, Harker thought to himself, he'd known this man for less than a minute and already Chloe was having to referee.

'Or infamously perhaps,' Doggie quipped. The joke induced a brief smile from Mr Stanton as Doggie introduced himself with a wave of his hand. 'Thomas Lercher, and it's lovely to meet you both.'

'But his friends call him Doggie,' Harker interjected with a smirk, and immediately received a dirty look from the dean.

'That's true, but my *real* friends call me Tom, so please feel free.'

'Oh, I get it, like that dog, the lurcher? Very funny.' Mr Stanton even nodded approval. 'And you are?'

'I'm a good friend of Alex here,' Doggie offered, then continued with a sly grin, 'and I'll be best man at the wedding.'

His appropriation of the role garnered a look of surprise from Harker. 'That's still to be decided,' he muttered.

Doggie appeared unfazed. 'Alex may seem at first a bit of a sourpuss, but I assure you he's a lot of fun once you get to know him.'

As the group chuckled in unison Harker began to feel his blood boil. He had managed to go from being a complete stranger to a palpable idiot in less than a few minutes. As Doggie continued to charm the pants off Mr and Mrs Stanton, Chloe grasped his hand in reassurance.

'Mum, Dad, I want to run some ideas by Alex for our wedding. Are you OK here for a minute?'

'Of course, sweetheart,' Mrs Stanton replied, and with a firm tug Harker was escorted by his future bride towards the church's main entrance.

'I thought you told them weeks ago,' he said once they had stepped out into the warm evening air.

'I wanted to tell them face to face, Alex.'

'Well, thanks a bunch for telling me. I felt like a complete moron in there.'

'Come on, it wasn't that bad,' replied Chloe. 'Anyway, if you hadn't barged in unannounced, it wouldn't have been a problem. My plan was to tell them before dinner tonight and then they'd meet you and, voila, things would have gone perfectly.'

Harker merely grunted at her scheme, then looked back through the open doorway to see Doggie complimenting Mrs Stanton on her wonderful pashmina shawl. 'Doggie seems to be a hit with them. I think you're marrying the wrong guy.'

Chloe draped her arm around his shoulder and kissed him on the cheek. 'Dad's always been cagey around my boyfriends. When I was a teenager he used to wait up late until I got dropped off at the end of the night, then come out and tap on the car window with a golf club when he thought it had been parked for too long. I think he's stayed pretty calm considering you just sprung our wedding on him.'

It was a fair comment, and even though Harker felt there was now a mutual dislike between the two men, he'd be able to rectify it over the coming days – and if not, then so be it. He was marrying Chloe whether Frankie boy liked it or not. What was he going to do, wrap a golf club around Harker's head? *Give it a try, Frank.*

Harker was responding in disgruntled acquiescence when a man wearing a charcoal-coloured suit and a red tie hurried up the path towards them.

'Alex, we need to talk.'

Xavier Botha was someone Harker now considered a good friend – and a necessity, as Sebastian Brulet would put it. Ever since Harker's run-in with the fabled and psychotic cult of Mithras a few months earlier, the Grand Master of the Knights Templar had been unusually protective of his men out in the field. The revelation that the cult's leader, Father John Davies, was Harker's uncle had not helped either, and had only added to the personal nature of the danger he was in. In the last few months there had been no further information on the where-abouts of the man's followers, including Stefani Mitchell, the woman who had conned Harker into believing she was a Templar and had begun leading him down a dark path. Couple that with the cult's assassin Avi Legrundy's threat on Harker's life, and Brulet had insisted that a Templar security detail be at his side until the '*Red Death*', as she was known, was tracked down and brought to heel. There would be, without question, an empty cell waiting in one of Her Majesty's prisons for the dreadlocked killer – for a long stay.

Botha, however, was one of the best, a South African who had been born into the Templar family, and as such was someone Harker and Brulet could count on one hundred per cent. The fact that he was built like a brick shithouse helped and, even though he stood only five foot five inches tall, his expertise with weapons and training within the UK counterterrorism services, amongst other intelligence agencies, made him a highly formidable asset within the organisation.

'Sorry for the interruption, Chloe,' Botha said with his usual gracious demeanour, 'but I need to borrow him.'

To Chloe's credit she didn't bat an eyelid but simply offered Harker another kiss on the cheek and a wave of the hand before heading back inside the church. 'Just have him back by dinnertime,' she said.

'I'll do my best,' Botha replied.

The two men stood alone in the small graveyard in front of the church.

'What's going on?' Harker asked, noticing how wide-eyed the young Templar looked.

'We've got a location. We have to go.'

This reply now had Harker looking wide-eyed too. 'Where? When?'

'Just now and you're not going believe where.'

'Well, go on,' Harker urged impatiently, irritated at being left out of the loop yet again today.

'Only twenty minutes away from here. They're holed up at the moment, but there's no telling for how long.' Harker sifted the answer through his mind as Botha continued enthusiastically, 'Either it's a one hell of a stroke of luck they're so close, or—'

'Or they've been keeping tabs on me this whole time,' Harker replied, feeling a sense of excitement and dread rolled into one.

'Exactly,' Botha replied. 'Seems it's either now or never.'

Harker needed no further encouragement. 'Let's go,' he growled, and without another word they began walking swiftly down the path towards the modest gravel car park ahead, before the familiar voice of Doggie called out, 'Alex, where are you going?'

'Get the car started, I'll be there in a moment,' Harker instructed his companion before turning back towards the church. With a nod Botha took off at a jog.

'They've found them,' Harker explained to Doggie, surprised by the growing excitement he felt. 'They're only twenty minutes away.'

'That close! Bloody hell.' Doggie looked shocked.

'I know – and there's no time to waste.'

'Then you'd better get going already.'

Doggie was already waving a hand in the direction of the black four-door Range Rover now pulling towards the car park exit. 'And don't worry about her father. By the time I've finished schmoozing him, he'll reckon you're the gold standard amongst sons-in-law. You just take care of yourself.'

'Cheers, Tom,' Harker replied and he was about to head for the waiting car when Doggie offered one last piece of advice.

'And for God's sake, be careful.'

'You too.' Harker nodded towards the church where he could just make out Mr Stanton in deep conversation with Chloe, no doubt discussing her poor choice in men. 'I'll catch up with you later.'

Harker turned to the waiting Range Rover, his mind focusing on the job at hand. How long had they been following him? He knew the dangers and had realised they would track him, but to now be so close meant an attack was not just on the cards, but imminent.

Harker slid into the front passenger seat, slamming the door behind him. Inside he found Botha at the wheel and two other members of his security detail, both Templars suited from head to toe in black Kevlar body armour, sitting patiently in the back seat. Not a word was said and within seconds they were driving at high speed towards the motorway.

The sun was already going down over the trees and melting into a dark red hue amongst their branches. As he watched the countryside go by, Harker began to mull over the nature of this trip. He'd be lying to himself if he pretended he didn't have a pang of nervousness in his stomach, but he couldn't allow himself to indulge in such a feeling right now. He was the Templars' Jarl, a role that carried great weight within the Order. Many people now relied on him to make the right decisions, and although tonight was not a regular part of his job, it was nonetheless a sobering reminder of the position he had accepted. Tonight's events would put the problem to bed for good, and he knew it.

Either with success. Or with his own death.

Chapter 3

Dark clouds shrouded the sky above as Harker warily made his way towards the run-down brick building, each of his steps slower than the last. This abandoned farmhouse appeared more like a demolition site, and even though the storage sheds were still intact, it would need more than some TLC to bring it back up to working order. The cement rendering on the exterior walls showed years of erosion by the elements and much had fallen away, leaving piles of rubble strewn on the grass below. Curiously the building had no windows so far as Harker could see, and with its solitary metal door in the middle and a flat metal cast roof extending over the deserted structure, it looked more like a giant oven than the farmhouse Botha had informed him it was.

A rustling in the bordering hedgerow sent him down on one knee and he paused in the silence to scan the shadowy undergrowth for any sign of movement. Satisfied it had been nothing more than a gust of wind, he stood back upright only to realise that his overcoat had dipped into a muddy puddle, and he cursed himself for not changing garments beforehand. For a suit, tie and overcoat were hardly the best outfit, given where he was, but there had been so little time. And time, as Botha had insisted, was of the essence.

Harker once again began to navigate his way along the cracked tarmac path. Apart from the creepy surroundings there was something else that didn't feel right here, and as he quietly approached the metal door, it dawned on him what that was.

There were no sounds of wildlife.

It was strange, because at the edge of the property he'd heard a chattering of nocturnal animals doing their nightly rounds, and even what sounded like a tawny owl cooing its presence into the night air. But now… just silence.

It wasn't until he reached the door itself and saw the faded red lettering above it that this suddenly made sense.

'Tockenham Abattoir,' Harker muttered quietly to himself. Animals weren't fools and the constant smell of death usually meant that most of them kept their distance from places such as this. But given that it must have been abandoned years ago, surely it would have been reclaimed by the various countryside species by now. Unless someone was still using it for something.

Harker grasped the metal door handle and gave it a light yank, but nothing budged. It was obviously locked tight, so he now headed around the side of the building to explore further, maintaining the same meticulous stealth he had adopted so far. If this was the place, then the last thing he needed was to alert anyone to his presence.

Not yet, anyway.

With the last traces of sunset cresting on the horizon, he could make out the shadowy outline of additional buildings connected to the 'oven', and a row of rect-angular warehouses with what looked like corrugated sheets making up their exterior walls. An educated guess suggested holding stalls for doomed animals past. Poking his head over the top of the closest one, Harker found it as deserted as he had expected. The floors comprised only dry, caked mud and clumps of blackened dung, no doubt a parting gift from its previous occupants.

With nothing else to see, Harker was about retrace his steps back to the front entrance, with the idea of attempting to pry it open somehow, when something else caught his eye and he squinted up inquisitively. Just above the bushy treetops to his left rose the hazy silhouette of something and so, with footsteps carefully placed through assorted debris, he made his way to the edge of the trees and peered around – to spot something that brought him to a standstill.

A crumbling, three-storey Victorian house loomed ominously in front of him like a monumental warning to anyone that came across it. It wasn't a wide building but it towered upwards to a sharp, sloping, slate-tiled roof, with boarded-up windows at each floor level. From the roof two large cone-shaped turrets rose proudly, like pointed ears, which added to the sense of foreboding. The highest point of the structure was at the far right, where a tall brick chimney rose a metre higher even than the top of the turrets. In better days this place would have been an impressive residence, but the passage of time and lack of maintenance had transformed it into a deathtrap that only a fool would enter now.

And I am that fool, Harker mused as he tentatively advanced towards the derelict building after slipping past the loose-mesh fence that stood untidily around it. Whoever had set it up clearly had no real wish to prevent exploring teenagers from entering it, probably hoping the collapsing look of the place would do that job for them.

Parts of the brickwork had long since fallen away, revealing sections of desiccated wooden beams, but the most troubling sight of all was at the mid-point of the façade, where the foundations had weakened enough to cause the right-hand turret to lean inwards precariously.

As the sunset in the distance now extinguished any final vestiges of perceived safety, Harker moved closer to the doorway-sized plywood board covering the building's main entrance. He carefully laid a hand upon its grainy surface and then gently shoved against it. It didn't budge an inch, probably nailed shut from the inside. Noting all the windows were similarly boarded up, he slunk around to the rear of the house, keeping a safe distance from the wall for fear of bumping against it and bringing the whole structure down on top of him.

As he turned the corner at the rear, a light blinked somewhere off to his right, and he instinctively pulled back and slammed against the brickwork, wincing as he glanced upwards, half expecting to glimpse a shower of bricks dropping towards him. Thankfully there were none to be seen.

With renewed caution Harker peered again around the corner to spot a thin gap between the boards covering one of the ground-floor windows, through which a sparkle of light emanated.

The house was occupied.

He crept cautiously over and pressed his eye to the gap, but the narrow angle offered nothing more than a view of the entire length of the interior wall. So he moved further along the building's rear until he finally came across what he was looking for. The back door was covered in peeling green paint and although it bore a number of jagged scratch marks across its surface, which briefly caused Harker concern, at least it wasn't boarded up. After taking a deep breath to steady himself, he reached for the handle and applied a light pressure.

The door itself offered no resistance and Harker glanced inside. Once satisfied the room beyond was empty, he headed further into the house.

The kitchen he found himself in was as much of a wreck as the building's exterior. All the fittings had been ripped out at some point, leaving patches of fresh wallpaper where years of sunlight had not faded the colours. The bright lightbulb hanging above showed that at least the building had electricity, but given the wretched state of the interior, it was a wonder why. Deeper within the house the sound of footsteps answered his question and Harker leaned up against the only other doorway in the room to hear more clearly. He froze as the sound stopped as quickly as it had started. Apart from a few aching groans from the house itself there was now complete silence, and he cautiously poked his head around the partly open doorway and surveyed the connecting passage.

The adjoining hallway was just as charming and offered the kind of squalor and privacy that only a crack addict could truly appreciate. It was completely void of any decor, with only dull and scuffed dark brown floorboards, but these seemed appealing compared to the moss-coated, floral wallpaper hanging in tattered strips off the walls.

On the far side of the hallway a single stairway led up to the first floor. The whole space was covered in dust and decaying brown leaves that had presumably been blown in from some other part of the building. What really caught Harker's eye though was the collection of boot imprints disfiguring the floor, along with a pair of narrow tyre marks that could have been made only by a wheelchair.

And they all led to one place: a crusty-looking doorway positioned directly under the rising staircase.

With a light step Harker slowly moved over to it and inclined his head towards the low doorway.

The scuffle of shoes on the other side of the room had him jerking backwards, and he leapt into the stairwell, then lay back against it, using the bottom of the end bannister as cover when the door was flung open and someone burst through it, slamming it behind them and letting out a frustrated yell.

Harker couldn't see the individual's face but he already knew who it was, for those greasy dreadlocks were a dead giveaway. He reached into his coat pocket, pulled out the oversized black pistol and rose to his feet with the weapon aimed directly at the newcomer's neck. 'Legrundy!' he shouted, then watched as she froze before slowly turning to face him.

Avi Legrundy, the butcher and fanatical assassin for the Mithras cult, looked momentarily shocked, but as she gazed upon Harker with those cold, dead eyes he remembered so vividly, a sneaky smile crept across her face.

'Alex Harker!' she declared, now seemingly happy to see him. 'I wasn't expecting to see you again so soon.'

That acknowledgement confirmed what Harker already knew and he offered simply a nod of his head as the psychotic killer remained motionless. 'I've been tracking you for a while,' he declared.

She appeared unmoved by his admission. 'And I you, *brother.*'

The fact that she believed the pair of them were somehow connected left a sour taste in Harker's mouth and he moved off the staircase and approached to within a few metres of her, the gun still aiming in her direction. 'I'm not your brother, Legrundy, but I am here to put an end to your madness,' Harker replied firmly, and he moved over to the main boarded-up window and slammed his foot into it, loosening all the nails and sending the section of plywood tumbling downwards into the darkness outside.

'There is a back door, you know,' Legrundy said condescendingly, as Harker moved back to face her directly, the barrel of his gun aimed at her chest.

'Anyone else here?' he asked, and the question received a slow shake of Legrundy's head.

'You know I work alone, Alex.'

'Not any more. Your work permit has been rescinded.'

Legrundy looked at him blank-faced for a moment before she burst into a fit of genuine laughter. 'Dat, Professor, is adorable,' she mocked, and continued to laugh out loud, so much so that she leant forwards, gripping her stomach tightly. 'I'd wager you've been saving up that little line for a while now.'

Sadly Harker had indeed mulled this line over in his head many times, yet now that he had actually spoken it, he had to admit she was right: it did sound pretty stupid. But he refused to let it show and he now dipped the barrel of the gun towards the floor.

'On your knees,' Harker ordered calmly as he pulled a set of handcuffs from his back pocket and threw them on the wooden boards. 'It's over. Put them on, arms behind your back.'

The sound of a creaking floorboard erupted from somewhere in the room behind her, and Harker immediately directed his weapon at the door – just as Legrundy began to smile, revealing those bright, pearly white teeth of hers.

He shot her a distrustful look as the door slowly swung inwards. The long barrel of a Steyr AUG assault rifle was pointed at him, as its owner, a stocky man with a thick neck and hairy forearms, moved slowly out from the shadows beyond and into view. Simultaneously a blonde-haired woman with a ponytail appeared from the kitchen doorway, holding the same type of rifle aimed directly at him. Harker swiftly moved his sights back and forth between the two intruders as they took up position on either side of Legrundy.

Each of them was dressed like a tramp in filthy trousers and a heavy jacket riddled with rips and stains, and the man wore a black skullcap with the message "No Fear" embroidered on the front.

Harker felt his heart begin to beat faster as Legrundy calmly reached down, picked up the handcuffs and threw them back at him, so they came to a rest inches from his feet.

'Now drop the gun and *you* put them on,' she hissed through tight lips, while she motioned to the two gun-proficient tramps standing next to her. 'Alone? I'm afraid I lied to you.'

As she looked on with a grin spreading across her face, Harker held his now somewhat pathetic-looking pistol up in one hand and, after raising his free palm towards them submissively, slowly reached into his jacket pocket and pulled out a small teardrop-shaped piece of plastic.

Legrundy stared at the seemingly inoffensive item as Harker pressed it twice with his thumb and then dropped it to the floor. 'I'm afraid I lied as well.'

A tiny, bright red laser dot appeared on Legrundy's chest even as another two appeared on the gun-toting tramps' jackets, and she immediately snapped her focus towards the open window from which Harker had kicked the plywood board covering only moments earlier.

'It's over, Legrundy,' Harker yelled, moving quickly to one side of the window. 'Tell your friends to put their weapons down.'

The dreadlocked assassin scowled at him as the two armed tramps, rifles still raised, both looked to her for instructions. As Harker watched the killers' eyes begin to squint, he already knew the answer.

It was a look that Botha and his team clearly recognised as well through their telescopic lenses, and a barrage of tranquilliser darts slapped hard into all three of them, before Legrundy displayed her usual instinctive prowess and dived head first through the kitchen doorway and out of sight.

Harker was already on the move as both gunmen ripped the darts from their bodies, and he flung himself low out through the open window as the sound of gunfire opened up, a bullet just grazing the heel of his shoe. The impact flipped his foot forward and sent him tumbling onto a pile of rubble below with a painful thud.

The gunfire fell silent and a scuffling of boots could be heard as the tramps scarpered for cover. Harker leapt back to his feet and limped to one corner of the house, rubbing frantically at where a sharp edge of brick had jammed into his thigh during the fall.

Above him the exchange of gunfire started up again, but it had to be blind fire because there was no way Botha and his team could be seen in the darkness where they had taken up position as Harker initially approached the abattoir buildings.

Ignoring the stinging in his leg, he stumbled to the back door in time to catch sight of the shadowy silhouette of Legrundy slipping in between a fence and an old storage shed, heading towards the corrugated holding pens he had encountered earlier. Immediately he began to chase her, but was stopped dead in his tracks when the female tramp appeared at the back door with her rifle aimed directly at him.

Harker had been caught cold, but instead of feeling the impact of a bullet in the chest, he watched as the woman's rifle barrel suddenly tipped downwards and her eyelids began to droop.

The tranquilliser.

Without hesitation Harker leapt forward and slammed one side of his pistol against the woman's face. With a nauseating crack as her cheekbone gave way, she crumpled to the ground. He then kicked the rifle away from her quivering, outstretched hand and took off into the darkness, in the direction of the holding pens, still gripping his pistol tightly.

With the only light coming from the kitchen doorway, it was difficult to get his bearings. After slamming his kneecap into a corner of the shed, with a muffled yelp he came to a stop at the first holding pen, dropped to a painful crouch and peered over the partition. The blurry outline of the pens lying beyond began to come into focus as Harker's vision acclimatised, and as he watched for any signs of movement. The night air fell quiet.

Back at the house a couple more gunshots rang out, followed by a subdued groan. Satisfied that Botha had the situation under control, Harker turned his attention back to the enclosures ahead of him. The tranquillisers had worked even faster than Botha had suggested and though Avi Legrundy might be tough, she wasn't invincible. Therefore she couldn't be far away, and so he began creeping deeper into the maze of rusting and disused pens, his pistol aimed forward, its barrel quivering due to his own shaking hands. This wasn't due so much to the adrenalin coursing through his veins as to his own nerves getting the better of him, so he loosened his grip on the gun and, with gritted teeth, moved onwards.

Each footstep made a squelching sound in the muddy earth. Legrundy would most likely hear him coming, so he decided to throw caution to the wind and call out after her.

'There's nowhere to go, Avi,' he bellowed, using the assassin's first name almost cordially, even though he knew it would make little difference. 'That tranquilliser has enough stopping power to bring down a fully grown rhino, so don't try and resist it. I promise you won't be hurt. The Templars aren't killers like your beloved cult of Mithras.'

The mere mention of the Templars produced a wheezing groan from somewhere near the last holding pen, and with his gun still outstretched Harker approached the last corner and peeked around the edge warily.

Avi Legrundy lay slumped against the corrugated fencing, saliva dribbling from one corner of her mouth. But that icy glare was far from gone and she stared at Harker with a sincere and burning hatred. 'I'll phll uuuu.'

Her words were unintelligible and Harker moved over and knelt down next to her, his gun now dipping towards the floor. 'I can't tell what you said, but I'm sure it was something unpleasant,' he replied acidly as she hissed more words that sent spittle running down her chin.

'I said, I'll kill you.' Much clearer now.

Legrundy's right arm swung towards him, but it was a sluggish blow, and Harker easily intercepted it with his free hand by grabbing and holding her wrist, exposing the four-inch, serrated steel Tekna knife held loosely in her palm.

'You're seriously like a stuck record, Avi,' he remarked bluntly before pulling the weapon from her hand and throwing it across the floor, well out of her reach. 'Your mantra's becoming old and predictable.'

Legrundy managed only a quiet grunt of anger before finally succumbing to the chemicals in her system. Her eyes fluttered momentarily then closed as she fell into a deep, drug-induced sleep.

He expelled a relieved breath, then sank back on his haunches as he stared down at the sleeping woman. She had been responsible for so many deaths, and those were only the ones he knew about. How many others had succumbed to a painful and miserable death of the kind that this Mithras assassin had dished out during her lifetime? How many final images had been of this face he now looked upon with such distaste?

As Harker gazed down at her motionless body, he heard a rustling sound behind him and jumped up to see Botha making his way over with a 9mm semi-automatic Beretta firmly gripped in one fist.

'Where is she?' he demanded anxiously, then his shoulders relaxed as he caught sight of the incapacitated Legrundy splayed out at his colleague's feet. 'Move,' the Templar ordered, and he pushed Harker to one side before pressing his fingers against the assassin's neck.

'She's out cold,' Harker assured him calmly, now feeling pretty pleased with himself for having orchestrated such a successful plan.

But Harker's moment of personal pride was brought to a swift end when Botha stood back up and gave him a firm slap around the face.

'What the hell was that for?' he exploded, but Botha seemed unmoved by his indignation.

'I should never have let you go inside first,' the Templar growled, as Harker rubbed at his cheek. 'My job is to protect you at all times and that came far too close. Another few seconds and you would be lying dead back there in that house, and all for the sake of satisfying your ego.'

Since acquiring his own personal protection unit three months earlier, Harker had found the line between his personal space and being smothered by security becoming increasingly blurred. With the Legrundy pledge to kill him hanging over his head like the sword of Damocles, of course he had appreciated the protection thrust upon him by the insistence of the Templars. But he had always known that once Legrundy was finally tracked down, he would need to confront her face to face. This wasn't ego per se, but rather a real need to see it all through to the end, considering how much she had put him through, not to mention the people he cared about. Not so much ego but a sense of justice.

As Harker stared into Botha's unyielding gaze, he now felt a mild pang of discomfort. *OK, maybe ego had come into it… by just a sliver.*

'Anyway, it's over now,' Harker offered as he glanced down at Legrundy, who was now sleeping like a baby without a care in the world.

Botha's expression began to relax and with a long outward breath he nodded agreement. 'OK. I'll have someone package her up, but right now we have to get you back inside the house.'

The last suggestion had Harker immediately looking around him in concern. 'Are there more of them?'

Botha shook his head. 'No, I don't think so, but there's something inside you need to see.'

'What is it?'

'Not exactly sure. I only caught a glance at it as I headed back here to find you, but it made an impression on me.'

Harker eyed the Templar with curiosity because Xavier Botha was a man prone to understate rather than exaggerate the facts, not unlike most Englishmen purported to do until the world-renowned stiff upper lip mentality had relaxed in recent decades. If Botha admitted it had made an impression on him, then it was important.

'Show me,' Harker urged, then gave Botha a firm slap across the face.

'What was that for?'

'That was for allowing me to enter that place all alone.' He gave a sarcastic smile and, as Botha's nostrils flared, started back towards the house.

'Cheeky bastard,' the Templar cursed, but with a smile, then headed after him, leaving Legrundy to continue dreaming whatever twisted things ran through her warped mind.

The body of the female tramp was still lying where Harker had left her, although now handcuffed. He stepped over the motionless woman and then back into the kitchen, while Botha ordered one of his men to secure Legrundy immediately.

'In here, Alex.' Botha gestured him into the room Legrundy had emerged from.

The room itself was just as shoddy as the rest, in keeping with Legrundy's shabby-looking armed guards. Only a few shreds of the floral wallpaper had survived on the walls here and the floor was filthy with an assortment of dust, dead insects and pellets of rat crap, giving the whole place a kind of public-toilet vibe.

'Take a look at this.' Botha gestured to the nearest wall, where a large world map had been tacked up, with a solitary, thick, red dot drawn on it to mark a location.

As Harker got closer he realised the mark had not been made by any pen. It was a single spot of blood that had left a thin drip line running down the surface of the poster. 'What is this?' he wondered as he began noting the location marked by the sickly blotch. 'Gibraltar,' he muttered to himself as Botha also now showed interest.

'I've no idea what it means, but it was that table full of stained cutlery that caught my attention.'

'Cutlery?' Harker turned away from the map to look over to where Botha was pointing on the far side of the room, where a scratched wooden table stood with blood-stained tools spread carelessly over it. The glinting blade of a butcher's cleaver stood upright at its centre, having been rammed into the surface, and as Harker moved closer he recognised the other scattered implements. If you ignored the blood splattered amongst them, it was a collection that any professional gardener or butcher would have been proud of.

'What the hell have they been doing here?' Harker muttered, almost not wanting to know.

'I don't know, but nothing good.'

Harker was leaning over to inspect the implements further when he heard a low-pitched groan to his left. He spun towards it, then discerned the outline of another doorway in the gloomiest corner of the room.

Botha had his pistol drawn already and aimed towards it. With a nod to Harker, who had similarly raised his weapon, he made his way over there and gently grasped the handle. With a glance back at Harker, he easily wrenched open the door. Harker's nose immediately wrinkled at the smell of urine intermingled with blood that wafted through.

The room itself was little more than a closet in which sat a man wearing blue jeans and an ill-fitting, grey T-shirt many sizes too big for him. He was tied into a wheelchair, his face covered by a brown woven sack over his head.

Harker initially flinched at the sight, but on noticing the man's legs twitch he dashed forwards even as Botha holstered his gun and wheeled the man further into the centre of the room. The hood was peppered with blood spots but it was the severed stump remaining where his right hand should have been that made Harker recoil, even as the bound figure now began to shake violently while emitting a high-pitched whimper.

Gulping apprehensively, Harker grasped the top of the sack and slowly pulled it off. What he saw had him once again recoiling, dropping the sack to the floor, but this time in astonishment because he had not seen anything like this before.

It was a man, that much was clear, but his features were unlike anything Harker had seen previously. The forehead was double the size of most people's, slanting back at an unusually steep angle, and the ears were large and bulbous like a veteran boxer's yet possessing no earlobes.

The cheekbones were so thick and pronounced that both eye sockets appeared buried deep into the man's face. And stranger still, the eyes weren't round but teardrop-shaped, elliptical almost, and now focused on Harker in desperation and pain.

'In here,' Botha called out through the doorway as Harker hastened back to the implements table and swiped up a small hunting knife, the only blade not already covered in blood. 'I need help, now.'

One of the Templar security team appeared at the doorway but only managed a few steps before the bound man's bizarre appearance had him gaping in stunned silence. Meanwhile Harker slipped the knife under the white plastic cable ties restraining the prisoner, slicing through one and then the other.

Free of his bonds, the man peeled himself off the seat like a dead weight, and tumbled straight into Harker's waiting arms with a groan.

'What are you waiting for?' yelled Botha and only then did the Templar rush to the man's aid, as the other member of the team appeared in the doorway, looking equally appalled by the spectacle.

Botha shot Harker a look of confusion over the man's bizarre appearance but he said nothing as his teammate pulled a roll of bandages from his black flak jacket and tossed them over to Botha, who began addressing the fellow's bloodied stump.

'You're safe,' Harker murmured, but the man appeared uninterested. Instead, he raised his remaining hand upwards and motioned for Harker to move closer.

Normally Harker would have done so without pause, but he caught sight of the man's surviving hand and hesitated, his eyes widening in surprise. Not at the blood encrusting the man's fingertips, but rather at the fingers themselves. There were *five* of them – not including the thumb.

As Harker gazed at the surplus digit with a blank expression, it was Botha who, in concern, swiftly snatched the man's hovering wrist and held it tightly while the fellow hissed in pain, before shaking his head.

'I don't think he wants to hurt us,' Harker uttered quietly, recomposing himself, as Botha, eyes still full of suspicion, finally released his grip and returned to his bandaging task.

The man weakly grasped for the side of Harker's cheek and gently pulled it towards him until Harker was within inches of those trembling lips. His words were spoken in nothing short of a whisper but they were unlike anything Harker had heard before. Yet, as he continued speaking, a few words started to become recognisable.

'What's he saying?' Botha asked, having finished bandaging the man's wrist, but Harker waved his question aside in frustration as he attempted to focus on what was being mumbled.

The man managed one more sentence before finally succumbing to his injuries, his arm slipping back down by his side as his body began to shake violently.

'He's going into convulsions,' Botha stated sharply, turning to the two other members of his team as Harker held the victim tightly. 'Get the car up here on the double and call Great Western Hospital. Tell them we're bringing in the victim of a car accident.'

'Car accident?' Harker asked as the men disappeared through the doorway. Botha offered him a stern glare. 'If you want to explain to the police how this man came to lose a hand, then by all means go ahead.'

'I don't think it's his injury they'll have an issue with,' Harker replied, glancing down at the strange-looking person still clasped in his arms. Apart from those obvious physical abnormalities, the man's skin appeared a light green olive colour, and only now did he notice the double row of teeth, one behind the other, set into his lower jaw. 'What the hell is he?'

Botha looked just as confused, shaking his head as his two teammates returned and carefully plucked the man out of Harker's arms, before moving him out towards the front door.

'What did he say to you?' Botha asked, still clearly shocked at the fellow's appearance.

'I'm not entirely sure,' was all Harker could offer. This merely drew anger from the Templar bodyguard.

'Not entirely sure? I thought you were supposed to be a textual archaeologist. Aren't languages your thing?'

'It's not that simple,' Harker snapped in response, irked by the insinuation. 'It's not a language I've heard before, but I did detect some similarities to Mesopotamian languages.' Harker then fell silent as possibilities churned through his mind, and after a few seconds his eyes began to light up as he finally pieced the mumbled words together.

'Well?' Botha demanded, in fact more annoyed by his own surprised reaction to the wounded man than Harker's need for additional time to come up with a translation.

Harker spent a few more moments mulling it all over before latching on to the best answer he could offer. 'There are only a few words I recognised. *The dawn*... no, the dusk... *now the dusk is upon us and*... and... *with it the birth of man*... no.' He gave a frustrated shake of his head. '*The rebirth of the civilisation. We have now returned.*'

Chapter 4

'What the hell is that?' asked the surgeon, as the strange-looking humanoid was wheeled into the operating theatre on the third floor of Great Western Hospital by two male nurses.

'I was hoping you could tell me, Dr Cordon,' Botha replied, shooting Harker an uneasy glance. 'But it looks as if he's been tortured and lost a lot of blood.'

'And also his hand,' Harker managed to add.

'That I can see,' Dr Cordon said as the nurses heaved the body onto the operating table with deep grunts. It had needed three of them to lift the deceptively heavy patient onto the gurney at the hospital's side entrance.

'Leave us to it. Now,' the doctor added, before the operating theatre's double doors slammed shut and left them both outside in the hospital corridor.

'How do you know this doctor?' Harker asked Botha, more than a little concerned by the looks the humanoid had received from the medical team.

'It's not going to be a problem. The staff here are friends of ours.'

The connotation of a Templar association immediately had Harker puzzled. 'Are you telling me we just happen to have our own people here in this hospital, right at this moment?'

Botha looked somewhat miffed at whatever insinuation Harker was making, and he instinctively scanned the empty corridor before replying.

'Alex, how long have I been on your protection detail?'

'Just over three months.'

'That's right. And my main protocol is to keep you safe and alive, correct?'

Harker gave a simple nod and let the Templar finish.

'Then how unprofessional would I be not to know the nearest hospital to your location at any given time? Besides, we have a small medical unit – composed of our own people – on standby at all times in case anything should happen to you. They move, posing as a consultancy team, to whatever hospital I request so as to raise as little suspicion as possible.'

This last admission had Harker's mouth drop open slightly. He knew the Templars were keeping a close eye on him but had never imagined this level of diligence simply for his protection.

'I had no idea.'

'And neither should you. That's for *me* to worry about,' Botha replied with a stern grin. He leaned towards him. 'I sometimes wonder if you realise just how important your role as Jarl is to the Templars, Alex.'

Botha made a good point because, despite gaining access to every secret the Templars possessed, Harker had maintained a level-headed approach to his recent appointment. It was an importance that, unfortunately, was not observed to quite the same degree by Chloe. On the way over to the hospital he had called her to apologise for not attending the family get together. Chloe had been understanding but had made it patently clear that she was not at all happy about it. Still, Doggie would hold the fort for him – although whether that was a good thing was yet to be seen.

'I really do appreciate everything you do for me, Xavier,' Harker replied sincerely, and received a simple nod from Botha, just as a muffled sound of organised chaos could be heard from the other side of the operating theatre doors.

'I've never seen anything quite like that thing.' Botha turned to face him. 'Those oversized eyes...'

'Forget the eyes. How about the five fingers!'

Both men now stared at each other in confusion.

'It looked barely human,' Harker ventured, but this observation received a more than disconcerted look from Botha.

'Let's just wait and see what the doctor says, shall we?'

'And Legrundy?' For the first time since discovering the strange humanoid, Harker was considering the Mithras killer's role in all this. 'Where is she now?'

'She's being taken to a safe house for the time being, but hopefully she can shed some light on all this.'

'Good luck then,' Harker snorted dismissively. 'She's as tight-lipped as they come.'

Botha was already nodding in agreement. 'Maybe, but we'll see.'

His menacing tone had Harker eyeing him suspiciously, because the Templars weren't torturers – even when dealing with someone as vile as Legrundy – but there was something in the man's voice that hinted nothing was off the table.

This awkward moment was broken as the operating theatre doors were pushed outwards and one of the nurses appeared.

'I think you'd better come in, gentlemen.'

The operating theatre was a flurry of activity as a team of three nurses worked on their new patient. Poised above him, Dr Cordon, wearing green scrubs and a surgical mask, was already securing two defibrillator pads to the man's chest.

'Stand clear,' the surgeon warned, as the short drone of an alarm signalled that the charge was ready.

The patient's body rose upwards as the pads released an electrical charge, his muscles tensing briefly before relaxing back against the table. Dr Cordon checked for a pulse. Whatever he felt made him pause and, after a puzzled glance towards the nearest nurse, he repeated his order for a second time.

'Clear.'

Another charge surged through the patient's muscles, and once again his chest rose upwards momentarily before sinking back down onto the operating table, as the team checked again for a heartbeat.

Nothing.

With a gloomy expression, Dr Cordon looked in Botha's direction and shook his head. 'He's gone, so I'm calling it. DOA.' But rather than raising the blanket to cover the deceased's head, he instead beckoned over one of the nurses.

'Get me the ultrasound, please, quick as you can.'

Within moments the nurse had wheeled the scanner over and placed the transducer into Dr Cordon's waiting hands. With the flick of a switch the scanner's monitor flickered into life.

Now brimming with curiosity, Harker moved closer to the operating table to watch as Dr Cordon gelled up the tip of the transducer and ran it across the dead man's chest, and the screen began to offer an interior glimpse of the body.

'What are you looking for?' Harker asked, as Botha now joined him.

'Hold on and I'll show you,' the surgeon replied. He brought the transducer to a halt directly in the middle of the dead man's chest, his gaze locked on the monitor. 'That's unbelievable.'

Dr Cordon instinctively stepped back from the monitor, and Harker pushed forward to get a better look. Even though his medical training was limited in the extreme, there was no denying what he now saw.

'He's got two hearts,' Harker declared flatly, whereupon the surgeon managed a nod. 'Is that... normal?'

'Obviously not, Alex,' Botha replied sarcastically, peering at the screen, and both he and the doctor glared at Harker as if he were an idiot.

'What I mean is have you ever seen that before?' Harker persisted, and this time received a more understanding look from the surgeon.

'I've never seen... I've not even *heard* of it occurring, except in conjoined twins.'

The three men glanced at one another thoughtfully, whereupon Dr Cordon began to move the transducer lower down the patient's abdomen. 'Everything else is normal, so far as I can see. The kidneys, liver, lungs are a bit larger than normal, but apart from that...'

His hand came to a stop and then hovered above an area on the lower left hand side of the stomach, before moving the instrument further around the patient's flank. 'There's something else in there,' he muttered. He plucked a scalpel off the metal side tray and began to make a shallow incision, from the centre of the sternum, in a C shape running all the way down to the waist. He then began to separate the skin from the muscle, with gentle flicks of the scalpel, until an entire flap of skin could be rolled back.

By now Harker felt pretty sure he was about to throw up, but as Dr Cordon lightly scraped away yellow patches of fat to reveal something else on the inside of the skin, his queasiness turned to fascination. There were markings, tattooed in black ink, on the inner surface of the skin itself.

'What the hell is that?' Botha asked loudly even as Dr Cordon continued to scrape away yet more fatty tissue, and in so doing revealed more of the tattoo.

'It's some kind of writing,' Harker replied, already beginning to recognise some of the letters. Dr Cordon scraped off the last pieces of tissue to reveal the markings in full. There were five lines' worth, meticulously drawn, but what really stood out was the symbol that enclosed the text. It looked like a simple bag, with looped handles at the top, and the written lines were all contained inside it.

'Is that a shopping bag?' Botha asked, instantly feeling foolish for having suggested such a ridiculous thing. But he was right, for it did look like the kind of item one might carry groceries in.

'It's cuneiform script,' Harker replied, moving hesitantly closer to the creature's exposed flesh.

Botha was now looking confused and he shook his head. 'Cuneiform? Sounds French. What is it? A French shopping outlet?'

'No, you fool,' snapped Harker, getting a dirty look from Botha for his dismissiveness. 'It's an ancient form of writing – the oldest, actually – but I don't recognise the words. Just as importantly, how did he manage to tattoo it on the inside of his skin?'

The three men gazed at each other vacantly, as the three nurses behind them looked on with blank expressions.

'I've absolutely no idea,' Dr Cordon replied, as someone began pounding on the doors. This had all three men startled and they turned in unison to see it open slightly and a face peer through the gap.

'Ah, there you are.' Dean Thomas Lercher offered them a courteous smile as he pushed his way into the room. 'Alex, what are you doing here?'

'What am *I* doing here? What are *you* doing here? What about the family meal with Chloe?'

Doggie waved a hand in front of him dismissively. 'It's going fine, don't worry. But after your rather cryptic phone call to Chloe, I wanted to check you were OK.'

Harker's call had been anything but cryptic: he was at the hospital, he was fine, but he'd have to miss the meal with Chloe's parents. In truth this intrusion was more likely due to Doggie's need to be in the middle of everything, a theory that was confirmed within moments.

'So you've not been in an accident then. That's a relief.' Doggie gave a sigh as he let the doors swing shut behind him and headed over to join the others with a look of eager curiosity, raising his shoulders like a schoolboy in the playground wanting to get in on whatever was being discussed. 'So, what's going on?'

Before Harker could answer, the dean caught sight of the abnormal-looking body they were all standing around, and came to an abrupt halt, his eyes widening like saucers.

'What the hell is that?'

Instinctively both Harker and Botha formed a barrier in front of the operating table but Doggie swiftly circumnavigated them and came to a stop at the foot of the table.

'Good god, Alex,' he gasped, raising a hand before his mouth in obvious revulsion at the sight. 'What on earth are you up to? And could someone please tell me why this man's skin has been peeled back?'

Doggie now focused his attention on the patient's unique appearance. 'Is he human?' the dean enquired in a daze, his hand dropping from his mouth.

Given the bizarre appearance of the dead man's face, it was a reasonable question. Botha only offered a shrug of his shoulders, and it was Harker who replied. 'Yes… we think so.'

'But he's got six fingers!' Doggie exclaimed in an unusually high tone of voice, before noticing the other arm was a stump. 'And what happened to his other hand?'

Although he appeared grossed out by the spectacle he was clearly also fascinated. Then he pointed to the tattooed writing. 'And what is that?'

Dr Cordon immediately pulled the skin flap back across to hide the writing, which elicited an immediate and unamused glare from the dean.

'I take it we're all *friends* here,' he said resentfully.

'Friends' was Doggie's latest code word for Templars, and Botha, looking unhappy, expelled a frustrated sigh.

'We are indeed, Dean.'

That was all the reassurance Doggie needed and he sauntered over to Harker's side as Dr Cordon pulled the flap back open. 'So, what have we got here, gentlemen?' he began sternly, instantly settling into lecturer mode.

Telling Doggie to get lost would be a waste of breath, and anyway the man could prove to be of some help to them.

'You tell me,' Harker suggested as the dean looked closer, wrinkling his nose.

'Interesting. I would say, at a glance, it's a type of cuneiform – but not one I recognise.'

'That's was my thinking too,' Harker said, now pointing to the bag symbol encompassing the entire tattoo. 'And that surround?'

At the sound of a vibrating mobile phone, Botha reached into his pocket and then without a word made his way out of the operating theatre into the corridor outside.

Doggie continued to examine the markings more closely. 'Well, it represents some sort of bag, doesn't it, Alex?'

'Yes, that much I guessed. But what is it?'

Doggie thought hard about this for a moment, then he stood up straight and made a clicking noise with his tongue. 'Well, I'd say that if the writing is a shopping list, then this was a person in tremendous need of a pen and paper.'

The joke did not amuse Harker or Dr Cordon.

'Sorry, Alex, just my attempt at bringing some levity into the situation,' Doggie said gingerly. 'It's not every day one is faced with a corpse missing one hand, five fingers on the other hand, that doesn't even appear to be human.'

Harker's continued silence spoke volumes and, with an embarrassed gulp, Doggie resumed his more professional manner.

'I don't know what that means exactly, but basically cuneiform was the written text of the Sumerians or the Mesopotamians – two of the oldest civilisations ever to grace the earth. They invented the wheel and were the first to develop agriculture and animal husbandry, as you well know, Alex. It's from them that earliest human civilisation sprang, but our lack of precise archaeological knowledge of them means they enter only as a footnote in most history books.'

'They were also the first to introduce the twelve-month calendar,' Harker pointed out, as Doggie nodded in agreement.

'Very true, using the lunar cycle. But in general they remain a somewhat mysterious group…' His words trailed off and then his eyebrows lifted upwards. 'You should go and speak to Barbara Holtz, who's still one of the leading scholars when it comes to cuneiform and the Sumerians. You remember her, don't you, Alex?'

Doggie's last sentence was delivered with one eyebrow raised teasingly. 'I believe she's based in Gibraltar, if memory serves,' he continued.

Harker's eyes narrowed at the mention, but before he could answer, the doors swung open and Botha reappeared, waving his mobile in one hand.

'One of my boys found something back at the old house,' he began encouragingly. 'On that world map we found, with the bloodstain marking Gibraltar. There were three names written underneath it in black biro. Easily missed until they shone a torch onto it.'

'Barbara Holtz being one,' Harker remarked, receiving a surprised stare from Botha.

'Yes, Dr Barbara Holtz. How did you know that?'

'Just an educated guess,' Harker replied, with a glance over at Doggie as Botha continued.

'The other two were Dr Michael Wexler and Dr Marsouk Khan, both archaeologists.'

The two names elicited no spark of recognition from either Harker or Doggie. Botha continued, now scrolling through the screen of his phone.

'Dr Khan was found dead at his home after suffering a heart attack, some two weeks ago, while Michael Wexler's body washed up on the shores of southern France the day before yesterday… the working assumption being suicide.'

Harker felt his heart begin to beat faster. This wasn't due to shock, because he had never met these men, but rather the feeling of a connection being made – like holding a piece of a puzzle whose precise location on the board had yet to be discovered. Completely nonsensical maybe, but a powerful feeling nonetheless. 'Do you happen to know what they were working on?'

'Doesn't say, but I'm sure we can find out,' Botha replied before dropping the phone back in his pocket. 'Though I'll bet the blood on the map matches our friend's here.'

They all glanced over at the corpse lying on the table with the dried blood on its remaining fingertips.

'Whatever the Mithras cult were looking for, they obviously got it out of him.'

As Harker mulled over what any of this could mean, it was the surgeon who now sought to bring the gathering to a close.

'Well, gentlemen, I intend now to do an autopsy, so unless you revel in the sight of blood, then I would suggest you leave the room.'

'Of course, Doctor,' Harker said with a gracious nod. 'I'd be very interested to know what you discover and also I'd appreciate a detailed photograph of that tattoo. Xavier here can give you my contact number.'

With a thumbs-up from Cordon, Harker nudged Doggie out into the corridor, whilst Botha stayed behind to hand over the relevant details.

No sooner had the doors swung closed behind them than Doggie had grabbed him by the lapels, his professional demeanour entirely vanished. 'What the hell is going on? You take off from the church in pursuit of Legrundy and next I find you deliberating around the bloody corpse of… whatever that thing is with its skin peeled off.'

Even though the dean appeared furious, he was, as usual, consumed only with curiosity. So Harker simply grasped his friend by the arm and guided him along the corridor. 'I'll tell you all about it in the car, but I need you to go back to the meal now and keep everyone happy.'

This request brought Doggie to a complete halt, and he stubbornly crossed his arms. 'There's not a chance I'm going back there. It's a total nightmare.'

'But I thought you said everything was going great!'

'Well, it is, for me,' Doggie said tentatively, nevertheless managing a smug smile. 'They've really warmed to me. But as for you? Well, let's just say that charm you're usually renowned for hasn't hit the mark.'

Harker let out a groan and dropped his chin momentarily to his chest, before looking back up at Doggie with a rather pathetic hint of desperation in his eyes. 'Her mother seemed to like me.'

He received a wince from Doggie and a slow shake of the head.

'Did her father mention me?' Harker asked, his eyes beginning to glaze in defeat.

'Well, not by name, but he did refer to "that bloody man" quite a few times.'

Harker's shoulders slumped and he rubbed at his forehead in frustration. 'Christ, you'd think I robbed her old man blind or something.'

Doggie gave a short chuckle. 'What can be worse than stealing away a father's only daughter? And, just for the record, I told you that arriving unannounced at the church was a bad idea.'

Harker was doing everything in his power not to clasp his hands around Doggie's throat and throttle him, when Botha came striding towards them.

'Hold up! Where exactly are you going?' Botha asked.

'I'm going to pay Barbara Holtz a visit once Doggie discovers her location in Gibraltar,' Harker replied, and received a confirming nod from Doggie. 'Is the jet available?'

'It's at Bristol Airport – only thirty minutes from here.'

'Good. Can you let them know I'm on my way? And once I get her contact number I'll text it to you. I think it would be best if you could get someone to keep an eye on her, just in case. Pull a few strings with the local police, if you have to.'

'Will do,' Botha replied, before swiping at his phone screen. 'Consider those strings already pulled.'

'You may as well tell them there'll be two passengers.'

He looked over at the dean, who stared back. 'I'm coming with you,' he announced.

'No, Tom, you should stay here.'

Doggie was now looking mutinous. As Harker considered the request, he turned his attention back to Botha. 'Can you let me know what you manage to get out of Legrundy, please? I need to know what that thing in there is and where it came from.'

'You and me both,' the Templar replied resolutely. 'But, as you said yourself, she's the tight-lipped sort.'

Both men contemplated each other silently for a few moments, before Botha reached out and tapped Harker on the forearm. 'Officially, now that we have Avi Legrundy in custody, my protection duties are over, but I'm happy to join you if needed.'

Harker felt tempted for a second, but Legrundy needed to be interrogated, and there was no one better suited to the job than Xavier Botha. Besides his military training, the Templar had been fully schooled in psychological interrogation techniques by the best in the business – Mossad, the Israeli secret services – and if anyone could get information out of the Mithras assassin, it was him. 'Thanks, but I want to deal with this myself,' he decided at last.

Botha nodded, appearing oddly pleased by this response. 'Yeah, you're a Jarl all right, Alex Harker. Godspeed, and if you do need me, just make a call.'

'Thanks, Xavier. I owe you one.'

Botha smiled and, with the mobile pressed firmly to his ear, he headed back towards the operating theatre, before glancing back over his shoulder. 'You owe me more than just one,' he said with a grin, then disappeared inside, leaving Harker and Doggie standing alone out in the corridor.

'So,' Doggie began with his arms crossed, 'are you going to tell me what happened tonight or what?'

'I'll tell you in the car.'

'No, you'll tell me on the flight – everything about your little jaunt to apprehend that evil hag Avi Legrundy.'

Harker eyed his friend sternly but his expression quickly softened and he offered him a conciliatory nod. 'But you must do as you're told, understand?'

'Absolutely,' Doggie agreed excitedly, showing more enthusiasm than Harker was comfortable with. 'Besides, given Barbara Holtz's total disdain for you, I think you'll find my being present a serious advantage.'

Even as they headed in the direction of the lift, Harker began to look sceptical. 'I'm sure she's already forgotten about all that business.'

'Oh, Alex, when will you learn?' Doggie said with a condescending tone in his voice. 'We men are the ones with poor memories. Women never forget a thing.'

As the lift doors slid open and they stepped inside, the last thing on Harker's mind was not his own safety but that of Barbara Holtz. If the death of those archaeologists, Wexler and Khan, was anything to go by, then her life could be in real danger. But *why* was still a mystery to him. Neither did he have any idea yet what that six-fingered humanoid was, and at this point in time he did not want to entertain the wild suppositions which, if he were honest, were running riot through his mind. If not human, then what? No, he would wait for the results of the autopsy before he even considered entering that doorway, and instead focus on the job at hand. Given that Legrundy had gone to such tortuous lengths to get hold of Barbara Holtz's name and whereabouts, things did not bode well. What did the woman know? And what did it have to do with such a bizarre-looking... 'human' with the script of a language last spoken thousands of years ago tattooed inside its skin?

Like a dam suddenly breaking apart, a torrent of questions flooded into Harker's mind and he found himself pondering the Mithras cult itself. Where had it disappeared to in the meantime? *Vanished* was more like it. And given the Templars' intelligence skills, that was an impressive feat in itself.

As the lift descended Harker once again thrust such thoughts from his mind and focused only on certainties that offered him a semblance of reassurance. When it came to the Mithras cult and its fanatical followers, there was only one thing he could be absolutely sure of. And that was that whatever was going on, it would not end well.

Chapter 5

An icy, unforgiving gust of wind whistled in the man's ears like the screaming of a banshee as he fought his way up the snow-covered path, whilst struggling to carry the two cardboard boxes clenched tightly, one under each arm. The lull in the storm had spurred him to make the trip for supplies, and given the winds were now gearing up again for another blizzard, he allowed himself a satisfied smile in knowing that he had timed his trip perfectly. The cold mountains inland from the Côte d'Azur were a far cry from the French Riviera, but they did offer a perfect sanctuary for anyone keen not to be found.

And he did not want to be found.

The soaring peaks and valleys of the Alps provided protection from prying eyes in a terrain that only the hardiest or most foolish trekker would dare take on. Of course, the town nearby attracted a horde of tourists. But with the thick forest surroundings and being so far off the beaten track, the mountain chalet he approached did not witness many, if any, unexpected visitors.

Off in the distance the lone howl of a wolf could be heard just above that of the wind, and as the sun began to set, the man hurried up to the wooden steps in front of the building. The wolf population had made a comeback in recent years, but unlike the bloody attacks of centuries past, this modern breed knew well enough to avoid humans. He had noticed occasional paw prints in the snow during the past few months, but it was nothing to be concerned about – his rifle would see to that problem, if necessary.

He stomped his way up the wooden steps, each creaking under his weight, then turned the brass knob and pushed inside just as the prevailing wind began to step up a gear, its numbing bite only increasing in vigour. Slamming the door behind him with his foot, he expelled a sigh of relief as the warmth from the log fire in the hearth at the centre of the room reached him.

With the curtains drawn, the room was lit only by the firelight. He first took a moment to set the two boxes onto the pine flooring, then unzipped his thick, grey thermal jacket and hung it on a coat hook before reaching for the light switch.

'Why don't you leave that off for now?' An unfamiliar voice with a heavy French accent came from the other side of the room.

The man jerked backwards in shock against the door frame. Squinting through the gloom, he could see a pair of brown leather Timberland boots emerging from the shadows at the far end of the room.

'Milat?'

'It is good to know you at least remember my name, even though you've done everything possible to distance yourself from us through this facile game of hide-and-seek.'

Milat Berger now stepped out of the shadows into the flickering light of the log fire and offered a dry smile. 'You could not possibly have believed that you and your band of merry men and women could just up sticks and disappear like a fart in the wind after the mess you've caused, could you, John?'

Father John Davies had regained some of his composure and he took a step towards his visitor, but then came to a stop as Berger raised his open palm.

'That's close enough,' Berger ordered, and he shifted closer to the fire. 'There's much to discuss before we kiss and make up, and I would appreciate it if you'd allow me now to do the talking.'

Berger's features were now clearly visible, and his shoulder-length black hair glistened due to the excess of gel slicking it back over his skull. He turned his attention to the pair of fire tongs hanging from a hook on the chrome ventilation chute fixed above the fire. His hazel eyes appeared glassy in the firelight and his bushy eyebrows rose slightly as he calmly grasped the handle of the tongs and then dipped the ends into the burning red embers, whereupon he began to stoke the flames.

'Your misguided notion of family has us all perplexed, John. This obsession of yours with your nephew – this Alex Harker – is a curious one. And that you attempted to bring him into our fold was misguided, to say the least.'

It was clear Davies was desperate to state his case but, even though his lips quivered with a dogged frustration, he remained silent, allowing Berger to continue.

'But to think you would expose our very existence to a Templar after the lengths we have gone to in persuading them of our demise.' He winced dramatically, as if in despair. 'This is the part that troubles us most.'

Berger took a moment to set the tongs against the side of the fireplace, leaving the tips resting within the flames, and then made his way over to Father Davies, stopping within a foot of the man. 'What on earth were you thinking?' His raised eyebrow finally signalled the wish for a response, and Davies leapt at this opportunity with fervour.

'Where's everyone else?' he asked, referring to the full house he had left here.

'Oh, your little adopted family are safe, but I must admit they were somewhat put out by my arrival... initially. Especially that girl of yours, Stefani Mitchell. She's quite the fighter.'

This mention of Stefani had Davies gulping, and his eyes darted around the otherwise empty room for any evidence of his followers.

'As I said, they are fine. I have a few chaperones keeping an eye on them in the back room – so as to give us both time to talk.'

Davies seemed partially relieved by this answer, but Berger's cold, unblinking stare demanded answers.

'Let me say first that I'm sorry we took off, but I thought that putting some distance between us was the wisest thing to do, given everything that had already happened.'

'Don't lie to me, John,' Berger growled. 'It is most unbecoming. The truth is that you performed your disappearing act out of fear. Fear of the consequences of failing us by exposing what was not yours to reveal.'

Berger grimaced, then waved his finger reprovingly at the thought. 'You've always had delusions of grandeur, John – you thought your position within the Mithras was far more elevated than it had any right to be considered. And now all those flimsy supports have come crashing down around you.'

He clapped his hands together and heaved a deep sigh. 'Perhaps I myself am at fault for giving you such free rein.'

There was a flicker of agreement in Davies's eyes but it was immediately extinguished as Berger leant closer to him with snarling lips. 'Or perhaps you took advantage of that freedom, and now you fear the cost of your fickleness.'

Davies's eyes deadened and he gave a reluctant nod. 'You're right as always. I did. But you must believe that my motives in courting my own nephew were just. I thought he would agree and join us. After all, we are family, of the same blood, and such a bond would allow us to destroy the Templars once and for all.'

'Family? We, the Mithras, are your family. And did you really think revealing that archaic practice of the eating of the flesh would convince him? You idiot, we abandoned that inane cannibalistic tradition hundreds of years ago.'

Davies gaped, genuinely surprised at this man's knowledge of what had occurred, while Berger glared at him now with real menace in his eyes.

'And so, because of you, the Templars have realised we still exist. And on top of this cesspool of failure, your lapdog, Avi Legrundy has fallen into their hands.' Berger paused, his fist still raised, and squinted at Davies. 'And judging by your expression, you had no idea!'

Davies did indeed look shocked by the disclosure, and he stood speechless as Berger returned to the fireplace and began stoking the fire once again, eyeing the flames intently.

'Does Harker know about the project?'

His question had Davies shaking his head fervently and he hurried over to the fireplace. 'I told him nothing about that, I swear,' he grovelled.

Berger continued staring into the embers but after a few seconds he began to nod his head. 'Well, that's something at least, you damn moron.'

Davies's attention now turned to the hot tongs being twisted around in the flames, and the nervous sweat breaking out across his forehead did not escape Berger's notice.

'Come now, John, have some faith,' the man said, letting the tongs slip from his hands. 'We don't kill each other – even if that's something you seem to have forgotten yourself.'

Davies still looked very nervous as Berger placed his arm around the older man's shoulders and gave them a gentle squeeze. 'But you have just screwed up magnificently, and for that I want you back with us where we can keep a proper eye on you.' Berger's disclosure appeared to calm Davies. 'Your roaming days are over.'

'And everyone else?'

The question was asked in such a pathetic way that Berger let out a chuckle. 'Of course. But their time of running amok ends now, understood? From this moment on, both you and they will be kept on a tight leash, because the road before us has just become rockier, and because the project... its time has come.'

Davies's mouth dropped open and he shook his head in disbelief. 'What? That's impossible. It can't be.'

'Apparently it is,' Berger replied, clearly enjoying Davies's disbelief. 'I was given the word just a few short days ago and the galactic wheels have already been set in motion. A new beginning is upon us, and with it everything we know changes in one fell swoop. The good news for you though is that Avi Legrundy was able to pass on to us the information that was needed before she got caught. Not everything, but enough... although time is truly of the essence now, as you can imagine.'

Berger was smiling like the Cheshire cat. 'Who would have thought, all those thousands of years ago, that *we* would be the ones destined to be here at this very moment. The odds against it must be in the billions, yet here we are.' An unsettling and devious grin now contorted his lips. 'Time for a change of management, wouldn't you say?'

Davies looked shell-shocked by the revelation. Berger gave him another squeeze around the shoulders, then began to lead him into the kitchen and towards the back door of the chalet. 'How long do you have left on the lease for this place, John?' he asked, grasping the door handle.

'Another six months,' Davies replied.

'Good, that leaves more than enough time. Now, let's go and see your family, shall we?'

Davies still looked bewildered as Berger pushed open the back door and nudged him through. 'And here they are.'

Stefani Mitchell and the others from Davies's fallen clan stared at him with bulging eyes. Their mouths were wide open but not one of them could move or say a word due to the nylon ligatures securing them to the trees and the fact that their mouths were stuffed with rags.

'There you go, John.' Berger smiled. 'Your family reunited again.'

A rifle butt slammed down hard onto Davies's head, sending him tumbling down the back steps to collapse in a heap, and the man holding the rifle followed him down with the gun raised. Before Davies could react, he received another painful blow to the head from the rifle butt, and he lay helpless on the fresh snow as a plastic cable tie was slipped over his wrists and tightened.

The others were now screaming, but the noise was barely audible over the growing roar of heavy wind. Davies was hauled upright by the rifleman and a man appeared around the side of the chalet wearing a red puffer jacket and holding a Glock handgun aimed at the hapless group of bound prisoners. Davies was then summarily shoved up against the only unoccupied tree and tied to it securely.

'I thought you said you didn't kill your own,' Davies yelled over the howling wind.

For a moment Berger stood there motionless and expressionless except for wincing slightly as the icy evening wind lashed against his face. Then he said, 'We don't, but you and your pathetically weak group aren't part of us. I'm not sure you ever were, John, and you have let us down for the last time.'

As a dirty brown rag was thrust into the prisoner's mouth and a piece of duct tape slapped over it, Berger pulled out his phone and snapped a few pictures. 'Just for the memory,' he explained as another smile crept across his face. 'I'm sentimental like that. And as for your nephew, this Alex Harker, I'm sorry to say we'll have no choice but to kill him.' He raised one hand and clicked his fingers. 'And, just like that, the last of your bloodline will be snuffed out. Simply tragic.'

Berger turned to the rifleman and pointed a finger at him. 'Cut out their tongues and break all their legs,' he yelled above the wind. 'The chalet's rent is covered for the next six months, so once they're dead, the local wildlife should dispose of their bodies.'

Above the whistling wind the howl of a wolf could be heard. Berger raised his finger and pointed it at Davies. 'I'm not one for long farewells, so goodbye.'

With that he headed back into the house, calmly dialling a number into his phone. He waited to be connected as the sounds of moaning interspersed with the roaring of the wind could be heard from outside.

'It's me. It's done and I am heading back to you now… I know time is short but the lead Legrundy gave us is solid and I have just the man to follow it up… No, not over the phone, but you already know him. He's doing a piece of business for me even as we speak, but I'll call him soon… Don't worry, we'll get there in time.'

Berger finished the call and slipped the phone back into his pocket before heading through the chalet to the front door. He opened it halfway and paused momentarily. *It's a shame*, he thought, relishing the warm atmosphere of the room. *I really would like to know what will kill them first: the cold, or the blood loss, or the wolves.* He shook his head and proceeded outside, in the direction of the jeep parked just up a side road. *That would have been nice.*

Chapter 6

The little girl ran along the pavement in the French town of Le Havre, smiling in excitement and clinging to the dog lead as hard as her small hands could manage. At the end of it, the stout Papillon puppy seemed just as eager to be outside.

This latest addition to the family had been brought home just days earlier, and so far it was proving much more fun than Cassius, their balding, half deaf, half blind cat with only three teeth left – but sadly a full set of sharp claws.

How was it possible, the little girl wondered, to have a pet that was only good for scratching her hands whenever she tried to stroke it? No, Alphonse here was definitely much more fun, and he liked spending time outside with her, rather than wanting only to curl up on the sofa and stink up the house with a smelly litter tray, which she herself had to empty every day!

The girl came to a sudden stop alongside Alphonse as the dog became rather enamoured of a freshly painted lamppost.

Still smiling, she waited patiently as he did his business against it. *That's right, Alphonse. Do your thing, and when we get home we can go and chase that silly, boring cat around the house.*

The thought made her giggle, and when Alphonse attempted to drag her away, she pulled at his lead and wagged her finger. 'No, Alphonse, we have to wait here for *Maman*. She'll be here very soon.' As she continued to talk to her new best friend, she was oblivious to the loud voices emerging from inside the nearby jeweller's shop with the small, varnished sign reading 'Madame Bisset' hanging above it.

'Flawless, absolutely flawless,' Madame Bisset exclaimed loudly, sounding extremely happy. 'The fire within them is exquisite and the cut...'

Her customer, Herbert Pelosi, watched his potential buyer enthusiastically rotate the five-carat diamond between her fingers, as she scrutinised it with a magnifying loupe nestling in her right eye.

The woman lowered her hand and let the loupe drop into it. 'Where did you get these?'

A barely noticeable smile formed on Pelosi's lips. 'They weren't stolen, if that's your concern.'

'Ah, conflict diamonds. No difference to me.' The woman's head tilted back and she returned his smile. 'How many do you have?'

Pelosi nervously looked over at the intimidating six-foot man wearing jeans and a navy zip jacket, sitting spread-legged on the edge of the leather couch and staring at him as if he was a juicy appetiser ready to be gobbled up.

'Don't worry about him,' the woman said soothingly. 'He only gets involved if a deal starts to get lively.'

Her words seemed to do little to reassure Pelosi, but he gave an understanding nod as she leant across the oak partner's desk, her hands folded.

'So, how many of these do you have?'

The small jeweller's shop barely had enough room to accommodate all three of them given the glass display cases against every wall and the oversized desk they were sitting at. With a noticeably shaking hand, Pelosi reached into the pocket of his thick, grey duffel coat and pulled out a sizeable, purple velvet pouch. He carefully placed it on the table before her, then pulled on one of its drawstrings to release a batch of shimmering diamonds onto the green leather surface. 'Forty of them,' he said proudly, spreading out the stones with care. 'And all of the same quality.'

The woman's eyes lit up intensely and she returned the loupe to her eye and began moving it from stone to stone with enthusiasm. 'Yes, yes, these are excellent.'

A few minutes of silent examination followed, then Madame Bisset sat back in her chair and rotated the loupe between her fingers. 'I can offer you two hundred thousand.'

Her offer hung in the air like a bad smell and, still looking nervous, Pelosi gave a slight shake of his head. 'They're worth at least five.'

The woman stared at him blankly. 'Maybe in the shops, but I take a cut to get them there. And besides, let's not forget where they come from.' She looked over at the goon on the couch and he now sat upright slowly, glaring at Pelosi. 'Things aren't going to get lively, are they?'

Pelosi glanced over at the man and then gulped anxiously. 'Two and a half?'

She began to make clicking sounds with her tongue, swaying her head slowly from side to side. 'I don't think so but, if you insist, I could take these off your hands for nothing.'

The veiled threat was made worse as the man began to tap his large index finger impatiently upon his thigh.

Pelosi gulped again and his breathing began to quicken as he offered a nod. 'Two hundred thousand then.'

'Good decision,' the woman replied with an arrogant smirk. She then motioned to the goon, who stood up and unlocked a walnut panel in the wall behind him to reveal a small cast-iron safe.

'Now, let's seal it with a drink to show there's no hard feelings.'

She reached into her desk drawer and retrieved a half-empty bottle of cognac along with three crystal tumblers, which she set out before her. The goon's head re-emerged from the safe and he brandished a hefty stack of Euro notes.

'I have to say, you're a lot smaller than the usual delivery man,' the woman remarked, eyeing Pelosi's diminutive frame as she poured three glasses. 'Something of a draw-back in your business, I would have thought.'

Pelosi gave a weak smile, then he gestured to the pouch of diamonds still on the desktop. 'It's not about the size but the quality, wouldn't you agree?'

This remark had the woman grinning, and with a nod she held the tumbler of whisky out towards him.

But the offer received a wagging finger from Pelosi. 'I'm teetotal,' he said, whereupon the glass was retracted and she reached once more into her desk and placed a juice carton before him. 'Maybe this will be more to your liking.'

The goon, meanwhile, dropped the wad of notes in front of him, picked up one of the drinks and joined the woman in raising his glass. Pelosi tore off the straw, pricked it into the silver hole and raised the small carton in the air.

'*Santé*,' the woman announced before she and the goon both slugged their drinks down, while Pelosi gave a cautious suck on his straw.

'And one for the road,' the woman declared, picking up the spare tumbler and swigging it as quickly as the first. 'Now, I would be happy to take any more of these darlings off your hands if they come along,' she said, scooping all the diamonds back into the pouch. 'But the price remains the same, given their... exotic origin.'

Pelosi sat expressionless for a moment, as all signs of nervousness evaporated, then he placed his drink carton down on the table and clasped his hands together. 'I have to applaud your negotiating skills, but your lack of security surprises me.'

The woman immediately glanced over at the open safe, with its further bundles of cash lying inside.

'Not really, as you would need a blowtorch to get into that,' she replied confidently.

Pelosi's whole demeanour continued changing as he sat up straight in his chair, with both arms draped casually over the armrests. A look of disdain now crept across his features.

'That's not what I was referring to.'

The larger man was now starting to sweat profusely. His lips tightened as he lurched forward, gripping his stomach.

'This building's security was child's play and that lock on your desk isn't worth the steel it's made out of.'

As the goon now fell back onto the couch, writhing in pain, the woman also began to tremble. She stared over at the half-empty bottle, then seized it in her hand only to drop it to the floor before grasping at her chest.

'What did you put in it?' she choked out, as she now gripped her left arm, her whole body becoming rigid.

'In your case, I think a heart attack.'

Pelosi rose from his chair and casually plucked the velvet pouch of diamonds off the table, sliding them back into his coat pocket. He then pulled out a black plastic bag from his other pocket, sucked the last dregs of his juice and dropped it into the bag along with the stacks of Euros.

'Mr Berger sends his condolences, but he believes you've started to become too greedy,' Pelosi announced, stepping over the goon thrashing about in agony and beginning to bag the rest of the cash from the safe. 'And greed always leads to conflict, does it not?'

With the last stack of notes secured, Pelosi looked down at the convulsing woman, then he leant over and wiped away the single tear rolling down her cheek. 'First rule of business: the customer is always right.'

With a smile he turned and made his way past the now motionless goon to the opposite side of the desk. 'The second rule is never underestimate the competition.'

As he watched the last moments of life draining from the woman, the mobile in his pocket began to vibrate. He retrieved it and took note of the number displayed, before tapping the green accept button.

'Yes?'

'You're needed,' a voice said coldly. 'Is our business concluded?'

Pelosi looked down at the woman as her body slowly collapsed forward and her head struck the desktop with a hard thud. 'It is now, Mr Berger.'

'Good,' Berger continued. 'We need you here in the UK.'

Pelosi eyed his steel Tag Heuer watch and then made his way out of the shop. 'I can be there soon,' he said, only just missing the puddle of dog urine as he hurried onto the street, glaring menacingly at the giggling little girl holding the puppy's leash. 'Give me a couple of hours.'

There was a slight pause on the line before Berger's cold voice returned. 'Quick as you can, then. Your particular talents are required.'

Chapter 7

Dark blue waves lapped foamy brine against pale grey rocks below as Harker gazed out across the Strait of Gibraltar towards the northern tip of Africa, so clearly visible upon the horizon on this glorious morning. With only nine miles separating the two continents, it must have seemed such a tease to early African travellers yearning to know what lay beyond the towering limestone cliffs they could only see but not touch. Although in the modern era it was only a short trip by boat, back then it must have seemed like a formidable expanse that only dreamers might contemplate and only conquerors dare to attempt.

Harker closed his eyes and inhaled a deep breath of clean salty air, enjoying a moment of tranquillity before once again this was shattered by the sounds of raised voices from a blue Portakabin behind him.

They had taken the jet from Bristol after a frustrating delay due to engine problems, most of which time Harker had spent snoozing on an uncomfortable airport lounger, until the pilot had finally woken him and informed him the issue had been resolved. The good news, though, had become tainted when Doggie appeared, looking far more refreshed, and explained that they had both been allowed access to the far more comfortable business-class lounge.

'I didn't want to wake you,' was the dean's excuse, but the wry smile accompanying his apology had only served to rile Harker further. So he didn't feel too sorry for him when, during their landing at Gibraltar airport under a heavy wind, Doggie had gripped the edge of the armrest, his knuckles turning white, as their aircraft was buffeted back and forth until both its wheels touched the runway.

The trip had taken a little under three hours, followed by a short ten minutes' drive in a rental car to Europa Point at the southernmost tip of the Rock. There Doggie had insisted that Harker wait until he had cleared the air with Barbara Holtz. But after five minutes of raised voices, this didn't seem to be making any difference.

With his patience beginning to fray, Harker took a final deep breath of invigorating air and headed over to the Portakabin, which was guarded by a local policemen, courtesy of Xavier Botha. After an approving nod from the officer, Harker rested his hand on the door handle, then paused as he hearde paused at he dfjdefl; his name being yelled in anger for the umpteenth time. It was obvious now that Dr Holtz had far from forgiven him his past transgression, and with a dismayed shake of the head he swung the door open and entered.

Harker barely had time to close it behind him before a gravelly voice yelled at him accusingly. 'You've got a lot of nerve showing your face here, Alex Harker.'

Barbara Holtz was not a woman to be trifled with. Hailing from Glasgow, she had a brash, unyielding Scottish accent and – despite a five-foot-two physique – lungs that could have frightened a fully grown elephant seal during mating season.

'It's good to see you too, Barbara,' Harker replied, mustering a smile despite Doggie's discouraging frown.

'Not long enough since last time,' Holtz growled, taking a moment to straighten the blue T-shirt tucked into her worn khaki shorts. 'I hoped never to see your miserable-looking face again.'

When confronted with someone who would clearly have your guts for garters, there are only two things you can do: either grovel profusely or fight back in earnest. And given the woman's loathing for anyone showing the slightest weakness of character, Harker opted for the latter. 'Believe me, the feeling's mutual. But seeing as your life may be in severe danger, I decided it was worth making the trip.'

That single sentence produced more of an effect than Harker expected. Although she was still visibly fuming, Holtz's demeanour appeared to soften – although not by much.

'So you're the one to thank for the policeman at my door, are you? Yes, Tom here already told me.'

'As I was just explaining to Barbara, we believe the deaths of Dr Khan and Dr Wexler may not have been as accidental as they might appear,' Doggie ventured.

'Ridiculous! Marsouk smoked like a chimney, so he was just begging for a heart attack, and as for Michael...' Holtz paused, and for the first time she looked concerned. 'Well, he's been suffering from depression on and off for years.'

'So you did know them both?' Harker said.

'I took over their positions here in Gibraltar,' she replied glibly, resuming her defensive stance, 'and that's that.'

'Perhaps... or perhaps not,' Harker replied, whereupon she began to shake her head and clench both fists tightly.

'*Perhaps* rubbish, and anyway, I told you last time we saw each other that I never wanted to see your face again.'

The event leading to the breakdown in their relationship had been unfortunate but in no way deliberate on Harker's part. During a function at Cambridge University to honour a selection of renowned archaeologists from around the world, Harker had been asked to make a welcoming speech to his fellow scholars. The short speech had gone fine, and even received a few laughs in the right places, but it was the selfie he had taken whilst giving it, and then posted on the university website, that had caused all the trouble. The photo had not only included himself but also the next speaker, Barbara Holtz, waiting just offstage, who had arrived late for the event and was still frantically slipping into her evening dress. The white, shiny gleam of Barbara Holtz's bottom was captured in the lower left hand corner of the frame and the image had managed to remain on the website for a whole twenty-four hours before being noticed and then deleted by Harker himself. Unfortunately for Barbara, most of the evening's attendees – and pretty much the entire student body – had viewed it by then. She had never forgiven him, believing wholeheartedly he had done it deliberately. As university professors within the archaeology department, there had always been a healthy rivalry between them, but after the 'Moongate' scandal, as it became known, their relationship had descended into a deep hatred on Barbara's part. She had left Cambridge a few months later to focus on fieldwork, and even though her teaching position had always been considered temporary, Harker suspected her departure had been hastened by his embarrassing faux pas.

'Now, Barbara, I swear I never took that photograph deliberately. And as I've said so many times before, I am truly sorry about it. Isn't it time now we put all this behind us—' He stopped mid-sentence as Holtz's eyes widened at his choice of words. 'What I mean is can you please forgive me?'

Barbara Holtz eyed him with deep suspicion for an uncomfortable further ten seconds and then, with a shrug, she offered him a nod. 'Fine, Alex, but don't ever expect us to be great friends.'

As Harker mouthed a thank you, Doggie's face was already lighting up with satisfaction.

'You see, it's all now water under the bridge,' he said, before transferring his full attention to their hostess. 'No one even talks about Moongate anymore.'

That flinty-eyed look of annoyance was back and Holtz briefly rubbed her forehead in frustration before glaring back in Harker's direction. 'What do you want, Alex?' she snapped.

This was probably as civil as it was likely to get, so Harker grasped the opportunity before Doggie – now looking somewhat embarrassed – could manage to screw things up any further.

'I was hoping you could take a look at this.' He pulled out his smartphone, brought up an image of the tattoo Mr Cordon had sent him a few hours earlier, and passed it over to her. 'What do you make of it?'

At first Holtz gave the image only a fleeting glance, but then, squinting, she began to study the screen with closer scrutiny. 'Where did you take this?' she asked, not bothering to look at him but transfixed by the photo.

'It was taken from the body of a dead man,' Harker announced, not yet wanting to confuse the issue by describing the corpse's bizarre appearance. 'Tattooed on the *inside* of his skin.'

'What?' Holtz gasped, appearing uncharacteristically flustered.

71

'The man had clearly been tortured, and we believe he revealed your name, along with those of your former – now deceased – associates, to his tormentors.'

Holtz now glanced up at him in shock. 'Why?'

'That's why we're here, Barbara. We're hoping you can tell us,' Harker replied, making his way over to her and staring down at the phone. 'Do you know what it says, and what that symbol of a bag means?'

Holtz said nothing but used her fingers to zoom in on the writing.

'We believe it's cuneiform. Or some form of it anyway,' Doggie added, joining the group huddle, 'but not one we recognise.'

Holtz's lips now quivered as she read out each line in no more than a mumble, and as Doggie opened his mouth to say more, it was Harker who deterred him with a subtle shake of the head.

For over a minute they both stood as Holtz traced her finger across the text, line by line, until she reached the end of it. Then her eyes trailed away from the screen, clearly now in deep thought.

'You really think Michael and Marsouk were murdered?'

All Harker wanted to know was what the text actually said, but he realised the woman was now displaying a fragility he had never witnessed in all the time he had known her. 'Honestly? I'm not sure, but yes… maybe.'

There was now genuine concern in Holtz's eyes.

'What does it say, Barbara?' Harker urged gently, leaning in towards her ever so slightly. 'What do you know?'

She glanced back at him ashen-faced, then she walked over to her desk, plonked herself down in the seat and placed his phone on the table in front of her.

'Three months ago, Michael and Marsouk invited me onto a dig which was being privately funded. Marsouk left a few days later without giving a reason, but not before putting me in charge of the project. Michael and I have been working on it together, but a few days ago' – Holtz began to bite her lip anxiously – 'we had a disagreement over the direction the project was taking, and he chose to take a few days off to consider his position. Then I heard he had committed suicide. I honestly didn't know what to think. Michael always seemed tightly wound-up at the best of times, but I'm now beginning to think it could have been something to do with what he and I were at loggerheads about.'

Holtz was obviously feeling serious regret about something and Harker placed his hand softly on her shoulder. 'Barbara,' he asked in a gentle tone, 'what's going on here?' He then glanced over at Doggie, who was still lost in thought, probably mulling over any potential value to the university the text may offer more than anything else. 'Barbara?' he said again.

Holtz slowly looked up at him and her finger began tapping on the table nervously. 'I'm not meant to say… I signed a non-disclosure agreement.'

Harker could see she was truly uncomfortable and he now gently picked up the phone. 'Two people are already dead so I think it's time you signed a new nondisclosure agreement, with us.'

Holtz's eyes dropped down to the table for a moment, then with a deep breath she looked up at him. 'We found something at the dig. Something… exquisite… along with that same text.'

Her response was as vague as it was intriguing, and Harker now began to push a little harder. 'What exactly did you find?'

She continued to appear unconvinced, as if fretting over whether or not to say any more. But then she suddenly slapped her hand down on the table and rose to her feet. 'I think it's best that I show you.'

Before Harker could say more, she was heading for the door, only glancing back to give them a beckoning jerk of the head before stepping out into the morning sunshine.

Harker and Doggie scrambled through the doorway to find her gazing towards the blue expanse of the Strait of Gibraltar, her nose raised as she sniffed the air.

'So where is this dig site?' Harker asked, clasping his hands in anticipation.

Holtz offered him a weak smile, then raised one hand out towards the water. 'Right there.'

Doggie was squinting dramatically, darting his head back and forth in an attempt to gauge exactly where she was pointing. He had not yet clocked on when Holtz turned to face Harker.

'Tell me, Alex,' she said with a smile, appearing relieved to speak at last about the secretive dig site, 'how are your scuba-diving skills these days?'

Chapter 8

The water was far colder than it looked. Harker flipped backwards off the small dinghy into the calm brine of the Strait of Gibraltar and immediately pumped his fists in an effort to warm them. The wetsuit he had been provided with was doing its job, and although the diving spot was no more than thirty metres offshore, the morning sun had heated the neoprene somewhat during the brief trip, offering additional comfort. Wearing a wetsuit, especially one as thick as this, felt as if your whole body had been wrapped in multi-layered cellophane. On land it felt restrictive – every movement announced by the creaking of stretched plastic fibres – but still yielding to his movements. The tank, on the other hand, was another thing altogether. Heavy and cumbersome, like a backpack full of weights that could easily throw you off balance – and even topple you to the ground if your attention lapsed. Fortunately, once underwater, that all changed. The feeling of weight vanished and the tanks helped to keep one straight and level due to their streamlined design, and although the wetsuit could feel sluggish at times, it also offered a sense of protection, like a cocoon keeping you safe.

Of course, this was merely an illusion and the blade of an engine propeller would cut through it like butter, so when Harker noticed the underbelly of a boat streaming past in the distance, he began to get moving.

With a kick of his black fins he swam over to join Barbara Holtz, who was just below the surface and grasping the thick nylon shot line descending from an orange buoy into the darker water below. The addition of a full-face mask, with two-way radio incorporated into it, was crucial so far as Harker was concerned, and he was glad that this equipment had been provided. The reception could be crackly at times, and the noise of air being sucked in and out a distraction, but it was essential as it allowed the divers to converse underwater.

'You OK?' Holtz asked as he joined her and grabbed hold of the nylon cord as well.

'It's like riding a bike – you never forget,' Harker quipped confidently, even though it was almost five years since his last dive, and he was feeling a bit twitchy about the prospect. It was an odd thing because, despite suffering from mild claustrophobia since childhood, his diving had never been affected. Locked in a small room, the sense of the walls closing in on him was difficult to stave off, but out here in the water, surrounded by a vast expanse of hazy blue ocean stretching in every direction, there was only a sensation of freedom and complete free will to go wherever one chose. Or, more accurately, wherever Barbara Holtz now chose to guide him.

'Good, let's begin the descent,' she replied before letting the air out of the jacket, to descend at a slow pace. 'If you feel the need for stabilisers, then let me know. That's nothing to feel embarrassed about.'

Quite how the analogy of bicycle stabilisers could be applied here was lost on Harker, but he understood what she meant as he began following her down the rope into the dark blue depths and the buffeting motion of the surface overhead disappeared from view.

'I'm surprised it's been such a while since you last dived. You were always a keen one when I last knew you.'

'Just haven't had the chance,' Harker replied, his voice crackling through the two-way radio. 'The last few years have been… busy.'

'Well, at least you've got more spirit in you than Tom.'

Upon hearing that the dig location lay under almost fifty metres of water, Doggie had immediately opted to sit this one out. His offer to keep an eye on things topside had not come as a surprise, because his only experience of diving was in the deep end of the local swimming pool. He therefore chivalrously offered to take refuge in a bistro restaurant overlooking the water nearby, declaring that it would allow him a complete view of the area – for their own safety, of course – and this had nothing to do with the excellent cuisine and fully stocked bar.

'A prawn cocktail followed by pan-fried seabass is the closest I like to get to the sea, Alex,' had been his parting words as Harker had joined Holtz on the rubber dinghy. And it wasn't a bad thing either, for a fifty-metre dip was considered a deep dive by anyone's standards, and a lack of experience at such depth could quickly turn into tragedy at a moment's notice. It was not an environment for the timid or uninitiated.

'It's really not his cup of tea,' Harker explained, 'and given you won't tell us exactly what our destination is, I can't blame him.'

'Like I said, Alex, you have to see it with your own eyes. But trust me, it's worth it.' Holtz's voice crackled and the radio sounded more muffled the deeper they went, which was likely due more to the pressure in Harker's ears than any interference.

He offered an acknowledging grunt as they moved hand over hand down the rope, settling into a steady rhythm with one another. He had forgotten how exposed one could feel when descending through an open body of water, with nothing to ground you but the rope in your hand. All around him was just misty blue water, with only twenty or so metres of visibility. It was a sensation similar to that most first-timers felt, and which with further dives quickly turned into excitement and a sense of freedom. Unfortunately, Harker's five-year absence had him tumbling back now to the feelings of his first dive, and as something began to loom out of the shadows below him, he felt a pang of nervousness.

'What's that?'

Holtz gave no reply as they continued descending, and then, like an old fuzzy analogue television screen that gets ever clearer as the reception grows stronger, the object began to emerge from the hazy gloom.

The outline of a small shipping vessel came into view beneath them. A row of viewing windows ran along its sides and at the top was a captain's cabin with another, larger set of windows and one seamless steering window at its front. The hull had been painted a dark blue and was peppered with limpets and other crustaceans that had made it their home during its service life. In contrast, the top half was plain white, and the front portion of its bow was partially dug into the rocky shoreline, no doubt as a result of the impact, and this was only a short distance from a shelf edge which plunged into the darker depths of the strait itself. Its final resting place might have been fortunate, but the long gash through its side was anything but. The build-up of green algae on the ship's upper half suggested it had lain down here for quite a time, and it shone with an array of green flecks as the available light from above reflected off its slimy surface.

'It's the HMS *Veritas*,' Holtz explained as they continued slowly down towards the bow of the sunken wreck. 'It's a passenger ship which collided with a container ship just two months ago. Everyone was saved but, as you can see, the vessel itself was unsalvageable. The Gibraltar government agreed to leave it down here while we conduct our work.'

'That's the dig site?' Harker asked, surprised not only that this ship was such a source of interest but that the government had allowed a wreck to remain here, given the heavy traffic passing above it on a daily basis.

'It's not the ship itself we're interested in.' They continued deeper, down past the looming bow and towards the circular lead weight their shot line was connected to on the seabed. 'It's what it crashed into.'

Harker said nothing but instead scoped out the expanse of sunken metal. To some the whole sight might be daunting, and approaching an object so much bigger than oneself could make you feel naked and unprotected, but personally he was finding it invigorating. It also helped that no one had died in the accident, because frankly that would have creeped him out. As they reached the grey muddy seabed, he now had a view of what lay on the other side of the vessel, despite the swirling muck disturbed by their presence. There was barely a crack between the bow itself and the rock forming the shoreline and he now struggled to control his breathing as he gazed upon the sight. The ship's impact on hitting the limestone rock had left a scattering of jagged rubble below, revealing a sight that was as unnerving as it was fascinating. A large elliptical eye, four metres across, stared back at him. Although at first glance it appeared to have been engraved directly into the rock, it soon became evident that it was a separate structure embedded within the shoreline itself.

'Is that Egyptian?' Harker exclaimed in astonishment as he gazed at the huge eye and noted the shape reminiscent of a pharaoh's death mask such as adorned the numerous sarcophagi he had examined in the past.

'Not quite. Follow me,' Holtz replied, the radio's crackling now becoming more intense, and she began making her way around the left side of the ship to a secondary nylon rope which led directly inside the deep gash running the length of the sunken wreck. She waited for Harker to join her, then pointed inside. 'It's a bit tight here, so be careful.'

Holtz pulled herself effortlessly through the metre-wide gap and Harker followed, even as a feeling of dread started to take hold of him. He had never made a wreck dive before, and as he approached the dark opening, he was relieved to see a row of vacuum lights illuminating their way. The hull had been fully ripped out and appeared to be empty apart from a few scattered pieces of machinery and engine parts.

'We decided to cut through the hull so as to gain access,' Holtz explained, as they approached a square-shaped opening, its edges disfigured by the telltale drip marks from a welding torch. 'There was concern that we'd bring the whole thing crashing down if we attempted to pull the ship away from the rock.'

'What thing?' Harker asked, his breathing becoming heavy.

'This thing,' Holtz replied, coming to a stop by the square opening.

As Harker reached her, he could see what she was referring to. Past the cut-away hull a long stone corridor led deeper into the rock, constructed from individual rectangular blocks now visible due to the additional lighting that had been laid along the floor for the length of the corridor, like landing lights. The passageway itself rose a massive eight metres high and was some four metres across – it could have offered a truck easy access, had it not been underwater.

Holtz swam into this spacious opening and, without any need of instruction, Harker followed her dutifully. As they began to make their way along the mysterious, rectangular passage, he began to notice some sections covered in a tan-coloured plaster. The yellow light from the guiding vacuum bulbs gave the surface a slightly green tint, and the strange symbols covering it looked black in colour. They were like nothing Harker had ever seen before and he stopped to hover alongside them, attempting to recognise similarities with anything he already knew of.

'Keep moving,' Holtz urged him, glancing back. 'This is the least interesting part, believe me.'

Harker pulled himself away from his inspection and continued to follow her down the gloomy corridor, with only the yellow vacuum bulbs beneath them for guidance, since the sheer size of the space prevented their light from reaching the ceiling. It was like following a lit-up road, with no sense of the walls or ceiling.

After another twenty metres or so they reached the last vacuum bulb, where Harker could see a set of hefty, wide, stone-slab stairs leading upwards. He came to a halt as Holtz repositioned herself.

'We're coming out here,' she announced and Harker watched the bubbles from her respirator rise upwards and disappear through a silvery separation of water above. He then watched and waited as Holtz disappeared through it, before following her. With a kick of his fins he surged upwards and broke the surface to see her clambering shakily up the last few steps. Then she sat down on one, unclipped her gas tank and deposited it on the stone floor next to her with a clunk. She then pulled off her mask, placed it over the canister's nozzle and finally grinned down at him. 'Don't worry, the air's good here.'

With a nod Harker followed suit and, feeling the weight of the tank returning, crawled up the steps and sat down next to her, where he unclipped his tank and gently laid it on the top step, glad to be rid of its burden. Then hesitantly he slipped off his mask and drew in a deep lungful of air. It was musty and cold, like the inside of a mine shaft. Holtz stood up and placed both hands on her hips.

'Congratulations, Alex, you're one of the first people to enter this place in several thousand years.'

As Harker strained to see anything around them, Holtz moved over to the left and began fiddling with something. He heard a clicking sound and then the red glow of light filaments started to warm up, brightening the area before them. The bulbs gradually illuminated the walls they had been set against, and like during a briskly cresting sunrise, shadows and outlines he had not been able to make out began to slowly take shape. The glinting of the walls was the first thing he noticed, with the reflection of the yellow bulbs dancing off their shiny surfaces before giving way to an intense light.

Harker's heart began to beat ever more quickly in sheer awe, and he stood up as the entire room became flooded with the light reflecting off every surface.

Two gigantic ten-metre-high statues loomed before him. Their eyes were strangely elliptical in shape, and although the facial features were basically human, they were longer at the cheeks, with thick, unusually protruding foreheads. The necks were far thicker too, with their muscles extending halfway along the shoulders, and while the midriff was in proportion, the legs were far shorter and thicker than in an average human being. Each statue held a large bag with handles clenched in one palm, which was stretched out in front of it in a gesture of offering. The figures' complexions were not the shade of a standard gold bar, but an orange, almost honey colour, and the light reflecting off them seemed to fizzle in the yellow light as if it had a life of its own, sending a spattering of sparkles down onto the glossy surface of the floor below. The stone carving was masterful, with both muscles and skin appearing to possess weight, and there were even wrinkles at the bottom of the bag each statue clasped, indicating the weighty items they might contain.

'Those bags,' Harker remarked, 'are identical to the one on the tattoo.' He then turned back to take in more of the spectacular sight.

'Yes, they are,' Holtz replied. But as Harker continued to look on in wonder, it was not the bags that now gripped his attention. Of course, the statues were intoxicating in their beauty – you didn't need to be an archaeologist to appreciate that – but there was something else that caught his attention above all else. The statues' elliptical eyes were absolute dead ringers for the ones possessed by the strange-looking humanoid he had left back at the hospital.

It was only now that Harker turned his attention to the rest of his surroundings. The room itself was shaped like a pyramid sliced in half, with a flat wall running straight through the middle and at the far end the two statues stood in front. The three other walls, behind him and to the left and right, sloped upwards to meet at a single point in the middle of the upright one. Below them the floor appeared shiny and spotless, its polished granite surface seamless, as if cut from a single sheet of rock. And the near perfect reflection from it only served to add an extra sense of dimension to the room, like a giant, black floor mirror. The walls, however, were formed from a lighter, more crystalline type of rock and, although flat-surfaced, their glinting quality created a kind of starry effect as if gazing at a distant constellation. Without question it had been designed to impress anyone who entered. In fact, the entire room seemed designed for its effect on the point of view of anyone entering. The inward slope of the three side walls made the far wall appear as a sparkling black triangle, like a cross-section of a pyramid, with the statues standing guard in front of it. The floor was a mirrored highway to the pyramid, with the sloping walls above replicating a brilliant, star-filled sky.

Holtz now made her way further into the room and Harker, still dazzled by the sight, slowly followed her, trying to take in everything this magnificent space had to offer. There were no markings or drawings anywhere on the walls, but that was the whole point. The very room itself was the artwork.

As Harker took step after step, he noticed that his own reflection, which should have been directly beneath him, instead appeared way out in front, creating the illusion that he was walking on air. And, stranger still, barely a trace of water was left by his still drenched wetsuit.

'The floor is porous yet it manages to maintain its shine,' Holtz explained, clearly marvelling at the qualities of the material used. 'We had a geologist in here who couldn't tell us what it was, but he was convinced that it is not a naturally occurring substance. Alex... this material was *made* by someone.'

'What's a pyramid doing here in the Strait of Gibraltar?'

Holtz let out an amused chuckle. 'This is just the apex. So far as we can tell, there's another three floors below us, although we haven't accessed them yet.'

'Three floors?' Harker realised he was repeating her words like a parrot but he really didn't care. This dig was the most incredible place he had ever seen... And a pyramid of this quality, so far from Egypt?

'We've only been able to access them so far by underwater drones, but yes.'

'So they're all now flooded. Because of the ship?'

'Not sure,' Holtz replied, clearly enjoying Harker's enthusiasm at witnessing such a discovery. 'But we intend to find out.'

With no further explanation she headed towards the far wall, pressed her palm against it and a seamless doorway – ten metres high – slowly swung open to reveal a room on the other side, already lit with the same vacuum bulbs he had seen so far. Harker walked over to her, glancing up at the two intimidating statues flanking the doorway and, with an ushering hand from Holtz, he took a deep breath and headed on through.

Three uplighters had been placed around the room which, unlike the previous room, had vertical walls and a flat ceiling, all perfectly smooth with the same plaster as the other rooms. Harker gazed in wonder at the fine fresco that covered them.

'The state of the plasterwork is remarkable,' he declared – there were no cracks anywhere to be seen – and his observation had Holtz nodding in agreement.

'The whole place was airtight,' she explained, and she flicked her finger from one wall to the next. 'There was minor flooding when the ship uncovered this little baby, but so as far as we can tell this place has remained untouched since it sank into the sea.'

'Sank?'

'Yes, we've taken some ultrasounds around the whole area and at it appears at some point the limestone beneath it gave way, plunging the whole site into the strait itself. Our drone incursions revealed the lower floors sustained severe damage to the structural walls, but as you can see this area was unharmed.'

Harker now turned his attention to the host of images painted on the walls and it soon became clear he was looking at a story. The left hand wall bore a fresco of a city spread out on a number of islands, clearly a seagoing civilisation in the throes of being consumed by a giant tidal wave or tsunami. The right wall showed a peaceful green valley full of trees and vegetation, and at one end a huge tide of water cresting the mountains on either side as a foamy mass of turquoise blue water was about to come crashing down into the valley. In the foreground, groups of terrified onlookers cowered on their knees at the sight of their impending doom. A host of different animals – oxen, bears, lions and tigers – were all fleeing in different directions, and right in the middle a woman wearing a ragged-looking tunic cradled her baby protectively, with her eyes closed.

The middle wall, though, was the most fascinating of the three. Directly in the centre stood a gleaming gold pyramid with light bursting upwards from its apex, creating golden clouds which hung in a clear blue sky. On one side of the pyramid a line of men and women in tattered rags stood in a line. The old man at the very head of the queue was not dressed in rags, though, but in a brilliant, golden robe with intricate, bronze stitching, and had his hand outstretched towards the final individual on the other side of the pyramid, whose hand was also outstretched but holding a bag with handles identical to the one featured on the tattoo and on the statues in the other room. The fresco itself was an incredible piece of artwork but it was not the artist's talent that captured Harker's attention but rather the individual holding this bag. The strange-looking man was three times as tall as anyone else depicted, and he sported those now familiar elliptical eyes. Like the statues too, his neck muscles were tremendous and, though with the same short, stocky legs, he towered over everyone in the line before him. From his peculiar eyes a narrow beam of silvery light shone directly onto the bag itself, which he was in the process of passing down the line of waiting people to the robed man, whilst the image of a giant elliptical eye sat at the apex of the pyramid, shooting a ray of light upwards towards an orb-like planet high up in the sky above.

Harker expelled a light breath in awe as Holtz now moved closer towards him. 'Incredible, isn't it?' she said, seeming utterly captivated by the images herself. 'And that – the eye symbol – replicates exactly the Egyptian hieroglyphic denoting the Eye of Horus.'

'The Egyptian god who protected the rulers of Egypt from on high,' Harker reminded himself, before pointing up to the only area of missing plasterwork, at the top left side of the central wall. 'What happened there?'

'I don't know,' Holtz shook her head, 'but the late Dr Khan told me it was like that when he first entered this place – a few weeks before I was invited to join the dig. We did, however, collect some loose material from the broken edges.'

From the fact that she was now chewing at her bottom lip, Harker already sensed what she was getting at. 'Have you dated this place yet with radiocarbon testing?'

She now stared at him worriedly, and her lips trembled as if she wanted to scream out her next words. 'We did some tests, yes, and we discovered that it's essentially a form of cement, but not like anything we use today – or we have ever come across before, for that matter.'

Harker was now nodding slightly, encouraging her to get to the point. 'And how old?'

'Ten thousand years.'

'What?' he gasped, genuinely shocked by this revelation. 'But Egyptian civilisation goes back only just over five thousand.'

'I know, and yet here we see the Eye of Horus thousands of years before it was thought to have been first used.'

'Jesus,' Harker muttered softly, as he now realised what this meant. 'There was a civilisation before us – but who?'

At this Holtz looked increasingly excited. 'Not *who*, Alex,' she said, pointing to the figure holding the bag, on the left hand side of the pyramid, 'but *what*.'

As Harker gazed transfixed at the thick-necked giant with elliptical eyes, Holtz moved over to the single electrical cable supplying power to the lights and prepared to unplug it, grasping it tightly in both hands.

'And whilst your brain is melting like a fried Mars bar, take a look at this,' she declared.

With a firm tug she pulled the connecting cables apart and, although Harker expected to be plunged into total darkness, instead the whole room was bathed in a multitude of colours, twinkling from the surface of the fresco itself.

'My God,' was all he managed as he stood back and visually devoured the dazzling images that radiated in a luminescent glow. Where earlier the image of the city being deluged by flood had been, another image could be seen painted *over* it that had been invisible under the light. It showed the same island city, but this time it was alive and thriving. Boats circled the metropolis and headed along the many waterways leading in and out of the island's centre, and it was dotted with lighting that looked more like the electrical type of the modern era than any oil lamps of old. The opposite wall also shone brightly, but in stark contrast to the impressive island city. Instead it depicted men and women living in caves and huddled around campfires, in a scene typical of the hunter-gatherers described in history books. Deerskins, stretched over wood tanners were being tended to, as other folks guarded the outskirts of the settlement with spears.

Finally Harker turned his attention to the middle wall and what he saw there brought an unsettled feeling to the pit of his stomach. Dozens of those same figures with elliptical eyes towered above crowds of normal-sized people in chains, while giant whips were lashed down upon them as they gathered crops or cut through thick tree trunks with long, two-man saws. On one side a man was being roasted on a spit over an open fire, and on the other was a wooden cage containing numerous prisoners, each clawing at their bindings in a futile attempt to escape. On the horizon, in the centre, stood the outline of a city radiating a sunny glow composed of thin beams of light, with a procession of people heading towards it, as yet more giants stood guard looking down at them, grasping enormous swords in their hands.

Harker gave an involuntary gulp as he glanced between the contrasting images of everyday life depicted on the outer walls and these images of suffering and bondage at the centre.

Still captivated by the sight, he now noticed for the first time an additional glow coming from above and looked up to see a dazzling display of pinpricks of light on the ceiling. It took him just a few moments to realise what they were. 'Constellations,' he murmured in no more than a whisper.

At which point Holtz raised her arm and pointed upwards. 'Orion's belt, Ursa Major and the constellation of Leo,' she explained, then moved her finger over to the star cluster in the centre of it all. 'I used a special program to determine the date when those stars would have been in those positions, and the dates revealed are even more intriguing.'

'When?' Harker asked, feeling that giddiness that only growing excitement can yield.

'Eleven thousand years ago – at least.'

This last statement was the most incredible part, and Holtz then took it upon herself to voice exactly what Harker was already thinking. 'That's right, Alex. Whoever created this knew exactly how the stars looked twenty thousand years ago.'

Harker turned to study the golden image of the giant holding the whip and a chill rippled through his body. 'And who were they?'

'They are the gods,' Holtz replied despondently, 'and if this image is anything to go by, they were here long before we were.'

Even though such conjecture would fit perfectly amongst the pages of a conspiracy theory magazine, even Harker had to admit it was fascinating. The construction of such architecture alone was thousands of years ahead of anything mankind had built, and the degree of knowledge needed to so accurately show the constellations far exceeded anything that ancient hunter-gatherers could have accomplished.

As Harker brooded the possibilities, Holtz set the two electrical sockets back together again and those unsettling images disappeared as the original frescos reappeared on the walls and the room was bathed in light once again.

'And then there's this,' Holtz said, moving over to the left hand corner of the room and reaching down to a small clay pot with silver stars painted on its surface, into which she dipped her hand and pulled out a round gold-coloured object about six centimetres in diameter.

'Coins. The pot is full of them,' she explained, whereupon Harker moved over to her and took the coin from her hand. Its surface was scratched and weathered and it appeared to have been handled many times before reaching its final resting place here in the clay pot. On one side it bore that same image of the unblinking elliptical Eye of Horus, but it was the other side that truly made him feel giddy. Its surface had been engraved with exactly the same image of a bag as he had seen in the humanoid's tattoo and, even though he couldn't decipher it, the cuneiform script contained therein looked remarkably similar, if not the same.

'What I'd like to know is how a symbol sealed within this place for eleven thousand years shows up now on a tattoo.' Holtz stared at him grimly. 'And just as importantly, who was the tattoo's owner?'

As Harker rotated the coin between his fingers, he refused to look up at her, for he knew it was time to come clean about that strange-looking creature they had found – but without mentioning the Templars or the Mithras cult, since their involvement would only bring more questions. Instead he decided to stay focused on the more immediate aspects of whatever all this might mean.

'What I want to know is what *you* think this is,' he said, giving the gold coin in his palm another shake. 'Is it currency of some kind?'

The look in Holtz's eyes revealed that she knew he was sidestepping her question, but with a sigh she took his arm and drew him closer to the central fresco. She knelt beside it, pulling Harker down with her.

'Not currency,' she said, pointing to the man in the gold robe being offered a bag by the giant, 'but an invitation.'

He craned his head closer to the image and spotted what she was referring to.

In the robed man's hand a single coin was being held outwards. It could have easily been mistaken for a ring at a distance, and though too small to carry any symbols on it, in Harker's mind it could be nothing else. 'An invitation to what?'

'To meet with the gods… our makers.'

He stared at her blankly, then back at the depiction of a giant staring down at the little robed man. In all of history there were three questions that had primarily occupied the human mind. Questions that, although unanswerable, nevertheless surfaced at some point in their lifetime within the minds of almost every person who ever lived.

One: Where did we come from?

Two: Are we alone in this vast cosmos?

Three: Is there something else after death?

As Harker stared at the fresco in front of him, he suddenly wondered if those first two questions might have just been answered here, and his mind began to contemplate the possibilities even as a rumbling began to shake the ground beneath him.

It was then that the explosions started.

Chapter 9

'We have to go – now!' Harker yelled, as another explosion ripped through the underwater structure with such ferocity that both he and Barbara Holtz were thrown to the floor. Up above, jagged cracks began to appear in the ceiling. 'This whole place is about to come down.'

The initial explosion had slammed both of them hard against the fresco, and even though this had left Holtz more dazed than it had himself, an absolutely firm shake of her head showed she had already recovered. 'I'm not leaving this site,' she insisted. 'The earthquake will pass.'

This response was admirable but ridiculous, and so Harker grabbed her roughly by the arm and dragged both of them to their feet. 'That's not an earthquake,' he explained. 'Those are controlled charges.' Even as he spoke the plaster of the astonishing frescos began to rupture and crumble off the walls, dislodged by the shockwave of the second blast. 'Can't you tell?'

Perhaps Holtz was in shock, but as Harker stared into her eyes frantically he could tell that was far from being the only reason for her refusal. She simply could not bring herself to abandon this remarkable archaeological discovery. But after a thick chunk of ceiling crashed to the floor just metres away, Harker delivered a swift, energising slap across the face that caused her eyes to suddenly brighten and any further resistance to fade.

Plumes of dust began to cloud the air and the tremors beneath them began to intensify. Harker pulled Holtz with him through the still wide open doorway and into the main chamber, just as the gigantic stone statue off to his right cracked at its base, explosively hurling fragments of stone in their direction, before lurching forwards, its immense weight succumbing to gravity.

'Down!' Harker yelled, and he dived off to his left, with Holtz clamped tightly to him, an instant before the stone guardian slammed down hard onto the floor and fractured into chunks, its torso eventually coming to a rest just metres from where they lay.

The impact left the glassy granite floor with a thin crack across its centre, and seawater began to spray up through the gap with such pressure that it hit the ceiling before splashing down all around them.

'We have to reach those air tanks,' Harker yelled over the sound of crumbling rock. With no need of further encouragement, Holtz jumped to her feet and this time pulled him along with her.

Together they clambered across the floor, navigating between splintered stonework from the fallen statue, each step proving a massive effort as the whole structure continued to shake violently.

'We have to hurry,' Harker yelled and Holtz, never letting up the pace, shot him a filthy glance.

'You think?'

Oh, now you want to get out, Harker thought as they pressed forward, each now pushing the other onwards. On reaching the temple's entrance, the sight that greeted them churned his stomach with dread. Water was welling out of the gap and beginning to flood the whole room, seeming to take on a life of its own as it bulged through the opening with the sole purpose of swallowing them whole. Whoever had set the explosions had counted on breaching the protective vacuum of air within the pyramid, and it was rapidly being forced out now, allowing fresh seawater to fill the newly unpressurised gap.

The sight of the two diving tanks just below the surface brought a moment of relief. But with no time to rejoice, Harker reached down and grabbed one of them as Holtz seized the other, and pulled on his mask and regulator just before the icy cold, rising water washed over them. The current was strong and Harker grasped the edge of a stone step with one hand to stop himself being swept backwards. He then felt a grip on his leg and looked behind to see Holtz clinging onto him for dear life. Thankfully she had also managed to get her mask on, but without fins it was near impossible for her to push forwards. He grabbed her wetsuit with his free hand even as the current tried to sweep them both back into the inner depths of the pyramid.

Harker felt his hand begin to slip due to the watery onslaught, so he let go of Holtz and managed to secure his other hand on the stone edge, feeling her grip tighten around his leg. She then clambered up to join him and they both hung there as if dangling from a cliff's edge, though horizontally, and as the seconds passed, the current began to weaken. This change was all Harker needed and he now propelled himself forward and downwards into the long entrance chamber, with Holtz still clinging to him.

'The water's easing up,' he said, and continued to drag himself forward, stone by stone. Then, without warning, the current pushing against him ceased and the water grew calm.

'The temple must be filled up now,' he said, looking back at Holtz who had finally released her grasp and now began to float backwards.

'Barbara!' he called after her, but there was no response, so he turned back, grabbed her by the wrist and hauled her towards him. Holtz's mask was scratched but still intact, and he could see the fog of her breath, although it was apparent from a deep cut on her forehead that she had been hit by passing debris.

'Barbara, can you hear me?' he said again, but with no response. 'Shit,' he said. The water was murky and dark up ahead but he could make out some dim vacuum lights that had not been destroyed in the explosion.

It was a miracle the entrance passage had not collapsed. Tugging Holtz along by the scruff of the neck, Harker began to navigate his way from one surviving light to the next. Although he knew where he was heading, he nonetheless felt unsettled. There was something about this enclosed, murky darkness that jabbed at his senses and he wanted to get out of there as soon as he could.

With Holtz still in tow, he slowly made his way along the string of lights, while his mind began to unleash a completely irrational series of thoughts and images. Like the jaws of a great white shark appearing through the muddy water, or some unknown sea beast released from the depths by the explosions and about to gobble him up with its razor-sharp teeth.

Of course this was absolutely ridiculous and sheer mind play, but as he pushed onwards, he couldn't shake the feeling that he was being watched... by someone or something. *Don't let your imagination get the better of you, Alex.* He felt a sliver of comfort in knowing that if some sea monster did come up behind him, at least it might take a chomp out of Barbara Holtz first.

Harker shook this shameful if understandable thought from his mind and instead focused his full attention on the dark passageway extending before him. Before long they had reached the entrance. The cut-out access to the sunken ship was still intact, for which he thanked his lucky stars. He grasped the metal edge and pulled himself and then Holtz through the gap, so they were back in the far clearer water of the bow section.

Given the force of the explosions, it was a wonder that the ship had suffered so little damage. This suggested the charges had been placed somewhere outside, but exactly where, and why, Harker was happy to leave a mystery until they got back topside.

'Barbara, can you hear me?' As he held her up to face him, he noticed her head tilt from one side to the other, the condensation of her breath still building inside the mask. This weak acknowledgement came as a huge relief and he now held her closer to him. 'You're fine, Barbara. We got out safely. Just a slow ascent to the surface now and it's over.'

Holtz managed a relieved groan, though her eyes remained shut, and satisfied that she was as stable as could be expected, Harker now cast his gaze around the dark interior of the ship's bow, simply getting his bearings, until he fixed upon the jagged rip in one side, which was the only exit he knew about.

With Holtz still held tightly in his grip, and renewed zeal, he began to swim towards the opening, but then stopped just short of it, feeling a strong need to look behind him. He detected no movement, but for some reason there was a tightening in his gut that left him feeling nervous. He scanned the bow space further, and where a few of the lights had cut out he spotted something that made him shudder.

It was only a kind of shadow, a movement of light at the darkened limits of his vision, but as he continued to watch, the movement became more visible. Then something glinting sent a scattering of reflected light across his chest. He stiffened as whatever was stirring back there came into sight and launched itself towards them.

Harker's earlier vision of a giant pair of jaws resolved itself into the form of a scuba diver wearing a black wetsuit. Harker's tensed muscles relaxed – until he spotted the source of the glinting: a long, serrated diving knife pointing directly at them.

He instinctively offered the universal OK sign, forming a circle with his thumb and forefinger, but the diver offered no response. Now he was just ten metres away, with the knife still aimed towards them, and Harker went into action. They were still within reach of the rip through the hull's side, so he thrust Holtz forward and pushed her through the gap into the blue ocean outside. He then grabbed the edge of the opening and began to pull himself through, glancing back in time to see the diver's blade moving towards him. Harker quickly grabbed the man's wrist and the two of them began grappling with each other in the confined surroundings of the ship's bow. The scuba diver was strong and with his fins had covered the distance between them in no time, but being barefoot for Harker had its own strengths. The two men stirred up a sphere of swirling bubbles, as each fought for an advantage, with all their focus on the knife. Harker raised one foot and jammed it into the diver's groin, and although there was not much weight behind it, he used the move to push off with his legs as hard as possible, shooting back through the hull's opening while leaving the diver curled up in a ball as he cupped his groin. Harker's foot had hit its intended target but that would be temporary, so once through the gap he swam to one side of the torn steel and waited.

Within seconds the diver reappeared, knife hand first, and Harker went for the wrist and tugged with just the right timing so that the diver's hand was wrenched back against the jagged metal of the hull, sending the knife drifting down to the ocean floor.

The diver grasped at his hand, momentarily in pain, but that was all the time Harker needed. He slipped his fingers underneath the man's mask and ripped it off, allowing it to fall back inside the ship as the diver now panicked. Trying to get his bearings amidst a flurry of bubbles, Harker grasped hold of Holtz, and then the nylon shot line, guiding them both upwards towards the surface.

Harker had barely gone a metre before he felt a hand grab his ankle, and he looked down to see the diver clutching at his foot. The man's mask now off, his long black hair waved back and forth in the current as he desperately tried to see through squinting eyes.

Harker kicked away frantically, but it made little difference as the half-blind diver began clawing his way up Harker's legs, then his torso, before reaching behind his own waist and producing a small pouch with a clip on it. He then thrust this forward and clipped it onto Holtz's belt. Then he yanked the small cord hanging from the pouch and with it came a popping sound.

Before Harker had time to figure out what was going on the pouch inflated to an oversized plastic balloon and immediately shot upwards, dragging Holtz with it.

As Harker watched her disappear from view, he felt the diver's hands now slip around his throat, but instead of fighting the grasp, he reached down and ripped the breathing regulator from the man's mouth, sending him once again into a panic. He gave a tug on the shot line, raised himself upwards and unleashed one final kick to his attacker's head, using it simultaneously as a launch pad to begin his ascent towards the surface.

Harker looked down at the man still scrambling around to find the regulator, now hanging at his side, and he continued to slowly make his way back up the nylon rope.

To ascend so quickly from this depth could have the gravest consequences by causing decompression sickness, also known as 'the bends'. Nitrogen taken into the blood and tissues needed time be released while the diver was rising to the surface, and coming up too fast could kill if the shock was severe enough. At the speed Holtz had been travelling, together with her semi-conscious state, she would need emergency treatment at the very least. As Harker continued his steady rise upwards, he hoped for the best.

He glanced back down, expecting to see the mystery diver preparing to make another attempt on him, but to his surprise the man was nowhere to be seen. If he had drowned, his body would surely have been visible, the currents not being that strong.

Who the man was he had no idea, but whatever those explosions were all about, it was a sure bet that the diver had been involved. It was a strange occurrence because, if he had been attacked on land by a man wielding a knife, it would have made more of an impact. But the sluggish-ness of movements underwater had numbed the whole experience and, even though Harker was still panting and

stunned by the attempt on his life, nevertheless he felt…
OK. Certainly not as adrenalin-charged as one should feel
when one's life was under threat.

Harker continued slowly ascending, surrounded by the
hazy expanse of peaceful blue ocean, and it seemed his
mind was the only thing racing. The bizarre discovery of
a pyramid was astonishing here at the tip of Gibraltar, one
of the busiest shipping lanes in the world. This ancient
construction had lain there beneath the water as if waiting
to be discovered, only then to be destroyed in one fell
swoop.

Others would surely go back and re-excavate the site,
but how much of it would now be left was impossible to
say. What Harker had seen there provoked more questions than answers, for the place appeared to be from a
time before records began, and far outside the recognised
timeline of human history. Had an entire era of civilisation
become lost in time? And more importantly, how did
it come about? The notion of ancient gods and – dare
he think it – extraterrestrials was not something he was
ready to seriously contemplate. Either way, whatever the
Mithras cult had become embroiled in here was something
too important to ignore.

Harker paused for a moment and fingered the edge of
the gold coin in his wetsuit pocket, relieved to find it had
not dropped out on his escape from the depths. Content
it was secure, he continued towards the surface, grateful
to be leaving the murky depths of the Strait of Gibraltar
behind him.

Chapter 10

It was early evening as the grey Transit van slowly rattled along the narrow country lane, scraping its way past an overflow of lush, green hedges before turning into a pillared entrance to the left. The driveway was a loose gravel path, crackling and popping under the van's weight as it headed towards a small cottage situated on the far side of the grounds. With a well kept lawn, the entire property was surrounded by a row of lofty fir trees, allowing only the main entrance to offer any meaningful access and providing near total privacy for its occupants.

The van came to a stop, and a woman wearing a green Barbour jacket with jeans and black Hunter wellington boots climbed down from the driver's side. She paused to scan the open area for any sign of activity and, once satisfied she was alone, made her way up to the porch and knocked on the sturdy oak door.

There was nothing unusual about the cottage apart from maybe the black security bars at the windows, for with its red brickwork it looked like any other traditional residence around the small town of Devizes in Wiltshire.

The woman waited for a few seconds and was about to deliver a second knock when the sound of the latch releasing caused her to retrieve her fisted hand.

The door slowly swung open and a man poked his head out. 'Get lost, did you, Ms Kent?' James Willits asked with a smile, then he stood back and waved her inside. 'Xavier Botha is out on call. He's the one who summoned you, but he should be back soon. Come on, then.'

'Considering your last minute request, consider yourself lucky I got here so quickly.' Ms Kent's response was firm yet polite. Once she was inside, the oak door was closed behind her and re-latched. 'Has she said anything yet?'

Willits simply shook his head and began to make his way down a small lavender-coloured hallway lacking any pictures or decorations, with his visitor following closely behind. 'Apart from insults, racial slurs and death threats, she's not giving us much.'

Ms Kent managed little more than a conciliatory smile. There was far more on her mind just now than whatever bile the Mithras killer might be dishing up. 'Any news on the thing you found?'

Willits came to an abrupt halt, obviously surprised by how much his Templar counterpart already knew. As a rule there were no secrets amongst the Templars, but given the bizarre nature of the strange hostage they had found with Avi Legrundy and the close quarters in which the information had so far been held, he was surprised. 'So you've heard then?'

A dry smile formed at the corners of Ms Kent's mouth. 'Assassins and killers are one thing, James, but a living being with two hearts and the look of something extraterrestrial is not something you can keep quiet for long.'

The mention of the word 'extraterrestrial' had Willits frowning. 'We don't know what it is yet, but it didn't look human. The body is still at the hospital undergoing tests. Until we hear anything more, Avi Legrundy is all we have to proceed with. And as I said, she's not talking.'

He continued deeper into the cottage with Ms Kent still in tow. 'We tried sodium pentothal on her earlier this morning, but all she offered us was a step-by-step guide on how to skin a person alive without actually killing them. It seems she's highly resilient to truth drugs.'

'Charming' – Ms Kent raised an eyebrow – 'and clearly well trained. It's a shame we can't just use torture on her.'

This comment caught Willits off guard and he shot her a concerned look, but the mocking expression he received in response made him grunt. 'Life would be a lot easier if we were as brutal as she is. But even if that were so, I doubt it would make her any more talkative. To her credit, she's a tough one. I'm hoping an autopsy on the creature's body will give us something to work with, but until then we're basically on babysitting duty. I'll feel better once we get her somewhere more secure.'

'I'm not surprised.' Kent nodded in agreement. 'From what I've heard she's a big fish – quite the catch. Do you think the Mithras will try to get her back?'

'No doubt about it. Whatever she was up to was at the behest of her masters,' Willits replied. 'But there's no way they can now know where she is… not yet anyway.'

There was an urgency in his tone and Ms Kent addressed it immediately. 'I've managed to organise a more secure location for you,' she said, getting down to the reason she was there, 'but the van is limited as regards space, so be warned.'

'I suppose that means there's no additional prisoner box inside, then?'

'You suppose right, James,' she replied as they headed into a stone-flagged kitchen where a black Aga cooker was radiating heat, with a collection of shiny pots hanging from hooks above it. 'I was able to acquire some waist shackles though. They should do the job.'

He appeared unconvinced as they proceeded into the adjoining back room, which had a stout metal door in the far corner. He clicked his tongue. 'I'd rather you'd brought a straitjacket and a muzzle as well.'

The thought of such drastic restraints brought her to a halt with a disbelieving shrug of her shoulder. 'Hey, it's Big Daddy!'

'Who's Big Daddy?' Willits asked, silently greeting the guard wearing a black flak jacket and holding a 9mm Beretta, who hovered at the side of the security door.

'You know, that wrestler back in the eighties... size of a bull?'

'Wrestling really isn't my thing, Ms Kent. Be warned. She may be petite, but I'd wager she's just as dangerous as this Big Daddy of yours.'

'I'll bear that in mind – and call me Dana.'

Willits nodded and smiled. He'd only known this woman for a few minutes and he already liked her. The Templar organisation was vast but its key members were a relatively small group, and only family members or those who had earned complete trust were awarded the status of associate. In practice, it meant that outside of the Templars' inner circle many contacts could be relatively unknown. But all shared the same belief in a higher power, whether Christian, Muslim, Jewish, agnostic or any other religion – with the exception of Satanists, of course. The common belief in serving all of humanity for the greater good, whatever the price, was of utmost importance, and a conviction shared by all that served, even if they had never met before.

'OK, Dana, let me introduce you, but the sooner we get her moving, the better.'

Willits swung the door open to reveal a black woman with dreadlocks sitting comfortably on a clean bed covered by a cosy looking white duvet, but handcuffed by one wrist to the headboard. The woman offered no smile and merely stared at them both in disgust.

'Say hello to Avi Legrundy.'

'Hello, Ms Legrundy. My name is Dana Kent and I will be escorting you soon to a new location—' Dana began, but her sentence was cut short when Legrundy spat out a glob of saliva which landed within inches of the new arrival's boots.

'Well, it's nice to meet you too. You'll forgive me if I don't offer you the same greeting.'

Legrundy stared at her with nothing short of absolute contempt as Dana moved to the far side of the room, well out of spitting distance. 'Fortunately I've brought a few fashion accessories with me.' She pulled from her pocket a white bag with a plastic-mesh protector at the front and let it swing gently between her fingertips. 'This should look lovely on you.'

Legrundy looked neither impressed nor intimidated but continued to stare menacingly with those icy cold eyes. 'Dat's a waste of time,' she growled, seemingly overemphasising a thick Jamaican accent in an attempt to unnerve her captors.

'Oh, really?' Dana replied confidently, bringing the swinging bag to a stop. 'And why would that be?'

Legrundy's smile offered a flash of pearly white teeth. 'Because you'll never get a chance to use it on me.'

This sentence had barely left her mouth when the overhead light cut out, throwing the room into darkness, which immediately had Willits grabbing the torch from his utility belt. He switched it on and aimed it directly at Legrundy, who had not moved an inch, and apart from wincing under the bright beam she remained calm and still.

'Sam,' Willits called out and one of the guards appeared at the doorway, his torch beam sweeping the room. 'Where's Brian?'

'He's still outside, patrolling the grounds.'

Willits snatched the Samsung radio off his belt and raised it to his mouth. 'Brian, come in.'

The was nothing but static silence from the receiver as he repeated the request. 'Brian, can you hear me?'

No response.

Willits swung his torch towards Dana to find that she hadn't moved except to draw her Glock handgun, while the face bag had been discarded onto the floor.

'Dana, you stay here and keep an eye on her,' he ordered, gesturing at the still smiling Legrundy. 'If she so much as moves, then shoot her in the kneecap – do you understand?'

Dana gave a confirming nod as he moved towards Legrundy and shone the torchlight directly into her face. 'Be smart now, Avi, unless you want to walk with a limp for the rest of your life.'

The assassin simply jangled the handcuff around her wrist. 'I don't think it's me you should be worried about, Templar. It's you dat's in trouble.'

Willits ignored the taunt and turned back to the guard who was still standing in the doorway. 'Sam, you're with me.'

Willits closed the security door behind them, then both men drew their weapons and began to venture back towards the kitchen, their torches poised over their wrists to illuminate each man's line of fire.

All the lights in the house had gone out simultaneously, and even with the curtains open the kitchen remained dark and full of shadows. The torch beams cancelled out most of the natural light penetrating from the evening sky as the two men stealthily made their way through the kitchen towards the door leading to the front of the cottage. There was no sign of an intruder.

As they reached the kitchen doorway Willits stepped to one side and Sam to the other, before Willits warily peered around the edge of the door and into the hallway beyond.

His circular beam of torchlight slowly swept from left to right, starting at one wall and passing over a walnut desk before he paused it at the cottage's front entrance. The door stood wide open, and as Willits looked out to the gravel path outside, his torch beam caught the tip of something protruding from the floor. He lowered his torch to illuminate a boot, then swept it across the motionless body of a man wearing the familiar black flak jacket of his colleague. Spreadeagled on the glossy red-tiled floor with his arms draped across his face, he appeared to have been dragged there by the wrists before being dropped where he now lay.

'Brian?' Willits called out in a hushed tone, but there was no response. He shot Sam a warning glance and gave a swift nod in the direction of their teammate's body.

Without hesitation Sam pulled back from the doorway, his torch aimed in the same direction as his gun, then he moved slowly out into the hallway and towards the body, as Willits covered him from the kitchen.

Whoever had taken down Brian could only be hiding in one of two places. Sam knelt down beside his fallen colleague, his Beretta still aimed squarely at the open front door, whilst Willits slipped to the left of him and shone his torch up the staircase.

There was no one to be seen, but he cautiously proceeded up the stairs and onto the landing. After checking that the few doors up there were still locked, he headed back down to rejoin Sam and check how badly Brian was hurt.

Someone was playing games with them. Dangerous ones.

'Is he alive?' Willits whispered upon reaching them both, still glancing back up at the staircase even though his gun pointed towards the open front door.

Sam's torch was now switched off and Willits could only just make him out on the floor. There was no response, so Willits asked again, this time with an impatient growl. But all he got back was a deep grunt, so with his gun still aimed towards the front entrance he moved over and knelt down beside them. 'Damn it, Sam, talk to me!'

Willits raised his torch and shone it directly into the man's face. The sight caused him to gasp. The long, thin metal shard of an ice pick was buried deep in Sam's eye socket, his mouth hung open, and his dead body was being held upright by man who appeared to be wearing identical clothing to his own and lying on the floor... and it wasn't Brian.

The face of Herbert Pelosi grimaced back at Willits before slamming a second ice pick, almost concealed in his free hand, deep into his neck even as the Templar swung his Beretta towards him and fired.

Back in the secure room, Dana jerked in reflex as the sound of a gunshot somewhere in the cottage shattered the silence. She kept her gun trained on Legrundy, who was still smiling unnervingly and barely blinking under the dazzling torch beam shining in her face. From far off came a loud yet stifled groan, followed by a slow thudding of footsteps which grew ever louder as they approached the far side of the closed security door.

Dana took a few steps backwards and, confident that the handcuffed killer would not be able to reach her, pointed both torch and gun towards the door.

'James?'

Her breathing was getting heavier and although the barrel of her gun remained steady and unwavering, her heartbeat raced as adrenalin flushed through her system.

'I'm hurt. Don't shoot,' called a voice in little more than a moan. Then the door handle clicked and it slowly swung open.

James Willits was standing there, his stance rigid, and with blood running down his neck. His eyes kept fluttering.

Dana immediately raced over to him. 'What happened?'

'Oh, what I expected,' was the response, but it came without Willits moving his lips, and she now caught sight of the business end of a 9mm Beretta poking out from underneath Willits's arm and pointing directly at her midriff.

A blinding flash from its muzzle momentarily illuminated the whole room, whereupon a hand swung out and slapped Dana's gun to the floor and Willits's body dropped face first onto the carpet with a thud.

Pelosi stood in the doorway, still holding the Beretta and stained with the blood of his victims. He watched Dana stagger backwards, the torch dropping from her hand, before she lurched forwards, clutching her chest, and collapsed in a heap next to Willits.

'About time,' Legrundy said from the gloom as Pelosi calmly picked up the fallen torch and made his way over to the bed.

'You're lucky they didn't discover that tracking device implanted under your skin, or I'd never have found you at all.'

Legrundy instinctively rubbed at a small scar between two of her knuckles. 'I told them nothing,' she said defensively.

He shone the torchlight onto her face. 'From what I understand, that's not really the issue, is it?'

The smile on the woman's face began to fade and she actually now looked apprehensive as Pelosi continued, his face hidden in the shadows. 'Your obsession with killing Alex Harker has clouded your judgement, Avi. All you had to do was deliver the package to us and then you were free to do whatever you wished. But instead you decided to try and kill two birds with one stone, and in doing so allowed that very package to fall into the hands of the Templars.'

Even though Legrundy could not see it clearly, Pelosi was shaking his head in disappointment. 'You know how important that strange little being is to us, because without it the project is doomed to failure… So, they're not happy.'

Legrundy's apprehensiveness was now changing to real anguish and her eyes widened, despite the brightness of the torchlight. 'I still know where to look. It marked a place on the map.'

'Which I suppose the Templars also have in their possession,' said Pelosi. 'Well, you had better give me that location, hadn't you because, thanks to you, this Alex Harker has a head start on me, wouldn't you say?'

A Samsung smartphone was chucked into her lap and Legrundy immediately began tapping away at the Maps app.

'And how about our little friend? Do you know where he is?'

'I heard one of them mention a hospital, but I don't know which,' Legrundy replied, without looking up from the screen. 'But it has to be nearby as he'd lost a lot of blood.'

Pelosi waited for her to finish, then he snatched the smartphone from her hands and peered at it. 'Looks like I'll need to catch a flight, then, doesn't it?'

'Everything I've done was for the good of the Mithras. And if you'd just get me out of these,' she rattled her handcuffs, 'I can still be of help.'

Pelosi seemed unconvinced and replied in a chilling whisper, 'What is that mantra you're so fond of, Avi? *All debts must be repaid.*'

It was clear from her puzzled expression that this was not the rescue Legrundy had been hoping for, and her jaw began to tense. 'I have more information to give you.'

Pelosi laid the torch on the lacquered bedside table, then he sat down on the wooden stool next to it. 'Oh, I know,' he remarked, shoving the gun into one pocket and retrieving a knife from another. He pressed a button and the blade flicked outwards. 'You'll explain everything.'

Legrundy's look of real fear was a sight few, if any, had ever witnessed. As she watched Pelosi tap the blade gently against an open palm, she began to rattle her handcuffs again. 'Undo these tings. You 'ave nothing to fear from me.'

Pelosi emitted a playful chuckle and nodded as if in agreement. 'I know I don't, Avi. And as for the handcuffs, well, once we've had a further chat you can have faith that I intend to let you stretch your wings' – he leant towards her and into the direct light of the torch, his teeth clenched tightly and with drops of his previous victims' blood now visibly spattered across his face – 'and soar like a bird.'

Chapter 11

'And with respect, Alex, that's why I don't ever go scuba diving,' Doggie said, sitting back in his seat looking rather cavalier about the whole matter.

'To be fair, Tom, the chance of one being blown up and then running into an underwater knife-wielding killer is a rare possibility.'

'Maybe so, but tell that to Barbara Holtz. Poor woman could have been killed.'

As soon as Harker had reached the surface, he was greeted by a coastguard dinghy that had been dispatched within minutes of the explosions being heard. Such a timely response was impressive by anyone's standards, for they had already picked up the unconscious Holtz and administered what medical assistance they could. She was suffering from severe decompression sickness, as Harker had predicted, and had been rushed by ambulance to the only hospital in the area with a hyperbaric oxygen chamber, whose waiting room they now sat in, waiting for news.

After changing back into dry clothes, Harker had met up with Doggie, who had heard the explosions along with everyone else and had immediately come looking for them. They had driven straight to the medical centre, arriving just in time to be interviewed by the local police, who were understandably treating the explosions with extreme seriousness given that the whole of Gibraltar had experienced the tremors. With Barbara Holtz in no shape to answer questions, Harker was their main source of information, and given the bizarre nature of their experience he had decided to keep the details to a minimum. Holtz had been highly secretive about the archaeological dig, and although she had government approval, the police appeared to have been totally unaware of the site.

In his statement Harker had not lied per se, but simply chosen to omit certain aspects of what had happened. He described himself as a former colleague who had taken up the offer to survey the underwater site and was in the process of consultation when an earthquake had rocked its foundations. On passing through the narrow exit of the dig, Dr Holtz had become entangled with a pressurised buoy used to retrieve artefacts from the depths, and had been tragically dragged too rapidly all the way up to the surface.

Of course, the clearly deliberate act of sabotage and the underwater knifeman remained at the forefront of Harker's mind, but he figured that Holtz would be able to explain things as she saw fit when she was able to speak again. Hopefully, that would be in as little as twenty-four hours if the doctor's assessment was accurate.

The only problem was that her eventual statement could clash with his version of events, but he would have to sort that out when the moment came. Anyway, he was determined to be the first person she saw on waking, and that was the reason he and Doggie had been holed up here for the past six hours. Holtz had been reluctant to reveal who it was that had commissioned her work at the site in the first place, but one thing was as clear as day: there was far more going on here than she had yet told him. The only absolute Harker could be sure of was that someone did not want the underwater site to be seen by anyone else, and it was essential he found out why. How this connected to the Mithras and that strange being with two hearts they had found was still a total mystery, but one whose solution preoccupied him.

'Fancy another coffee?' Doggie asked, getting to his feet and stretching his arms. 'There's a Costa Coffee around the corner, and it beats this filtered gunk they're serving here.'

'Sounds good,' Harker replied, flexing his own shoulders. 'Large skinny latte, please.'

'Skinny! You're not overweight, Alex. Why not live a little?'

This comment made Harker chuckle. 'Perhaps that's why I'm *not* overweight.'

Doggie appeared unconvinced but held out his hand limply, with a roll of the eyes. 'Fair enough, give me a fiver and I'll see what I can do.'

That the dean made far more money than he did was known to both of them, so Harker stared at him. 'You know, Doggie, you really should try to be a bit more generous… maybe live a little.' He said it with a sarcastic smile.

Doggie shook his head and leant towards him to say, 'Perhaps that's why I'm never broke.' This was Dean Thomas Lercher, scholar, colleague, trusted friend and a complete cheapskate. Harker pulled out his wallet and handed over a crisp five-pound note. 'Knock yourself out with that, O generous one.'

With a satisfied look Doggie whipped the money from Harker's hand. 'Good, I'll be back in a minute and then I want to hear all about that pyramid again... especially the frescos.'

'Shh,' Harker uttered quietly, anxiously looking around to make sure no one was in earshot.

'Sorry, I meant the archaeological site,' Doggie corrected, then slipped the note into the pocket of his green tweed jacket and performed a gracious and mocking Victorian bow. 'I shall be away but a moment.'

Harker watched the dean saunter off through the medical centre's double doors, almost clipping a lone individual who was entering. The man was short, but with his shoulders held back he exuded a sense of authority that belied his stature. His eyes darted back and forth anxiously as he made his way up to reception, before they settled on Harker and a glimmer of recognition flashed across them.

There was an odd momentary pause as their eyes met, and for a brief second Harker felt as if this stranger was about to rush at him. His whole body tensed in readiness, but instead the man's lips twitched apprehensively and he opened his mouth to speak.

'Professor Harker?'

Friend or foe? Who knew, but Harker's knuckles continued to tighten regardless, as he offered a slow nod of his head. 'Yes?'

The stranger's expression immediately relaxed and his eyes widened in relief. 'It is indeed you – good. The photo I received was less than satisfactory.'

The stranger then pulled out his mobile phone and held it up to display a rather undignified image of Harker in mid-conversation at some event, with his mouth hanging open and his eyes in mid blink.

'Do I know you?'

'No, not yet,' the man replied, popping the phone back into the pocket of his light tan suit. 'My name is Harold Cortez and I'm the Minister for the Environment here in Gibraltar. May we speak?'

As the man waited for a reply, Harker was already glancing back towards the entrance for any sign of additional security as befitted a minister, but there was none to be seen.

Cortez picked up on this immediately. 'If you're looking for security agents, Professor, I can assure you I am quite alone. This is Gibraltar, not Whitehall, and besides you're not in any trouble... so far as I know.'

Cortez extracted a business card from his wallet, which he slowly passed over, allowing Harker to note the official UK coat of arms preceding the minister's name, so relieving any concerns he might still have.

'Professor Alex Harker,' he introduced himself, shaking the minister's hand. 'What can I do for you?'

'Just a moment of your time, please,' Cortez replied and glanced over towards the main entrance. 'Let's find somewhere a bit more private, shall we?'

The minister smiled reassuringly, extending his hand courteously towards the door, and so Harker followed him outside onto the entrance steps. Cortez peered warily down the road for a few moments, then apparently convinced that all was clear, he began to speak, his thinning grey hair blowing in the strong wind to reveal the edges of a poorly secured wig.

'I believe Dr Holtz is fortunately in a stable condition, but unable to speak for the time being,' he began, 'which at least is one positive aspect to this whole bloody mess.'

'She's expected to remain in the decompression chamber for some time, but yes, the doctor tells me she'll be making a full recovery,' Harker replied, while not allowing his eyes to stray towards the unconvincing weave covering Cortez's scalp.

'Good, I have a private security team arriving within the next ten minutes to ensure her protection,' Cortez announced confidently. 'It would have been much sooner, but I was dealing with the government's response to that *"earthquake"* that you were caught up in earlier. If only I'd known she'd brought you into this little cabal of ours, I would have demanded that we two met sooner. But given today's events, I suppose that is now bye the bye.'

'It was a very last minute thing, I'm afraid,' Harker replied off the cuff. The minister was clearly mistaken as to his actual reason for being here, and it was a misunderstanding that Harker was happy to exploit.

'Well, I should have been told, but there's no point in crying over spilt milk, is there? How much has she told you?'

Now Harker knew he was playing with an empty hand because, apart from seeing the pyramid itself, he was totally clueless as to what the minister was referring to. And so, with a shrewd look on his face, he leant in closer. '*Everything*. Although she was definitely most diplomatic when speaking of your own involvement.'

This answer received a look of scorn from Cortez. 'Well, firstly don't judge me, Professor. I took the money for purely patriotic reasons, that I can assure you, and let me also say that every penny was allocated to the Gibraltar coffers.'

The suggestion of a bribe drew no reaction from Harker, who instead gazed at the minister sympathetically. 'Given the nature of the site we discovered, I would say the donation was more than justified.'

This appeasing comment had Cortez looking more relaxed as he offered a self-satisfied nod. 'Good – and I want your detestable bosses to know that the destruction of that site had nothing to do with me whatsoever.'

Bosses, Harker thought, proceeding to play along with the charade. 'You should know that they're not happy, Minister. Perhaps it is I who should be asking exactly what do you know?'

There was an air of threat in his question, which instantly garnered the reaction he was hoping for.

'I can assure you no one else knew about the site – as I promised – but the whole of Gibraltar would have heard those explosions. And you should know that there are Royal Navy divers combing the area even as we speak. If they do find anything it will be hard to keep a lid on it, but rest assured I have already interceded to put myself in the middle of it, so any findings have to go through me first. I will of course come up with a cover story, but it won't be easy.'

On the outside Harker managed to maintain a solid poker face, but inside he felt almost giddy. Indeed, he felt like a spy extracting information. Of course he still had no idea what the point of all this was, but nonetheless he seemed to be a natural at this kind of game and this confidence allowed a smile to appear at the corner of his lips.

'You find that funny, do you?' Cortez asked angrily.

'Not at all, Minister. Just glad that you're on top of this bungled situation. I'm sure you're aware of the financial backing and support we can provide if your cover story doesn't stand up to scrutiny.'

Harker was already cursing himself for having perhaps pushed this façade too far, but the look of nervous panic spreading across the man's face quickly reassured him.

'I assure you it will. I'm a man who can be counted on to honour our agreement, but I expect you to keep your word too. I want my pictures back – and any copies – as soon as this is all over, as was promised.' A frown appeared on Cortez's forehead. 'I take it you've already seen them?'

This last question had Harker utterly stumped 'Ahh, yes... those.'

Cortez now looked embarrassed. 'So you have, then. Well, let me say, Professor Harker, that regardless of whatever money is offered, I find blackmail one of the most dishonest of all crimes. It would destroy my reputation and my family – and that cannot be allowed to happen.'

Finally Harker twigged what the minister must be referring to, and it was clear that, whoever those 'bosses' were, they had caught Harold Cortez doing something he should not have been doing and used it as leverage in demanding his help and discretion regarding the dig site. Of course the important aspect, *why*, was all he really wanted to know. 'Yes, Minister, a highly compromising position to be found in... and mightily unusual I would add.'

Cortez's nervousness suddenly evaporated and he stood there stout and proud. 'Having one's buttocks spanked whilst being ridden like a horse is simply role play, Professor, and nothing more. Whilst the blinkers and chomping bit were merely for a touch of realism.'

Harker's face firstly went blank, then he couldn't help smirking childishly, but Cortez dismissed this reaction with a grunt.

'I want those pictures back when this is done. No ifs and no buts.'

'You'll have them back as promised,' he assured him, pushing an unwelcome image of Cortez from his mind and concentrated on squeezing more information out of the minister. 'I assume it was explained to you why all this secrecy was necessary in the first place?'

'No, it wasn't, Professor Harker,' Cortez huffed, 'and I don't want to know. Your lot blackmailed me into keeping that underwater site under wraps – and I have done so – but now it's time you answered some of my questions. What the hell happened down there?'

It was evident the minister was as much in the dark as Harker himself, and he now saw no reason to keep hidden the events that had recently transpired deep in the murky waters of the Gibraltar Strait. 'Someone exploded a set of charges and almost killed us in the process. Then, on the way out, we were attacked by a diver with a knife.'

Cortez looked shocked by the revelation and his eyes narrowed. 'Military?'

'I don't know, but he managed to attach an inflatable buoy to Dr Holtz and as a result... well, you know how she is.'

The last piece of information had the minister looking bewildered. 'This is getting out of hand, Professor,' he said, his hand shaking ever so slightly. 'I was asked to keep this archaeological site off the records and that's one thing, but if we're now talking attempted murder, then that's not something I can be a part of, and neither will I – photos or not.'

It was refreshing to see this man displaying some moral courage and for some reason it made Harker feel he needed to come clean. 'Mr Cortez, there's something I have to tell you and you may not like it. I'm not the man you think I am.'

'What?' Cortez's face screwed up like that of a bulldog chewing on a wasp. 'Then who are you exactly?'

'I came to find Dr Holtz, not the other way round,' Harker explained, as the minister's cheeks began to twitch in anger. 'She gave me a tour of the site, but that's as far as my involvement goes in whatever is happening here.'

'You sneaky bastard,' Cortez fumed, infuriated at the realisation he had just disclosed his secret penchant for equestrian activities to a complete stranger.

'I apologise,' Harker waved a hand in the air, 'but I have to know what's going on here, and believe me when I tell you it has nothing to do with your personal proclivities – which won't go any further, you have my word on that.'

Harker's openness did little to assuage the minister's growing anger and he continued to glare. 'So who the hell are you?'

'You know who I am: Professor Alex Harker, Cambridge University.'

'Yes, I know that. How do you think I got your photo? I pulled it off the web. I mean what are you doing here?'

'It's a long story, but I met with Dr Holtz of my own volition.'

Cortez slumped slightly as if the wind had been knocked out of him. 'When I heard you and Dr Holtz had both been pulled from the water by the coastguard, I just assumed you were one of her recruits.'

'Recruits?'

'Yes, Dr Holtz has had a few archaeology buffs brought down here over the past few months. After Dr Michael Wexler left so unexpectedly, I just assumed you'd been brought in to replace him.'

'Didn't you wonder why he left?' Harker was surprised at how little the minister seemed to know about anything.

'When one is being blackmailed, Professor, one tends not to pry too much,' Cortez replied bitterly. 'But I did at least demand to meet them beforehand, to give them my official permission to visit the site.'

Harker eyed the minister suspiciously, but he needed no longer than a few seconds to decide that he was being told the truth. Yet there was still something he needed to know. 'Does the word "Mithras" mean anything to you?'

Cortez remained blank faced, then shook his head. 'No, doesn't ring any bells. Should it?'

'Obviously not,' Harker replied with a growl, his frustration seeping to the surface. 'Well, if you can forgo any legal comeback claiming I was attempting to blackmail you, then I am happy to forget we ever had this conversation.'

The compromise was met with a firm nod from Cortez and Harker was just about to thank him and leave when something buzzed past his ear. He jerked his head to one side and rubbed at it with the palm of his hand, assuming it to be a flying insect. But as he looked towards the minister he realised exactly what it was. A thin line of crimson trickled down Cortez's face from forehead to nose, and his eyes now seemed vacant as Harker spotted the small bullet hole where his forehead and the hairpiece joined. With a twitching of his shoulder, the minister's legs gave way and his body crumpled to the ground.

Harker spun around in time to catch sight of a silencer poking out from the rear passenger window of a black 5 Series BMW, which was even now shifting its aim towards him. He leapt off the steps of the medical centre, ending up in the middle of the road just as another shot pinged the tarmac inches from his shoe. His heart now racing, Harker lunged across the road to reach an angle behind the car where the gun couldn't get a clear shot without shooting through the vehicle's rear window. Then he jumped to his feet and took off down the street.

Behind him could be heard the sound of screeching tyres, but he had gained a good head start and reached the corner of the building just as another shot was fired, slamming into the nearby brickwork, a spattering of fragments catching him on the cheek.

'Jesus Christ,' he yelled and came to a sharp halt so as not to slam into somebody heading the other way.

'Nope, just me,' Doggie said with a smile before Harker tore the cardboard tray from his hands, sending hot coffee everywhere, and propelled him backwards.

'Run, Tom, *now.*'

If there was one thing you could count on Dean Thomas Lercher for, it was self-preservation, and so he quickly followed Harker along the side street, off to the right and onto a narrow walkway, as the sound of tortured rubber careened away in the distance.

'What are we doing?' Doggie yelled, as the two men raced along the narrow path.

'We're being shot at!' Harker yelled back. The dean seemed unfazed until a further shot clipped the nearby wall just as they dived into the nearest side alley.

'We're being shot at!' Doggie yelped in sheer terror, picking up the pace.

'I know,' Harker growled angrily. 'Just keep running!'

The sound of the car had faded, the alleyway too tight for it to follow, but this respite had no effect on Harker and, as they entered the small hospital car park, they continued sprinting towards where they had left the rental car.

Harker reached it first, but in the heat of the moment he slammed his arm into the driver's door, knocking the key from his hand. With clenched teeth he grabbed it off the ground, jammed it into the lock and dived inside, while Doggie flung open the passenger door and leapt in to join him.

'What the hell is going on?' Doggie yelled, as Harker started up the engine.

'They just shot the minister,' Harker wheezed, struggling to catch his breath.

'Minister? What minister? I thought I was just getting us coffee!'

Harker ignored him, slammed the gearstick into first, and revved up towards the exit before coming to a screeching halt.

The black BMW was sitting in the road opposite, its engine purring lightly. Harker glared towards it, but all its windows were blacked out, even the windscreen. As he snatched a look off to his right to ensure the coast was clear, the BMW began revving its engine lightly, as if challenging them to make a break for it.

'Doggie, sit right down in your seat. This is going to get a little rough.'

Doggie nodded compliantly and sank into his seat. Then, as Harker tightened his grip on the steering wheel, a police car slowly appeared around the corner and made its leisurely way towards them, the two officers inside looking relaxed as if just going about their normal duties.

'Doggie, sit up now,' Harker said, now sounding much calmer. The dean peered over the dashboard and began to wave frantically. 'Stop that!' Harker ordered, slapping the man's hands away, leaving Doggie looking absolutely bewildered.

'Are you crazy, Alex? Flag them down, for goodness' sake.'

Harker ignored his plea and instead slowly pulled out of the exit, right in front of the police car, and continued up the street at a steady pace. As he approached the traffic lights at a T-junction, he came to a complete halt, even though the lights were showing green. In the rear-view mirror Harker could see the black BMW still waiting patiently. As the yellow, blue and white police car passed by, the BMW pulled out and began to follow, as if in a convoy. Timing would now be crucial. As the police car came to a halt behind them, it honked its horn because the lights were green.

'Change, damn it,' Harker muttered, giving an acknowledging wave to the boys in blue. Just then the lights turned yellow and he pulled off to the right, leaving the other two cars behind him. Within fifty metres, Harker had the accelerator pressed to the floor. Despite a good lead they would be hard-pressed to outrun the BMW in this clapped-out, ten-year-old Fiat, but given the airport was less than two miles away, they still had a shot.

'Why on earth didn't you stop and get help from the police?' Doggie roared, anything but happy with the decision. 'Those people were shooting at us. Have you lost your damn mind?'

'That's exactly why I didn't flag the cops down, Tom. The lot in the BMW had just murdered Gibraltar's Minister for the Environment, so do you honestly think they wouldn't add a couple of policemen to the body count?'

Doggie took in this terrible information and then began to shake his head in bemusement. 'What the hell is going on?' he yelled, slamming his fist against the dashboard. 'The last thing I knew is we were about to enjoy a nice latte.'

'Not any more,' Harker replied, glancing in the rearview mirror to see the black BMW turning onto the main road some distance behind them, while the police car went trundling off in the opposite direction. 'Hold on.'

At the next junction Harker turned right with such speed that the whole vehicle groaned as it struggled to hold the road, then he gathered speed with each gear change, like a professional racer. He found it fascinating how the fear of being shot focused the mind, as he sped onwards, each minor bump threatening to overturn the car like a bouncing ball, its suspension straining under extreme stress.

To anyone who has not visited the Gibraltar, it might come as a surprise that pretty much every road there leads to the airport. But as Harker rounded the last corner, he realised the mistake he had made in his eagerness to escape. The entrance to the Dudley Ward tunnel loomed ahead, and as they passed inside it a feeling of dread settled in his stomach. This was not only the longest way round but it afforded nowhere to go but straight ahead. Logistically it was the worst route he could have taken.

The Fiat's engine whined in protest as Harker held the pedal to the floor. They would make it out of the tunnel in less than forty-five seconds, but the BMW had already appeared behind them and was closing in fast, and now gunfire from an automatic rifle began to rip through the air.

'Get down,' Harker yelled as a spray of bullets shattered the back window. One passed between the front seats and collided with the radio, sending shreds of plastic and metal flying everywhere. Harker slid down in his seat and began weaving back and forth across the painted road dividers as a second burst rang out. If their pursuers got alongside them, the tyres would become a prime target, so Harker continued to block their attempts to catch up every time he heard the BMW begin to accelerate, while the thud of spent bullets hitting the boot vibrated through the vehicle.

After several failed attempts to overtake, the BMW now changed tactics and slammed into the Fiat's rear. A punishing jolt threw both occupants forwards, and even though they were keeping as low in their seats as humanly possible, the blow appeared to infuriate Doggie. In a moment of madness the dean sat up, and with a furious expression stuck his head through the shattered passenger window and shook his fist at the BMW.

'You bunch of degenerate reprobates!' he yelled.

Harker slid one hand off the wheel and pulled his companion down just as another burst from the automatic sent bullets thudding into the back of the car. 'You idiot! What the hell are you doing?'

'I'm getting angry,' Doggie ranted, and for a moment Harker had no recognition of the man alongside him. He had never seen the dean behaving so manically, but then again he had never seen him being shot at either. His friend had transmuted from a mild-mannered gent to a road rage nutter in less than a second.

'Do you feel better now?' Harker yelled, clutching the steering wheel with both hands again.

Doggie slid himself further down towards the footwell and glared at Harker with fire in his eyes. 'You bet your sweet bottom I do. Now drive, you bastard, as I refuse to die in Gibraltar.'

In that instant of staring into his friend's eyes, Harker realised that Doggie was cracking up. And as another burst of gunfire slammed into the car's bodywork, who could blame him?

With Doggie now crouched in the footwell, Harker glanced back at the road in front and felt his heart skip a beat as – with lights flashing – an oncoming Ford Fiesta loudly honked its horn. Harker jerked the steering wheel to the right, missing the car by inches.

The Fiesta clipped the side of the BMW and sent it slamming into the rock face, crumpling the right side of the bonnet, which in turn locked the right wheel in a cloud of smoking rubber.

At a glance, the Fiesta itself looked relatively unscathed, but the damage done to the BMW's wheel had it screeching to a long drawn out halt. With the accelerator still pinned to the floor, Harker pulled the Fiat further away, and by the time they saw sweet, welcoming sunlight at the tunnel's exit ahead, the BMW was over fifty metres behind them with black fumes now billowing out of its bonnet – or what was left of it.

Apart from some seriously loud hyperventilating from Doggie, both men remained silent for the rest of their short journey to the airport.

Harker's whole body now ached. Although neither of them had suffered a bullet wound, he felt like he had been hit by a freight train. Adrenalin was keeping him going, but their tight escape had more than frayed his nerves and his thinking. His objective was simple: get to the jet and safety.

He finally pulled up on a grass verge no more than twenty metres from the check-in point, then turned off the engine which spluttered to a halt. The airport seemed unusually quiet but it would not be too long before someone noticed a bullet-ridden Fiat with all its windows shattered. With luck, they could be in the air within ten minutes, hopefully before news of the minister's assassination caused a massive security crackdown on the Rock. So he knew they had to keep moving, even though his palms felt glued to the steering wheel and his muscles had tensed to snapping point.

Harker looked over to see Doggie appearing calmer though still pretty wired. He tapped the dean on the shoulder. 'We have to get moving.'

Doggie attempted a nod, but his head jerked violently back and forth instead. Nevertheless, he pulled himself upright on the seat and expelled a shuddering sigh of relief. 'How are you going to explain the state of this car, Alex?' he said, scanning the multiple bullet holes just about everywhere.

'We'll just dump it here, Tom. It's now the least of our problems,' Harker replied. He managed a mild smirk as his pounding heart began to settle. 'Besides… it's registered in your name.'

Chapter 12

'Jesus Christ, Alex, do you realise how serious this is? It's the lead story on all the news channels.' On Harker's phone screen, John Schroder's frowning face moved closer. 'Every law enforcement agency in the UK will be all over this faster than shit through a goose. You can't just brush the death of a government minister under the rug. There's going to be real scrutiny from all sides, I can promise you.'

In all the years Harker had known John Schroder there were few times he had seen the man so worked up, and they had been through some pretty rough scrapes together. The MI6 officer was one of the smartest, craftiest men Harker knew, and he possessed an ability to compartmentalise his experiences that allowed him not only to be a reliable and clear-thinking asset within the intelligence community but also to maintain his cover as a Templar agent.

Harker had once goaded him about his status as a double agent within MI6 and it had not gone down well, ending in an abject apology. Schroder was a loyal British subject, beyond reproach, and given that he considered his membership of the Templars to be on the side of good, his dual roles rarely, if ever, came into conflict. But this was different. The death of a UK minister and apprehending those responsible would be the top priority, and though the two men trusted each other, Schroder's currently suspicious expression was something Harker couldn't ignore.

'I had nothing to do with it, John,' Harker replied, struggling to not look guilty under Schroder's sceptical glare. 'Harold Cortez approached me and he got shot during that conversation. I only just managed to get away safely myself.'

'And me as well,' Doggie interrupted, pointing to himself excitedly. Clearly the adrenalin was still running strong.

After abandoning the bullet-ridden rental car they had managed to get to the Cessna jet without complication, and had been safely in the air before news of the minister's murder hit the media. Their flight plan had been filed with the UK as its destination, but twenty minutes into the flight Harker was still deciding what their next port of call should be when Schroder had called.

'How did you know I was in Gibraltar anyway?' Harker enquired.

'How did he know *we* were in Gibraltar,' Doggie interjected, but his trivial pique was dismissed sharply by a flick of Harker's hand.

'Your babysitter, Botha, let me know,' Schroder answered, with no sign of his frustration fading. 'And when I heard about the minister's death, I had the unsettling feeling you might be involved – and I was right.'

Harker ignored the 'babysitter' reference and sighed. 'I've never lied to you, John, and you know that. But I'm right in the middle—' He glanced over at Doggie, who had folded his arms combatively. 'I mean, *we're* caught in the middle of something. Wrong place and wrong time.'

'I doubt that, Alex, as you have a talent for being in the wrong place at exactly the *right* time. What the hell is going on?'

'After we found Avi Legrundy… did you hear about that?'

'Course I did. Botha brought me up to speed,' Schroder replied. 'The last time I checked, he was preparing to move her to a more secure location – until we decide what to do with her.'

'Good. Well, she had a map on her directing us to a certain Barbara Holtz, who is – was – working at an underwater dig site in Gibraltar.'

There was a pause as Schroder's mouth tightened. 'An underwater dig site? I haven't heard anything about that.'

'You and everyone else,' Doggie once again interjected, as usual keen to be part of the conversation.

'It's true,' Harker continued. 'Cortez was being black-mailed to keep it all hush-hush. At least that's what he told me before someone took a potshot at him.'

'What kind of dig is it?'

'You should have seen it, John – a pyramid, right under the Gibraltar strait.'

'A pyramid?' Schroder looked bemused.

'I know, it sounds so unlikely, but what's more is that the carbon dating suggests it's around eleven thousand years old.'

'That's impossible,' Schroder remarked dismissively. 'The Great Pyramid of Giza wasn't built until 2,500 BC.'

'Exactly,' Harker replied, suddenly becoming excited at the thought, 'so it shouldn't even exist. And it appears to have served as some kind of hub or beacon for people in search of it.'

'A hub? But for what?'

'We don't know. We were still debating that when someone brought down the whole site with some detonation charges. We only just managed to escape, but whoever arranged the explosion also sent a diver down to finish the job. As a result, Dr Holtz is lying unconscious in a decompression chamber even as we speak.' Harker now pulled out the gold coin he had taken from the site and twiddled it between his fingers. 'We also found this down there.'

Schroder moved even closer to the screen, his eyes squinting, 'What is it?'

'Honestly, John, I'm not sure,' Harker replied, putting it back in his pocket, 'but it's inscribed with the same text as the tattoo on that body we found with Legrundy.'

'Bloody hell!' was Schroder's reaction.

'I know, like I said, we only just managed to escape. I was later approached by Harold Cortez at the hospital where Barbara Holtz had been taken. He didn't have much to say except about himself being blackmailed into keeping it all a secret.'

Harker considered explaining how his own intelligence skills – or tradecraft, as Schroder would have put it – had managed to extract the necessary information, but the MI6 officer appeared far more interested in the why.

'Blackmailed? How?'

'He was compromised by photos showing him indulging in what you might call equestrian-themed sex games. I don't think you really want to know the details.'

Schroder raised an eyebrow. 'Really? Well, each to their own.'

'I didn't get the name of his blackmailer, but this whole rabbit hole quest started with Avi Legrundy, so I'd bet a pretty penny that they're part of Mithras.'

A silence now fell momentarily, as Schroder gazed away from the camera thoughtfully.

'If that's true, then it would seem we've landed right in the middle of whatever the Mithras are currently up to,' Schroder replied finally.

'And it would also seem that they're mopping up any loose ends – including Mr Cortez.'

'And you as well, Alex,' Doggie added.

Schroder nodded in agreement. 'We already knew Legrundy had been out to get you since you foiled their plans for recruiting you. And if you're right about all this, then she's inadvertently drawn us into whatever other plans they have. Which turns her into a real liability for them.'

The mention of Legrundy's role had Harker thinking busily. If the Red Death's obsession with Harker's payback had unwittingly encroached on what the Mithras were now up to, then they would surely make an attempt to retrieve her, rather than risk leaving her in the hands of the Templars.

'We need to contact Botha and give him a heads-up,' he decided, and this suggestion was met with a firm nod from Schroder. But before the MI6 officer could reply, a voice crackled from the main screen located at the front of the cabin.

'Apologies for the interruption, gentlemen, but I asked the pilot not to bother you whilst you were in full flow.'

They all knew that voice and simultaneously turned towards the screen. Harker positioned his phone so that Schroder could also see it.

'Truly fascinating. And as usual, Alex, you've ended up right in the centre of things.'

Sebastian Brulet, Grand Master of the Knights Templar, gave them a courteous nod. The unusual sheen of his very white skin appeared to gleam more brightly due to the hue of the screen.

'Sebastian,' Harker acknowledged, happy to see his old friend. 'How have you been?'

'Better than you, I'd suggest – given your adventures of the past few hours. Are you and Dean Lercher both well?'

'We're fine,' Doggie replied, with a certain pride in the fact, and he sat up straighter in his chair.

'Yes,' responded Harker, 'if you don't count almost being blown up and witnessing the murder of a UK government minister taking place right in front of me.'

'And having to make a daring escape from killers armed with AK-47s,' Doggie added with pride.

'Yes, Dean, I'd heard. And given the circumstances, I can only say how happy I am to see you both appearing unscathed.' Brulet gave them a reassuring smile. 'I only wish Mr Cortez could have been so fortunate.'

There were many good things one could say about Sebastian Brulet, for he was kind, considerate, charming and staunchly loyal to those around him, but he possessed some qualities that only become apparent when meeting in person. For one, there was his uncanny ability to command respect without saying a word. It was an innate charisma. You either had it or you didn't, and Brulet had it in spades.

Of course, his eyes inspired a sort of fascination in anyone close enough to see them. His pupils were not round but cross-shaped, due to a hereditary genetic condition. It was thought that generations ago this mutation had been a factor in his family being chosen for prominence by the Knights Templar. Those peculiar eyes were now staring at them from the screen.

'What do you think is going on here, Alex?' the Grand Master asked, as a lock of white hair escaped his ponytail and was brushed to one side.

'Apart from the discovery, which would literally tear apart archaeological timelines, I'm not really sure… yet. But given the lengths the Mithras appear ready to go to in order to cover it all up, I would guess that it's something we should definitely be scrutinising. Then there's that strange… man… we found with Legrundy.' Harker was still uncertain what to call the humanoid. Even considering its physical similarities with those frescos back at the dig site, especially the eyes, he wasn't ready to accept such implications – let alone the 'god' aspect Barbara Holtz had referred to. But now he decided it was time to at least put it out there and gauge their reaction.

'We found a series of frescos at the dig site, inside the pyramid itself, and it may sound crazy, but there were some similarities in them with… the humanoid.'

Brulet frowned. 'What do you mean, similarities?'

Harker was still wondering how to phrase his thoughts when Doggie just came out with it. 'Alex thinks that strange-looking fellow you recovered is an alien. He also thinks the frescos refer to some ancient alien civilisation that came to Earth, whereupon humans declared them to be gods.'

'Tom, that is not at all what I think!' Harker exploded, feeling his cheeks begin to flush. He was an archaeologist, not a conspiracy nut. 'I'm just looking at the evidence, and from what I've seen so far, it would seem that… that…'

'That extraterrestrials have been guiding us human beings for at least eleven thousand years,' Doggie concluded sarcastically, with a little chuckle.

Harker could feel his blood boiling. It had been a long time since he and Doggie had tussled seriously and, although they rarely argued, when they did so it was explosive, and he felt his anger begin to spill over. 'You know something, Tom? You've been acting like a bloody idiot ever since we got shot at back in Gibraltar.'

Doggie was already rolling his eyes. 'What, you mean about half an hour ago?'

'Half an hour is enough, Thomas,' Harker replied scathingly, deliberately reverting to using his friend's full name, 'You know what I think?'

'Do tell,' the dean groaned.

'I think you cracked somewhere along the line. I think, while those bullets were flying overhead, something in you snapped. You've been as bitchy as hell ever since. And what was with the "You bunch of degenerate repro-bates"?' Harker recalled mockingly before jabbing a finger towards a small stain alongside the zip of Doggie's trousers. 'And let's not forget how you wet yourself.'

Doggie's mouth dropped open and he looked abso-lutely livid. 'How dare you accuse me of incontinence! These are coffee stains.'

'Oh, really. That's funny,' Harker said, still gesturing to the offending area, 'I've never had yellow coffee before.'

'Enough,' Brulet roared, and both men immediately went quiet. 'Please, gentlemen, you're behaving like chil-dren. Could I offer some suggestions?'

Neither man offered any sign of consent but they did remain silent with their eyes now glued to Brulet.

'Alex, how long exactly were you down there?'

'How long where?'

'The dive, Alex. How long were you down there?'

'Umm, about forty minutes, give or take.'

Brulet raised his head knowingly. 'And how long before you stepped onto this plane?'

This simple question had Harker realising what the Grand Master was getting at. 'Probably not long enough,' he said.

As any diver would know, a certain period of time should elapse between diving and flying, so much so that there were charts specifically devised as necessary guidance for anyone planning such an endeavour. It concerned the body's reaction to pressure and if it wasn't followed could have serious consequences.

'I would suggest, Alex, that you're suffering from a mild case of decompression sickness. Symptoms would include nausea, irritability, and perhaps also some dizziness.'

Harker slumped back in his seat and rubbed his forehead. 'I do feel a bit light-headed,' he confessed.

'And Dean Lercher,' Brulet continued, 'I would suggest that you may be suffering from shock. You wouldn't be human if you didn't. Why don't you go and get yourself a Coke? I'm sure the jet is adequately stocked. The sugar will help. While you're doing that I'll ask the pilot to drop down to a lower altitude and reset the cabin pressure accordingly.'

The screen went black. Doggie silently made his way over to the flight cupboard, pulled out a Coke and began slurping it, as the jet started to descend.

'You all right?' Schroder asked suddenly over the phone as Harker lay back in his seat and closed his eyes.

'I'll be OK. With everything going on, the precautions slipped my mind.'

As Doggie took the seat opposite and continued gulping at his drink, Brulet reappeared on the main screen. 'You'll be fine, gentlemen. Now just relax and let me do the talking.'

Harker and Doggie gave each other a conciliatory nod and Brulet proceeded to take the reins.

'When I saw the pictures of that humanoid, I must admit the thought of something otherworldly did enter my mind, but I settled instead for some kind of terrible genetic experiment having caused the poor creature's bizarre appearance. Given what you have learnt since, I now believe we should keep an open mind – no matter how unconventional things may seem.'

Brulet's broad-minded approach came as a relief to Harker, who found himself nodding. He realised that his head was beginning to clear, even if he was still feeling off colour and physically drained.

'With that said, we should be asking ourselves three questions. One: if we take this assumption to be correct, then where did this creature come from? Two: why is it so important to the Mithras? And three: how do we find out this reason?'

'Well, I can't answer the first two,' Schroder said from Harker's phone screen, 'but the third I can be of help with.'

'Please do, John,' Brulet replied, as Harker began to readjust himself in his seat, feeling better with every passing second.

'As for the two doctors working with Barbara Holtz, I dug up the autopsy photographs of Dr Khan – and trust me, he's dead. But Dr Michael Wexler is another thing entirely. I tracked his credit card and it was used just yesterday.'

'He's alive?' Harker was startled.

'I don't have photographic proof, Alex, but there is a chalet registered in his name just three miles away from his last purchase. It's a good place to start.'

'Where?'

'The town of Zermatt, in Switzerland.'

Harker was already rising out of his seat, but he paused as Brulet spoke out to him, his voice crackling over communication static.

'You just take a further moment to rest, Alex. I will now inform the pilot, and I'm sure John will have the address and a rental car waiting for you on arrival.'

As Brulet began to wrap up the conversation, Doggie flung his hand into the air like an enthusiastic student. 'Talking about rental cars, what about the Fiat?'

'And what car would that be, Dean Leacher?' Brulet enquired.

'The one we left in Gibraltar, covered in bullet holes… and, more importantly, hired in my name! If it's found, the authorities will be after me like a ferret up a trouser leg.'

To Harker the expression seemed bizarre and rather archaic, but hey, it was Doggie, a man who wore Victorian-style cravats when his colleagues wore ties.

'I'll get onto that right away,' Schroder offered.

Doggie visibly relaxed as Brulet gave a final nod of his head. 'Good. Stay safe and let me know whatever you find out. Concerning the body of our strange friend, we have Mr Cordon currently performing some DNA tests. Once he's got the results, I will of course inform you all.' Brulet paused, and then let out a deep breath. 'If any of this bears out my suspicions, then I don't mind telling you, gentlemen, what a momentous discovery this will be. An intelligent, extraterrestrial life form right here on our planet.'

'*Dead* extraterrestrial life form,' Harker added sombrely.

'Nonetheless, Alex, that new knowledge could change everything.'

With a smile, Brulet leant forward and the screen went black. Harker turned his phone so he could speak again to Schroder.

'I've got to say, Alex, you possess a remarkable agility of mind when it comes to handling a good mystery... But, as your friend says, you can be a gigantic pain in the arse.'

'I aim to please,' Harker replied with a tight smile.

'Yeah, well your aim is completely crap. Now send me the location of that car.'

Harker stifled a chuckle. 'Duly noted, John, and thanks again.'

The call now ended, Harker typed in a message identifying the precise location of the abandoned rental car. After sending this, he sat back in his seat and tried to enjoy the soft humming of the jet's engines, while mulling over all that had transpired. What with his narrow escape from the pyramid, the extremely close shave with the minister's killers and a mild case of decompression sickness, he now felt totally spent. Still, they had managed to get out in one piece and, despite their little spat, Doggie appeared to be thriving on it. Truth be known, the dean had shown real grit during the car chase, and by grit he meant his old friend hadn't collapsed into a quivering wreck as might reasonably have been expected.

'You handled yourself well today, Tom,' Harker said, offering this compliment as though awarding a prize. 'You really held it together – and I apologise for having a go.'

Doggie leant forward with a grin spread across his face. 'Calmed down, have you now? And yes, I think I did.'

Then the smile vanished. 'And I apologise too. I didn't mean to make fun of you. But I'll admit my nerves have been overstimulated somewhat.'

His apology was about as good as it would get when it came to Doggie, and Harker smiled warmly. 'Apology accepted, Tom. Shock affects us all in different ways.'

'Maybe so, but I don't have to remind you that it's not the first time I've stood firm in the face of danger, my friend. Far from it.'

'Faced much gunfire before, have you, Tom?'

The intended jibe did little to knock the wind out of the dean's sails and he sat there proudly with a single eyebrow raised. 'I will admit my experience of being on the receiving end of a lead dinner is minimal, but every time I enter a charity event, address the University council to seek a budget increase, or deal with thousands of students all baying for my blood for whatever is the offence of that day, I can assure you it's all-out war.' He looked up stoically towards the ceiling. 'These things demand a stern resolve which a man can only draw from the depths of his own soul.'

'Looks like it's not the only thing that's got drawn out of you,' Harker mused with a smile, and gestured to the stain by Doggie's zip.

Doggie's eyes widened and he glanced down before crossing his legs. 'I told you it's a coffee stain. You should know that as it was you who knocked the cups out of my hands back at the hospital.'

'Of course it was. My mistake, Tom.' Harker was glad they were back to their usual banter. 'Interesting how coffee just keeps getting yellower these days.'

'Enough!' Doggie roared. 'I'll admit I may have relaxed a tad too much during our escape, but it only goes to prove my naturally steely nerve when faced with danger, to push ahead, no matter what.'

'Yeah… a stainless–steel toilet.'

'Oh, shut up, Alex. You try escaping armed killers when your bladder's full with four cups of coffee.'

'I'm just messing with you, Doggie. I know it's a coffee stain.' Harker was lying through his teeth. 'But you should buy yourself a new pair of trousers once we land… and a pack of Huggies while we're at it.'

Chapter 13

A strip of blue and white plastic tape cordoned off the crime scene as an officer wearing a white hazard suit and a mask positioned yellow markers around the body of Environment Minister Harold Cortez. A blue cover had been laid over the body itself but the concealment of such a bloody sight had done little to stave off interest from a crowd of nosy onlookers currently being held back by the police. Media cameramen bustled amongst them, doing their upmost to get a clear shot and so adding to what could only be described as a civilised frenzy.

With such commotion occurring right in front of the hospital, no one noticed the diminutive man in a lengthy tan overcoat who was jimmying the side fire exit with a crowbar. The lock finally gave way with a crack, and he glanced around to check if anyone had noticed before sneaking inside and pulling the door closed behind him.

The stairwell was cool and quiet as the little man slipped off his coat, turned it inside out to reveal a white inside, then slipped it back on. He pulled out a shiny metal stethoscope from his pocket, hung it around his neck, then made his way to the adjoining door and pulled it open a just a smidgen. The corridor was clear, as most of the hospital workers now stood around the main entrance, gawping at the events being playing out on the front steps.

There was a smoothness to the man's gait as he made his way along the corridor. He seemed in full control of every muscle and tendon in his body, like a dancer whose every movement is minimal and precise.

The intruder came to a stop at the end of the corridor, looked up to check one of the signs, and with a pleased expression followed its direction.

The nurse at the reception desk did not even acknowledge his passing by. Along with her immediate colleagues, she remained glued to the television screen where the headline 'Minister Gunned Down' scrolled along the news ticker.

Further on, he came to a halt at a set of double doors and, with one final glance back at the preoccupied reception staff, pushed one open and disappeared inside.

The room was dim, with only a single wall light illuminating a large cylindrical recompression chamber. He glided over to look through the small glass portholes fitted on the side.

Barbara Holtz lay there motionless, dressed in a blue hospital gown. Her breathing appeared slow but regular, and a light sheen of sweat covered her forehead. The man pulled away from the porthole, scanned the chamber's exterior for the red communication button and pressed it with his index finger, before once again turning his attention to the porthole.

'Barbara… can you hear me?'

Holtz remained still, so he spoke again, louder this time.

'Barbara, can you hear me? It's time for you to wake up.'

Her eyelids began to flutter, then slowly her eyes opened and she gazed up to see the smiling face of Herbert Pelosi at the porthole window.

'Doctor,' she said weakly, 'where am I?'

'You're safe, Barbara. You're in hospital. You took a nasty turn while you were diving, so we've had to put you in this chamber to treat you for decompression sickness.'

The news had her raising one hand and knocking it against the inside of the cylinder, in growing panic at the confined space she found herself in.

'Please relax, Barbara,' Pelosi said in a kindly tone. 'You're quite safe now, but we need to keep you here for a little while – until you're better.'

Holtz's hand dropped back to her side and she gave a feeble nod. 'What's your name, Doctor?' she asked, her eyelids drooping as she continued to relax.

'Oh, I'm not a doctor, Barbara,' Pelosi said with a smile. 'I'm an associate of Mr Berger and he wanted me to speak to you regarding your visitors at the site.'

The mention of that name had Holtz's eyes flicking wide open, and her breathing began to quicken.

'I didn't say anything, I promise.'

Pelosi maintained the smile but a frown was now forming across his forehead. 'That's not exactly true, is it, Barbara? I heard you gave a tour to Professor Alex Harker, didn't you?'

She shook her head. 'He's just a colleague and I only wanted his professional advice. It's for the good of the site.'

Pelosi's smile evaporated completely and he tut-tutted. 'Now, that's not what we agreed to, is it? Only people approved by Mr Berger were supposed to have access, and I think that was made very clear to you from the outset.'

Now wild-eyed, Holtz began shaking her head rapidly. 'No, no, I would never betray Mr Berger. I swear that on my life.'

Pelosi was already waving his hand in an attempt to calm her. 'We realise that, Barbara, but you need to tell me how much Harker knows.'

Hearing footsteps outside, Pelosi released the communications button and, like a cat, glided over and behind the door just before it was pushed open. A nurse's head poked inside and looked over at the recompression chamber. Pelosi was already extracting a leather-handled switchblade from his pocket, his thumb pressed against the switch, when the nurse disappeared back into the corridor, clearly satisfied that nothing was amiss.

Expressionless, Pelosi popped the weapon back in his pocket, stepped back to the chamber and pressed the button to resume their conversation.

'Now, what does Harker know?' he asked, without missing a beat.

'He knows that Dr Khan and Dr Wexler were both working with me, and I showed him the fresco and one of the coins, but that's all.'

'Does he know what any of it means?'

'No, I swear, he has no idea.'

Tears were now running down Holtz's cheeks, and Pelosi raised a finger to his lips. 'Shhh, Barbara, it's going to be OK. But we need to get you out of here. There are likely to be too many questions.'

The suggestion seemed to calm her and Pelosi reached for the blue pressure-control knob at the top of the chamber. 'I'm now going to slowly release the pressure inside the chamber. It may sting your ears a little bit, but I have another one waiting for you only a ten–minute drive from here. OK?'

His plan met with a wide–eyed scepticism from Holtz, and as he began to lower the pressure, the pain became obvious in her expression. With the valve all the way down, and Holtz's eyes fluttering, Pelosi reached over to unlock one of the smaller pressure valves leading from the chamber, then poked his finger inside and wiggled it. 'We'll have this finished in no time,' he declared.

Pelosi moved over to one side of the room, where he began messing around with a large steel washbasin, then he returned and plugged the pressure valve back into place.

'Shouldn't be long now,' he whispered before letting go of the communication button, as Holtz offered a groan. The change in pressure was already having an effect.

Water began seeping into the chamber through the pipe, and rose across Holtz's legs.

Pelosi pressed the communication button one final time, whereupon her groans turned into screams blasting across the intercom. 'Now, don't you worry about a thing, Barbara. Just let it happen,' he said with a smile. 'That nurse shouldn't be back here for a good thirty minutes yet, which gives us more than enough time to conclude our business.'

Just as with his entrance, no one noticed the diminutive man in a long overcoat exiting the hospital side door and hurrying off down the nearest side street. With the commotion still in full flow outside the main entrance, no one paid him a second glance. In fact, he would already be crossing the border into Spain before the drowned body of Barbara Holtz, mouth wide open in terror, would be discovered by the duty nurse.

Chapter 14

The hum of excited chatter and occasional bellowing laughter was oddly intoxicating to Harker as he and Doggie made their way up the cedarwood steps to the impressive wooden chalet. This residence had been dug right into the side of the mountain, and its two floors, balconies, overhanging roofs and multitude of large windows must have cost a fortune to build. Down below, the town of Zermatt glowed, nestling in a deep gorge amidst the Swiss Alps. It was home to not only the wealthy but to thousands of tourists who came each year seeking adventure and the skiing the nearby mountains were renowned for.

At the front door they both looked back down towards the twinkling lights, with the Matterhorn towering over the town like a guardian, its snowy peaks bathed in a silvery light from the full moon overhead.

'It seems Dr Wexler has done well for himself,' Doggie remarked, his tone tinged with a hint of bitterness that only a close associate could detect. 'On the other hand, it's probably rented.'

'Not bad for a dead man,' Harker replied before going straight to the crux of the dean's comment. 'Your own house is rather lovely too, Tom.'

'That's not what I meant.'

With a smile Harker grasped the heavy round knocker and gave it two hefty raps. He then took a step back and glanced down at Doggie's recently purchased trousers. 'Loving the new threads, by the way.'

On arriving at Heathrow airport during the evening, and expecting an hour's travel wading through the London traffic, Harker had demanded that the Dean use the first available clothing store to replace his stained trousers. Under duress Doggie had been frogmarched into an unknown establishment 'Bob's Best Buys' in the duty-free section, though judging by the scarceness of stock and '*Everything must go*' signs, Bob's business was not only going to the wall but his taste in fashion was the most likely cause. Doggie had opted for a pair of brown nylon trousers which, to be fair, was the best of a bad selection. It was remarkable to Harker how a simple change in trousers could transform the usually impeccable-looking Dean into a sad-looking bohemian with just a single purchase. The fact that they were two inches shorter than the Dean's inside leg measurement hadn't helped either. *Thanks for the memories, Bob!*

Above the sound of glasses clinking and the merriment inside, footsteps could now be heard approaching, and Harker took another step backwards as the door swung open to reveal an attractive woman in her fifties wearing an expensive-looking red dress with frills at the shoulders.

'Yes, can I help you?' she asked in French and using a haughty tone.

'We're here to see Michael Wexler,' replied Harker.

'You've got the wrong address. There's no one of that name here. And in case you haven't noticed, we are entertaining this evening, so I'll have to ask you to leave.'

Judging by the glassy look in her eyes and the way she swayed back and forth with each sentence, the woman in red was unquestionably on the way to having one hell of a hangover in the morning.

'We know that he's here,' Harker replied firmly, sounding like a man of authority. 'A serious situation has arisen and it's crucial we speak with Dr Wexler immediately.'

The woman continued to stare at him with that vague look which anyone who has spent a night of heavy drinking with friends would recognise, and their already uncomfortable conversation now descended into nothing short of a staring match.

As the two of them locked eyeballs, a man appeared in the hallway behind her and quickly made his way over, placing his hand on her shoulder.

'Thank you, Estelle, I've got this,' he said, adding a friendly tap. 'Why don't you rejoin the party. We're about to serve liqueurs.'

Estelle shrugged her shoulders and headed back inside, swaying down the hallway.

'Sorry about that, just my sister in full flow,' the man declared in an upper class English accent, before swigging an imaginary drink, 'if you know what I mean.'

'Not a problem… Dr Wexler?' Harker replied.

'I'm afraid not. My name is Wendel Hippendale, so you appear to have the wrong address.'

Fakest name ever, Harker thought, shaking his head at such a poor choice of alias. 'Well, *Wendel*, that's a remarkable coincidence, because you look very like Dr Michael Wexler.'

It was clear that Wexler not only had a penchant for choosing bad aliases but wasn't very good under pressure either, for his neck now began to twitch back and forth.

'Look, Dr Wexler, we know it's you,' Doggie said flatly as the fellow peered over their shoulders into the street behind. 'We can assure you we mean you no harm.'

Wexler was still eyeing them suspiciously. 'Who are you and what do you want with Dr Wexler?'

'My name is Professor Alex Harker and this is Dean Thomas Lercher of Cambridge University.'

The use of titles clearly had little effect on this man, so Harker sought immediately to get straight to the point. 'There's been an incident out at the Gibraltar dig site involving Dr Holtz, so may we have a word with you in private?'

Wexler's eyes widened with concern but still he gave a shake of his head. 'I don't know a Dr Wexler, or a Dr Holtz, I've already told you. You must have me mixed up with somebody else.'

'Such as a dead man?' Harker muttered cynically, both eyebrows raised. 'Come now, Michael, we know that's simply not true.'

The man just about maintained his composure as he glanced back and forth between them, but his thumb had begun to twitch awkwardly. 'Who are you exactly?'

Doggie now took the lead, and with a single stride he joined Wexler on the top step. 'We're men who believe in discretion, Michael,' he said, glancing over the man's shoulder towards the sound of company in the other room. 'And given what's happened, that's something you should value highly at this moment.'

Harker was impressed – the dean still had what it took – and Wexler's resolve visibly began to crumble.

'Fine. Then you'd better come inside, hadn't you?'

Their reluctant host stood back and waited for them both to enter the hallway, before closing the door firmly. He said nothing, but only beckoned with his finger for them to follow, then led them past the main room, allowing them a glimpse of Estelle downing a large glass of green crème de menthe as fifteen or so well-dressed guests egged her on enthusiastically.

'We can talk in my study,' Wexler explained as they followed him up a narrow staircase to the first floor.

The impressive paintings hanging on lilac-painted walls screamed wealth and taste.

'Is that a genuine Caravaggio?' Harker stopped before a painting of a naked young man hunched, holding a lamb in his arms, which was displayed in a gilt-trimmed frame illuminated by a rectangular brass display lamp.

'Ah, yes, the Apostle John as a boy, with the lamb of God,' Wexler replied, displaying a fleeting surge of pride in his possessions. 'You have a good eye, Professor Harker.'

Wexler continued to the end of the landing where he opened a door into the last room.

Doggie leaned in close to Harker's ear. 'I never much cared for Caravaggio.'

'Oh, I agree,' Harker whispered back sarcastically, 'I much prefer that poster of the Mona Lisa you bought in the Louvre gift shop.'

With Doggie looking mightily unimpressed they followed Wexler into his study and took a moment to take in the decor, while their host closed the door softly behind them. At the far end of the room stood a heavy mahogany partners' desk. Long green curtains hung alongside each of the two large windows overlooking the street outside. The crimson carpet seemed at odds with the lilac walls and the desk itself sat on a red and white Persian rug which seemed to clash with the chrome skirting board that ran around the edges of the room.

The doctor seemed understandably miffed by their intrusion but he extended an arm and gestured for his visitors to take a seat in the two Herman Miller office chairs on the other side of the desk.

'Thank you,' Harker replied as he and Doggie sat down. 'I appreciate our arrival must be somewhat disconcerting for you, given the… clandestine nature of the dig in Gibraltar.'

'Not to mention the exaggerated reports of your demise,' Doggie added with a wink.

From Wexler's blank expression it was evident the doctor was unwilling to reveal any information he didn't have to, and Harker settled back in his chair like a man in charge of the situation.

'Are you aware that earlier today that same underwater dig site was destroyed, and Dr Holtz herself is now in a critical condition?'

The seriousness of Dr Holtz's physical state was a deliberate overplay on Harker's part, but Wexler remained silent regardless, allowing his visitor to make his point.

'You should also know I was inside the pyramid when it collapsed. Or, more accurately, was blown up.'

There was still no reaction and so, like choosing the right bait for a fish to bite, Harker reached into his pocket and pulled out the gold coin Barbara Holtz had given him and then, very slowly for maximum effect, he leant over and placed it on the desktop. 'And then there's this.'

Wexler's left eye now began to twitch with undisguised interest and he stared down at it, then back at Harker, then down at the coin again. He calmly picked it up off the desk and held it between thumb and forefinger as he examined it more closely. 'Where did you get this?'

'I took it from the site, as you should know,' Harker replied as Wexler continued scrutinising the coin. 'Maybe we should start with what you yourself know, beginning with why you've faked your own death.'

Wexler looked irked initially, his lips tensing and his grip on the coin tightening. But as they sat there in silence, his expression began to soften and he replaced the coin on the desktop.

'I'm not sure I understand exactly how you've become embroiled in all of this, Professor Harker.'

'Please, call me Alex,' Harker replied, sitting up straighter in his chair.

'Very well, Alex. But seeing as you have me at a disadvantage, and in light of this,' Wexler tapped a finger on the coin, 'why don't we start at the beginning?'

Finally chose the right bait, Harker reflected.

'I was invited to the dig by Barbara Holtz because of my academic background in ancient texts,' he began.

'She said *you* invited *her*.'

'No, that's incorrect. She invited both myself and Marsouk Khan for the same reason, just over two weeks ago.'

This timeline contradicted Holtz's account, but Harker remained quiet and allowed the man to continue.

'It was a fascinating experience and like nothing else I'd ever seen – truly unbelievable, as I'm sure you'll agree. A complete rewriting of traditional historical teachings. Involving a previously unknown civilisation, and one – if the frescos are to be taken seriously – that explains much about history we don't understand.'

'How so?' Harker asked, despite not wanting to contaminate this explanation with his own views on the subject. Which were views he was not even sure of yet.

'Let's put that to one side for the moment,' Wexler replied, shifting in his chair, 'because, after the initial survey, we found something that at the time I did not truly appreciate the significance of. Both Marsouk and myself believed that this discovery should be made public, and we urged Dr Holtz to bring in the media, but she was adamant that the whole site remain a secret until we learnt more.'

'So, what did you discover?' Doggie asked, but Wexler merely waved his hand dismissively in the dean's direction.

'I'll get to that shortly, if you'll allow me to continue. Now, as I was just saying, Dr Holtz refused our request, and as the days rolled by it became an ever growing bone of contention between us. So, finally, I gave her twenty-four hours to agree to my request, or else I would go to the media myself.' Wexler began rubbing his forehead. 'Marsouk was found dead at his hotel eight hours later – an apparent heart attack, if you'll believe that – and I… well, I panicked. I took off immediately.'

'The reports claim your body was found washed up on a beach in the south of France,' Harker interjected, and Wexler offered a nod.

'My brother-in-law serves in the police force down there. I asked him for his help because my life was likely in danger, and he agreed. I then came straight here to Switzerland.'

'That story will never hold up in the long run, Michael,' Harker declared. 'If there wasn't actually a body, then someone will find out.'

Wexler shrugged his shoulders. 'It won't matter soon, anyway.'

This answer was unnerving and Harker shot Doggie a worried look. 'And why would that be?'

Wexler stared gloomily out of the window and down at the sparkling lights of Zermatt below. 'Because in a week's time everything we know, love and cherish will be gone… all in the blink of an eye.'

Chapter 15

'What exactly are you talking about?' Harker demanded sharply, getting to his feet. None of this made any sense to him. 'What did you find down there?'

Wexler seemed oblivious to his question and continued staring out of the window, but now up at the night sky. 'Do you know how legends are started, Alex?'

He hazarded, 'They're actually true stories convoluted over time, through retelling, until they take on a life of their own. Well, that's my take on it.'

'Exactly. I couldn't have put it better myself,' Wexler replied, turning away from the window to face him. 'It starts with truth – fact – that, over time, becomes more than what it once was. Each generation adding to it, a little bit here, a little bit there, until finally, when enough time has passed, the legend recounted bears only a glimmer of the truth that it once related to. It's all about time, you see. That's the important component.'

'OK,' Harker replied vaguely, beginning to frown in confusion.

'If enough time passes, then what was once legend is sometimes taken up as fact again – like Chinese whispers, when you think about it.'

Wexler rose from his chair and with an outstretched hand gestured Harker to return to his seat, before perching himself on the edge of his desk and continuing. 'If an apocalyptic event took place on Earth, say twelve thousand years ago, how would those who survived it warn the following generations?'

'Why would they want to warn them? It's already happened.' Doggie revealed his lack of interest in this bizarre conversation by flicking some specks of lint from his thigh.

'Ah, but what if they realised it would happen again – and perhaps even had happened before. Then what?'

Finally, Harker thought, *at last some foundation for a discussion*. 'Some kind of documentation would provide the most straightforward solution.'

'True, true. But how sure could we be that such documents would survive the passage of time? I mean, materials can break down completely and turn to dust within a few hundred, let alone thousands of years. Languages evolve and empires shift. No, how could survivors of such a catastrophe even hope to ensure that their warnings might stand a chance of reaching people so far in the future? Something physical would be a gamble at best. Would it not make more sense to embed the message in something intangible, which could survive down the ages within the minds of humankind?'

'You're talking about religion, aren't you?' Harker asked, now feeling genuinely interested.

'Precisely, Alex. How best to pass a message on to the future than through an ideology that countless humans hold so dear.'

Wexler made his way back to the other side of his desk and slid open the central drawer. He pulled out a large book with yellow sticky notes sticking out from the side, and opened it at the first one before motioning for them to approach the desk.

'In every religious doctrine there are certain similar, connecting themes. All of them describe a higher power, a god. They all comprise stories of man's realisation that this god is their master, to be served and worshipped.'

'And?' Harker was becoming mildly frustrated.

'And this,' Wexler replied, pointing to the reproduction of an oil painting depicting a gigantic flood, with naked people being washed away on cresting waves while a few clung to a small rock protruding from the surface, along with a single, bedraggled looking lion.

'Noah's flood.'

Wexler gave a grave nod of the head. 'In every religion, on every continent, the legend of a great deluge appears. It is described as being of such epic proportions that almost everyone and everything was washed away by it.'

The doctor now began flipping pages to each of the bookmarks in turn. 'The Bible, the Quran, Buddhism, Hinduism, Judaism all contain the story in their doctrines. From China to the Aztecs, Mesopotamians, Egyptians, Hawaiians, Aboriginals, Sumerians… and I could go on and on. There is not one civilisation on Earth whose mythology or religion doesn't describe the story of a great deluge – an apocalypse that wiped out humankind.'

Harker and Doggie remained quiet, uncertain as to what to make of this intense presentation. There was something in all this that they were still missing. Whether it involved a member of a doomsday cult or the guy who traipses the streets wearing a 'The end is nigh' sandwich board, they all shared one thing in common with Michael Wexler… that wide-eyed look of consuming obsession. And it was with that very gaze that he stared at them now.

'Well, that's all very interesting,' Harker began, scratching his cheek, 'and I will admit those frescos back in the pyramid did depict a huge flood of some kind, but I'm not sure that I...' He motioned to Doggie, looking equally bemused, and continued, '... that *we* know where you're going with all this.'

Wexler closed the book, reached into his pocket and pulled out a smartphone, which he began to tap on. 'Did you notice anything missing whilst you were inside that pyramid?' he asked, without looking up from the screen. 'Something that stood out? Something on the walls maybe?'

Harker was racking his brains when he suddenly remembered the one oddity that had stood out. 'There was a piece of plaster missing from one of the frescos.'

'Good, you noticed,' Wexler replied, now looking up from the mobile's screen. 'Barbara Holtz had removed it, but not before I managed to take a picture of it.' He passed the phone over to Harker.

The image seemed familiar to Harker, and as he used his fingers to zoom in, he started to recognise it. 'It looks similar to the Mayan Calendar, but the markings are different.'

'Yes, the famous Mesoamerican Long Count calendar that had every conspiracy buff on the planet thinking the world would end back in 2012.'

Harker remembered it well. Although he himself could not take it seriously, there were many who did, but as he had expected, that date had passed with nothing eventful transpiring.

'And your point is?'

'My point, Alex, is that this calendar follows the same countdown as used by the Mayans, with one notable exception. The day of reckoning begins rather closer to us now.'

'How close?' Harker asked.

With a sombre expression, Wexler's shoulders stiffened. 'In just under a week.'

As fascinating as this seemed, Harker was not about to put any real credence into whatever their host alluded to, but he decided to tread carefully given that a crazy, unhinged look was back in Wexler's eyes. 'That is very interesting, Michael, but there are the same types of prediction in most ancient cultures, from all over the world. What makes this one so special?'

'Swipe on to the next photo,' Wexler instructed, gesturing towards the phone.

Harker did so to find himself looking at an image of what appeared to be a series of dots surrounding a central orb.

'What you're looking at was found on that same piece of plaster, and right next to the calendar,' Wexler said, pursing his lips. 'Now, you tell me, what does it look like?'

Harker didn't need any time to reflect because he already knew what it was. The orb in the centre had pointed triangles protruding from its surface, clearly representing light, and the other dots – or smaller orbs – had been placed at various distances from it. Each was connected to a faint ring showing its rotation around the central orb. 'It's the solar system,' he said confidently.

Wexler nodded. 'And how many planets are there?'

Harker did a quick count and then, for the first time since meeting the doctor he felt a slight twinge in the pit of his stomach. 'Nine.'

'Nine,' Wexler repeated. And as the two men stared at each other, a frown spread across Doggie's forehead.

'Sorry, gentlemen, but am I missing something? Are we still on the subject of Noah and the flood and apocalyptic calendars, or should I just leave you boys to it? I'd be more than happy to go and join the party below.'

Wexler looked rather offended, then he pointed again to the phone. 'Well, if that doesn't impress you, then perhaps this will. Swipe to the next photo.'

Harker did as he was told and what he saw made him gasp. The photo showed the body of a man standing naked, but it wasn't the nudity that was disturbing, rather the large elliptical-shaped eyes, olive-coloured skin and six digits on each hand.

'Where did you get this?' he asked, as Doggie craned to take a look.

'I downloaded it from Barbara Holtz's laptop,' Wexler explained, looking thrilled with himself. 'Bet you've never seen anything like that before.'

Harker glanced over at Doggie, then passed it back to the doctor. 'Actually, we have... in the flesh.'

Wexler's mouth dropped open. 'Where?'

There was no chance Harker was about to reveal his Templar identity, along with the events that had transpired, but he felt, given Wexler had already seen the photo, that he should be told the truth – at least in part.

'It's a long story, but yesterday we actually found this creature with the same people who hired you to work on the site in Gibraltar.'

'Who are *they*?' Wexler asked, making it sound more like a demand.

'They are called the Mithras, and they're a very powerful and dangerous group of people.'

'The Mithras? From ancient Rome? That sect died out two thousand years ago,' Wexler protested, looking highly dubious.

'That's what I thought at first, but I can assure you they're very real indeed.'

Wexler's head bowed, deep in thought, before shooting back up again. 'And where did they find this creature from the photo?'

Harker shook his head. 'That's what we would like to know.'

'Alex thinks it's an alien,' Doggie added, but with no sarcasm in his voice this time.

'Not just an alien, Dean Lercher, but an Annunaki,' Wexler remarked. He opened another drawer in his desk and this time pulled out an even bigger book, flagged with the same yellow stickies, and began flicking through it until he reached the desired page.

'Once I saw that photo, I knew it was real,' Wexler said, and he slid the book around and pointed to a black-and-white picture of images carved into a stone wall. 'The Sumerians were the very people who invented cuneiform, and whose writing is on that coin of yours. They wrote of gods – the Annunaki – giants who towered over men and taught them the technology of the wheel, as well as astronomy, agriculture and animal husbandry, and provided mankind with the knowledge that was to become the very foundation of civilisation as we know it today. There have even been seals discovered depicting the number of stars in the solar system, thousands of years before the Western world even considered the science of astronomy.'

'I'm aware of the artefacts, Michael,' Harker interrupted. 'Most archaeologists are, but it's a long way from there to believing the creature in that photo – which I've seen with my own eyes, I might add – is not one of the Annunaki. Besides, it's only five feet tall.'

'Right,' Doggie said, with a hint of sarcasm returning to his voice, 'but of course it is nevertheless an alien.'

'The Annunaki were not aliens. And according to the Sumerians, when the time is right, and before a giant deluge descends to cleanse the Earth once more, the Annunaki will appear again to save humankind from such a terrible tragedy.'

Harker could see how committed to this belief Wexler was, but he thought it only right to be honest with the man. 'It could be difficult for them to do that, Michael, because the creature we found – this Annunaki – it died last night.'

The news hit Wexler like a brick in the face, and he stood there stunned before dropping heavily back into his chair. 'How?'

'We're not sure,' Harker lied, choosing to pass over the revelation of the torture Avi Legrundy had inflicted upon the creature. 'As of this moment it's lying on a surgeon's table at Great Western Hospital, in the UK – and having its DNA tested.'

Wexler looked almost broken-hearted as he retrieved a packet of Gauloises and a gold Dunhill lighter from his desk drawer and slipped a cigarette between his lips. 'Care for a smoke?'

Both Harker and Doggie declined his offer as the doctor lit up, sending a cloud of blue-tinged smoke into the air. 'Some people find these too strong but personally I enjoy the harsh draw.' He inhaled deeply. 'Everyone has their own preferred brand but they all come from the same source: the humble tobacco plant.'

Harker wasn't sure where this conversation was heading but both he and Doggie remained silent while Wexler retrieved a glass ashtray from the same drawer and placed it on the desktop, before lightly flicking ash into it.

'So many brands and such different qualities of tobacco, yet all coming from a single species of plant. Life on this planet is not much different,' he continued with a lick of his lips. 'So many diverse forms of life in all shapes and sizes and each as diverse from each other as animals are to vegetables, yet we all arose from the same place. It involves the same set of genes which, over time, has added layer upon layer of additional information to best suit individual habitat via the process of evolution.' Wexler began to rock back and forth on his chair. 'As I have already said, time is the key to everything, of course, because without it we are nothing. Everything we see in our reality has its origin in stardust, the prime ingredient of the cosmic soup that has given us every conceivable thing, be it this cigarette, the jacket you wear, the mortar that holds this house together, and the variety of life we see about us. All from a single source, and everything we hold dear, but without *time* it could never happen.'

Doggie looked unimpressed by the deliberate, long-winded route Wexler was taking, which was in his experience utilised by most university professors when trying to kill the last fifteen minutes on a Friday afternoon.

Harker, on the other hand, could already see what the doctor was leading up to. 'You're referring to the origin of life, aren't you?'

Wexler took another long drag, swaying his head from side to side. 'Not just life, Professor Harker, but the gods that created it.'

Harker's mouth dropped open and he glanced over at Doggie, whose eyes narrowed with disbelief, while Wexler took another long drag.

'An ancient civilisation that settled on our planet but became lost to time and history, a shadow civilisation, you might say.'

Harker gave an involuntary gulp and he, like Doggie, started looking more than sceptical. 'Are we talking little green men here?' he asked, clearing his throat with an uncomfortable grunt. 'Area 51? The Roswell crash?'

The hint of sarcasm in his tone had no effect on the doctor, and a smile formed upon the latter's lips. 'You've seen this creature with your own eyes and yet you doubt it? My own belief is that they are the parents of the human race, sent back down to us whenever their help is needed most, just as the ancient Sumerians believed.' Wexler took a deep breath. 'As I already said, gentlemen, over time truth becomes legend, and then legend becomes truth, and then reverts to legend again – and finally, superstitious nonsense.'

There was silence in the room and Harker looked on in bewilderment, because they had gone from apocalyptic floods to aliens, the Annunaki, and now the creators of humankind.

'That's quite a segue, Michael,' he said as Wexler finally stubbed out his cigarette in the and placed the ashtray back in the drawer. 'But if we can put aside the whole Sumerian aspect for a moment, what makes you so convinced this great flood, this planet-wide cataclysm, is about to take place?'

The doctor got to his feet and placed his hands on his hips. 'Because, as I said at the beginning of our conversation, the Sumerians believed there were nine planets.' Wexler strode over to the study door. 'If you have a few hours to spare, then there is someone I think you should meet. It's not too far, no more than an hour's drive, but it's cold so we'll need to get you some puffer jackets.'

Harker glanced at Doggie and nodded towards the door. 'Come on, Tom, I'll explain more on the way.'

With that, he followed Wexler out of the room, leaving Doggie muttering to himself, before he also stood up and hurried after them. 'Michael,' he called out, 'could I at least get myself some crème de menthe to go?'

Chapter 16

'Is the Council here yet?' Milat Berger snapped, smacking a pair of long leather gloves against his palm, whilst a young blond man removed the black Burberry trench coat draped around his shoulders and folded it neatly.

'They're already waiting for you, Mr Berger,' the young man replied with a respectful bow. 'It's the first office on the left.'

Berger dropped his gloves on top of the coat and, without a word, made his way down the corridor and into the room indicated. This small and unassuming office building was located in the suburb of Munich. Away from the city's busy central business district, its location was obscure enough to offer a satisfactory degree of anonymity and privacy for anyone visiting.

'My lords,' Berger began, with an elaborate bow. 'I hope I have not kept you waiting?'

The faces of three women and four men stared across at him from the split-screen wall monitor, three above and three below, while in the centre was an old man with a greying goatee and white crew cut. They all looked indifferent to the apology.

'You have been out of contact for longer than usual, Mr Berger,' the old man began, as the other six looked on suspiciously. 'We had hoped for an update on proceedings sooner than this.'

'For that I apologise, but events have been happening thick and fast,' Berger replied, maintaining his self-assured tone of voice.

'And what is the word on our old comrade, John Davies, and his pathetic band of idiots?'

'I took care of that personally, my lords. They won't be a bother to us any more,' Berger replied with a sly smile.

'And what about the gift for the coming celebrations?'

'That also has been prepared. I got your message in time so was happy to oblige. On the far more urgent matter of our project, you will also be pleased to know that although our plan is proceeding far more rapidly than anticipated, we are controlling it step by step.'

'Under whose hand?' asked a dark-haired woman in the top row.

'Herbert Pelosi, my lady, who is, I am sure you will all agree, someone we can place our faith in.'

It was clear from the Council members' expressions that there was no disagreement regarding Berger's assessment of the assassin, though the old man in the middle appeared unsure.

'I agree that your faith in Mr Pelosi is justified, for he is a solid and capable asset, but we have some reservations about strategy.'

'How so? We are getting closer to our objective, faster than we have over the past few months.'

'True, Mr Berger, but from what we understand, that is due more to this Alex Harker than to our own efforts. Perhaps John Davies was right about that one after all?'

Berger's lips puckered slightly, and although he did a good job of suppressing it, the old man noted it straight away.

'No one on the Council is questioning your tactics or capability,' the old man assured him with a gentle smile. 'Without you, we would never have been able to secure the site at Gibraltar, or keep it secret, and the work you have done there is something we can all have faith in. But you must admit that this precocious little professor appears to have a knack for unearthing things.'

'The coin, yes,' Berger acknowledged, his ego feeling slightly bruised. 'That idiot Barbara Holtz took him down there, against all protocol, but her mistake has now been paid for in full. And you know that the pyramid has been destroyed, and Mr Pelosi is keeping a very close eye on Mr Harker, so if he makes any further progress we will be there ready to take it from him.'

The Council members all looked encouraged by this answer, though collectively not entirely satisfied.

'Very good, Mr Berger. But given the importance of what he might find, meaning that which belongs to us, we feel that perhaps it is time to sharpen our sword.'

Berger thought about this for a moment, then nodded in agreement. 'Very well, my lords, but as you well know, this might only exacerbate our situation with the Templars.'

'We are well aware of the complications it may cause, Mr Berger, but it would have to happen sooner or later, would it not?'

'That much is true, my lords. I will arrange it immediately.' Berger nodded. 'And our man on the inside will make sure to keep us one step ahead of Sebastian Brulet and those zealot clowns of his.'

The old man looked concerned by this reply, and he leant in closer. 'Do not underestimate Brulet and the Templars, Mr Berger. They are a wily lot, and therefore to be taken very seriously. That is a lesson we have all learnt in the past, though, but one you have not yet experienced for yourself.'

'Of course.' Berger lowered his head respectfully. 'I will take all the necessary precautions. You have my word on that, upon the honour of the Mithras.'

The old man looked pleased at that and he finally began to smile, revealing a set of near perfect white teeth. 'When we have what we seek, I promise you that the Templars will pay their full dues in blood, and those that oppose our ordained greatness will be cast out like the sodomites they are.'

Chapter 17

The red cog-wheel train, the first of its type when it opened in 1898, wound its way slowly up the snow-covered mountainside to the ridge of Gornergrat, at an altitude of more than 3000 metres. The railway had been upgraded over the years to accommodate the millions of tourists who made the half-hour journey from central Zermatt for the stunning views of the Matterhorn and surrounding Alps. Sadly for the three men travelling in one of the carriages, there was nothing to see in the darkness outside, as thick clouds muffled the full moon's silvery embrace.

'So, is anyone actually going to tell me what's going on here, or should I expect to remain ignorant in perpetuity?' Doggie complained, having pretty much reached the end of his tether. 'Because if that is the case, I might as well have stayed back at the chalet.'

'As I said, Dean Lercher, you'll see in due course,' Wexler replied for the umpteenth time.

Seeing how annoyed Doggie seemed, Harker turned to him and said 'I'm not sure—'

'I knew it,' Doggie interrupted loudly. 'You haven't got a bloody clue, have you?'

Wexler merely smiled and continued to gaze out of the window into the gloom beyond.

Harker rolled his eyes. 'I was going to say I'm not sure, but do you know how many planets there are in our solar system?'

'Nine,' Doggie said with a shrug and was met with a shocked look from his friend.

'Jesus, Tom, it's eight. It *was* nine until they dropped Pluto a few years back for not being considered large enough. How did you ever become a dean?'

'I'm a dean of archaeology, not astronomy, Alex,' Doggie replied curtly. 'It's just not my bag, as you might put it.'

'Well, we've come this far, so what's the harm in going a bit further? Besides, he seems to know what's going on here better than we do.'

Doggie responded with a concessionary smile, where-upon Harker settled back into his seat and, with a playful smile, motioned to the darkness outside. 'So just enjoy the ride and take in these incredible once-in-a-lifetime views.'

For the rest of the thirty-minute journey, Harker found himself preoccupied with many questions. He had still not heard back from Dr Cordon, who was obviously taking his own sweet time over the DNA test on the humanoid. Botha hadn't yet called to tell him how his interrogation of Legrundy was progressing. And he had no idea why the Mithras had put so much time and effort into all this, not to mention where that creature – alien or Annunaki, if you believed Dr Wexler – had come from in the first place. By the time they arrived at their destination his head was swimming and he felt quite light-headed.

'Feeling OK?' Wexler asked solicitously as the train pulled up alongside the concrete platform of Gornergrat station. 'You look a bit rough.'

'It's just the altitude, I think,' Harker replied, not wanting to explain that he might be still suffering a mild case of decompression sickness. 'I'll be fine.'

'Some people can be affected by the sudden change in elevation, but you'll soon get used to it. Let's go,' Wexler urged. The train's doors slid open and they stepped out onto the cold mountaintop.

There was nothing beyond the station except a path that snaked upwards and, some hundred metres away, the grand, looming Kulmhotel. With its grey stone walls and large sun terrace facing the Matterhorn, it was the perfect place to enjoy the majesty of the surrounding Alps – in the daytime. At either end of the façade rose an impressive, round, stone tower, each topped by a small observatory.

'Beautiful, isn't it?' Wexler said as they approached the hotel's front entrance. 'On a clear day you can see for hundreds of miles, and there's nowhere better to view the Matterhorn.'

'It's quite something,' Harker agreed, squinting into the near pitch-black darkness. 'Really makes you think.'

Wexler swung open the door and allowed his guests to enter before following, then he made his way to the concierge's desk in the cosy reception area.

'You can buy yourself a Swiss Army knife if you want – there's a shop just around there,' Wexler said, pointing to a nearby door before speaking to the receptionist.

'Considering that man believes our world is going to end in just a week, he's acting mighty chipper,' Doggie whispered.

'Maybe he just wants to enjoy it all while it lasts,' Harker replied, getting an alarmed look from Doggie.

'You're not buying into all this rubbish, are you?'

'Of course not, but he is.'

Wexler returned from the reception desk and motioned towards a red door. 'He's in the restaurant. Follow me.'

The interior was stunning and not because of the quaint, Swiss-style, wooden chairs with hearts carved into their backs, or the white tablecloths with glinting cutlery neatly laid out at each place setting. Neither was it the red curtains at the windows nor the elegant bar running the length of the room. The stunning aspect was the view, now that the clouds had cleared and the giant peak of the Matterhorn was visible, rising above the mountain tops like a lone sentry keeping watch on all that happened below.

'Gentlemen, may I introduce Nicholas Wattling,' Wexler began, as a tall man in his thirties stood up from a table and offered his hand to Harker and then Doggie, who had barely taken his eyes off the wondrous view since entering the room. 'This is Professor Alex Harker and his colleague Dean Thomas Lercher, and they know what's going on.'

Wexler's blunt, straight-to-the point opening words had Wattling offering a half-hearted smile. 'Well, you better sit down then, hadn't you,' he said, his accent North American. 'I'm sorry to say I'm not as sanguine as Michael about this whole business.'

His words caused Harker to stare at him curiously, and Wattling added, 'I'm guessing maybe Michael hasn't given you the full picture.'

'Actually, it's been fuller than we'd expected,' Harker replied. 'It has something to do with a flood and… a ninth planet?'

Wattling gave a gentle nod. 'Overly informative, that makes a nice change, Michael. OK, then, you'll have to forgive us, Professor, but what I'm about to tell you is something that we've been keeping – how do you British say it? – under our hats for some time now.'

Harker could tell that the man was prickly, on edge, and he sought to soothe his nerves straight away. 'Perhaps it's best if you start at the beginning.'

'Very well, though I don't suppose it matters – not anymore.'

Wattling leant to one side and waved over towards the bartender. 'Another double Southern Comfort on the rocks, and...?'

'Not for me, thanks,' Harker replied, and Michael shook his head.

However, Doggie said, 'I've got a hankering for a crème de menthe, please.'

'A hankering? Wow, you really are an old-school Brit, aren't you?'

'Quite,' Doggie replied, as Wattling ordered the drinks, then turned his attention back to Harker.

'I'm an astrophysicist by trade, graduated from the University of Colorado. I've worked at NASA and more recently at the European Space Agency.' Wattling now looked over at Wexler. 'Michael and I are old friends, so when he came to me a few months ago and asked if I would run some simulations on a picture he'd found...' Wattling paused and wagged a finger at Harker. 'He showed you that picture of the planets and their orbits which they took from the pyramid, right?'

'Yes, he showed us.'

'Good. Well, I charted an exact orbital for that little ninth dot, in relation to the aforementioned image, and it turns out that the conspiracy nuts were right.'

'You found it? A ninth planet?' Harker asked, noticing that Wattling was slurring his words ever so slightly. He wasn't yet totally soused, but definitely on his way.

'Oh, I found it all right, and discovered that it orbits the sun every eleven and a half thousand years, before it then spins off back into space – until it returns the next time. It also comes a lot closer to Earth than anyone could have imagined.'

Wattling went suddenly quiet as the bartender approached their table and delivered the drinks, before returning to his station.

'How close?' Harker pressed, as Wattling took a hefty swig from his glass.

'It passes right between Mars and Jupiter.'

'Well, that's pretty far away, isn't it?' Doggie remarked, taking a generous chug of his own drink.

'It's not the planet but what it hits that's the problem.'

'The asteroid belt,' Harker guessed, feeling his stomach beginning to tighten.

'Bingo. It clips the edge of it, sending rocks flying off in all directions, including towards this little blue planet of ours.'

Harker and Doggie sat in stunned silence as Wattling took another swig, then began to manoeuvre his hand like a plane flying in front of him.

'And when they hit… BOOM. Humanity gets sent back to another Stone Age… if we're lucky.'

As Harker sat there feeling numbed by this revelation, Wexler leant over the table towards them.

'Don't you see? This is what caused the Great Flood ancient history tells us about. During the Ice Age, eleven and a half thousand years ago, these asteroids rained down onto Earth, turning billions of tonnes of ice into a global flash flood that swept across the planet, and almost wiped out the human species in the process.'

Harker felt like he was about to throw up, and he turned towards Doggie, who was also looking petrified, his mouth hanging open slightly.

Meanwhile, Wexler proceeded with his reasoning. 'Only last year they discovered a thirty-one kilometre wide impact crater underneath the Greenland ice sheet and, relying on the depth of the ice cores they're drilling, they are putting the impact date to around—'

'Eleven and a half thousand years ago,' Harker interrupted, though in no more than a whisper.

'Correct,' Wexler replied, with a smile that to Harker seemed unwarranted. 'I believe the last one wiped out the previous civilisations, those same ones who contrived to build the pyramid you recently visited. A civilisation we didn't even know existed... and who knows how many civilisations before that, in a recurring cycle of destruction and then rebuilding, over and over again.'

'Then why isn't there any other evidence of it?' Harker asked.

'Who's to say there isn't? Think about it. During the Great Flood how much would have been swept away, and is now quite probably underneath tonnes of seabed? We're taking about a flood that would have carved canyons within hours all over the planet, annihilating everything in its path. And ask yourself how much archaeology is carried out underwater... not much at all. There could be a treasure trove of evidence down there, just waiting to be discovered.'

The man's explanation was still far too loose for Harker, who was already shaking his head. 'But wouldn't NASA know about this? Wouldn't one of the observatories have picked it up by now?'

Wattling now stared at him in disbelief. 'Do you know how many objects are observable in the night sky? Hell, a meteor big enough to wipe out the planet could hit us and it's possible we wouldn't even know about it until the last second. Besides, maybe NASA and world governments do know but are keeping quiet. I mean, there's not much they could do about it at such short notice.'

Wexler seemed unmoved by his colleague's appraisal of the situation. 'Or is there?' he said, tapping the table with his finger. 'Could I see that coin again, please?'

Harker reached into his pocket and placed the disc on the table. Wexler picked it up and ran his finger across the inscription.

'Marsouk and myself spent months investigating this writing. It's a kind of cuneiform, although there are discrepancies in some of the letters.'

'Well, damn it, man, what does it say?' Doggie said impatiently, banging his glass down hard on the table.

'Please try to stay calm, Dean Lercher. I realise this is a lot to take in,' Wexler said before returning to the inscription. 'We weren't able to translate it all but basically it reads: "Before the chaos... when the planet returns... the power to stop the rising tides... faith in the gods and the wisdom to prevent. Trust in the Annunaki."'

Wexler looked around them excitedly. 'I think they were aware of what was coming. Maybe they were far more technologically advanced than we can imagine. And maybe they even possessed the technology to stop it happening again.'

Wattling had remained quiet, focusing on his drink, but now he finished it off and rolled his eyes. 'Christ,

Michael, will you give it a rest? This previous civilisation of yours, this shadow civilisation, they were not aliens. But for argument's sake, let's say they were, and that they had technology advanced enough to halt an asteroid… and remember that's a monumental assumption. Why didn't they use it to save themselves?'

Wexler looked unfazed by his friend's disbelief. 'I don't know, Nicholas, but what we do know is the Sumerians clearly believed that after the flood the gods set about seeding the rebirth of civilisation. It would have taken hundreds if not thousands of years to track down any survivors around the globe, before they could reach a point where rebuilding might begin again with their help. It wasn't just some religious tale they were describing. These beings appeared specifically to help mankind rebuild. And then, when they had passed on their knowledge, they disappeared back into the shadows, waiting until needed again… And we need them now.'

No one said a word. But despite the horrendous possibility of a cataclysm taking place within days, Harker couldn't help but smile cynically and shake his head. It was a response that Wattling echoed as he placed his empty glass back on the table. 'And if you believe that big pile of steaming bullshit, you'll believe anything. There's no secret Ark of Knowledge waiting to be found, no aliens waiting to offer us their help with technology able to stop a meteor, for fuck's sake. The only truth is that, in just under a week, civilisation as we know it is going bye-bye and there's nothing we can do except find somewhere to hide. Which is exactly what I intend to do. I'm going to drink myself stupid over the next twenty hours or so, enjoy the two beautiful observatories above us before they're gone, and then head underground and wait this whole shitstorm out. And with the grace of God, maybe, just maybe, we might emerge to see what's left.'

'Underground?' Harker asked, sounding more desperate than he intended. 'Where?'

'What many people don't know about Switzerland is that it not only takes the prize for the best chocolate, although I'm sure the Belgians would disagree, but also its underground nuclear bunkers. During the Cold War thousands were built here because this country has always stayed neutral in times of conflict. I know of one, where we've been stockpiling food and water to keep us going… if we survive the initial impact, that is.'

'Where?' Doggie asked, already gearing up to ask for a place.

Wattling looked hesitant at first, because he knew exactly where this question was leading, but after glancing at Wexler he shrugged his shoulders. 'Nearby, at a friend's. It's pretty deep and so offers us a chance – but depending where the asteroids strike that may count for nothing. Still, it's better than nothing… and no, we're already full up before you ask.'

Doggie expelled a nervous sigh and even though the gravity of the situation was suffocating, Harker couldn't help but think the other two men were being far too calm about the whole threat. Especially Wexler.

'If all this is true, and the world is about to end, then I have to ask why you both are looking so relaxed about it.'

Wexler maintained his smile and it was Wattling whose expression changed, and with his eyelids drooping lazily, he offered a grunt.

'Do I seem relaxed?' he replied and signalled to the bartender for another drink. 'As for Michael, ask him yourself… No, Michael, why don't you just enlighten our new friends about your warped philosophy regarding the meaning of life?'

Wexler patted his friend on the shoulder, then licked his lips in anticipation of giving an answer.

'Yes, I'll agree that I felt some trepidation when I first discovered what was about to happen.'

'You're not wrong there, buddy, you were close to tears,' Wattling confirmed, now tapping at his empty glass impatiently.

'But after that I came to the conclusion – more an acceptance, really – that this is all part of the galactic plan, God's very will, and therefore I can live with it.'

'Or die with it, as may be the case,' Wattling added as the bartender dropped off his latest drink and collected the empty glass.

'No, Nicholas, humanity survived last time around, and I think – no, I believe – that we will make it through this too, and see the new world that's then offered to us. And if the worst does come to pass, I can honestly say that not only have I enjoyed a wonderful life, but I will die in the knowledge that I – amongst only a few – have learnt the true history of this beautiful planet.'

Wattling was already shaking his head miserably as Wexler continued. 'As an archaeologist, what more could I ask? The price may well be high but I have learnt more about our ancient past in the last few months than my predecessors discovered in the past hundred years.'

This explanation helped Harker not a bit, and as he watched the still smiling, now annoyingly upbeat Wexler, he rested his chin on his hand and slumped forward. He realised he was actually buying into this stuff and felt truly terrified of what might come next. What about Chloe, Brulet, his former students… even Doggie and everyone else he knew and cared for? Wiped out with recurring accuracy on a galactic timetable that cared nothing about life or morality, but instead only obeyed the laws of astrophysics. What made things worse was that sinking feeling in his bones that there was nothing he could do about it. He and everyone else was now at the mercy of the universe, and it made him feel pathetically helpless.

As Harker sank deeper into despair, he began grasping at straws… something, anything. He needed to do something, no matter how crazy, other than simply accept it.

'Michael, you said you believe that these Annunaki – these gods of the earlier civilisation – possessed the power to withstand such a cataclysm. Why?'

Wattling rolled his eyes and stared into his glass as Wexler replied eagerly, clearly pleased that someone wanted to hear what he had to say. 'It was that fresco back at the dig site that got me thinking,' he began, resting his elbows on the table. 'It was the central scene depicting light, or maybe energy, pouring upwards from the tip of the pyramid and surrounding the burning sun like a yoke. Is it possible the Annunaki somehow managed to harness technology that we haven't? And if you consider the possibility of them being aliens, then who knows what majestic delights they might possess in their arsenal. Problem is that even if it were true, we've no idea where that arsenal is now. Flight of fancy, I suppose, but fascinating to consider.'

Or completely depressing, Harker reflected. Although Wexler was burning with bright-eyed enthusiasm, it did nothing to put Harker's mind at rest. He stood up and stretched. 'I think I need some fresh air.'

'Can't say I blame you,' Wattling said.

Wexler pointed to a green door at the back of the restaurant. 'There's a terrace out there. I'm not going anywhere, though.'

'Thanks,' Harker replied.

Doggie finished off his crème de menthe and stood up likewise. 'Think I'll join you.'

Harker headed towards the green door with Doggie in tow, exuding all the energy of a weary backpacker. With shoulders hunched he opened the door and they ventured out into the dark night air. It was freezing as they made their way past rows of glowing ornamental lights to lean against the wooden railing overlooking the Alpine peaks.

'At least the moon's come out,' Harker remarked, trying to sound cheerful.

'They could be wrong, you know,' Doggie said, still apparently rattled by the apocalyptic news.

'I'm thinking that too. So we need to get another opinion.' Harker found himself thinking of Chloe. 'If they're right, then so much for the wedding.'

'Yes, I never thought you'd go to such lengths to stop me being your best man.'

They both chuckled at that, letting out steamy breaths which evaporated in the cold night air. Even though they had been outside for just thirty seconds, Harker was already yearning for the warmth of the restaurant.

'We need to get more information out of Nicholas if we're going to verify all this for ourselves. Know any astrophysicists?' Harker asked.

'Quite a few, actually, all connected through the university. But let's say for argument's sake that it's true, then who do we tell?'

Doggie's question was pertinent but Harker didn't really have an answer. 'If we call the media it will become bloody chaos. Can you imagine? The social fabric of entire countries would break down within days, with armies being deployed… sheer anarchy.'

'I think you're probably right, but we have to tell someone – at least give people a chance to find somewhere to hide. Nicholas said himself he has no idea where the meteors will hit, and so thousands, if not millions, might survive.'

Harker thought about that for a moment, then he gave an accepting nod. 'We need to confirm it first, but then probably the British government is the place to start, and go on from there.'

Just speaking about this made everything they had been told feel all the more real. Harker expelled a deep breath. 'Jesus, it's so hard to even contemplate.'

'I know. What a time to be alive. Just a hundred years earlier and we could have lived out a long life completely oblivious to this approaching destruction.' Doggie was now looking understandably glum, and Harker gave him a gentle nudge. 'You, living in Victorian times? I can see that – you'd have fitted right in. You'd probably have got yourself elected a member of parliament.'

Doggie looked offended by the very idea. 'Do you mind? I'm a decent and respectable man.'

They both laughed out loud and Harker turned away from the railing. 'Come on, let's get whatever information we can out of Nicholas, and then make some calls.'

Doggie nodded in agreement, but as he turned to follow, he spotted something moving in the dark and nudged Harker, pointing out a man dressed in black creeping towards the hotel's front entrance.

'Well hello, it looks like we've got ourselves a ninja.'

Harker focused his attention on where his friend was peering, and noticed not only the oddly behaving individual but now he spotted others all dressed the same, who were emerging from the rocky outcrops surrounding the hotel. They remained hunched as they began to skulk towards the hotel.

'What are they doing?' Doggie gasped, seeing the leading figure now raise something in front of him.

Before the dean's question could be answered, all hell broke loose.

Chapter 18

The sound of gunfire cut through the crisp, and the muzzle flash from four barrels lit up the hotel building sporadically as Harker flung himself and Doggie down on to the terrace floor. Shattered glass crashing to the floor could be heard from the front entrance, before the sound of panicked yelling took its place.

'Shit, not this again,' was Doggie's only comment. As Harker hovered over him he could hear the guns start up again, now more measured and in shorter bursts, as if the attackers were going from room to room, dealing with anyone in their way as they went.

'Shh,' Harker urged, still lying on top of the dean while regaining his composure after the initial shock. In an open space surrounded by mountains, the gunfire could be heard echoing off in the distance, which only added to the overall eerie effect. 'Stay still.'

Judging by the dean's frozen demeanour he didn't have to be told twice, and Harker raised his head until he managed to get a clear view through the restaurant windows, just as the terrace door opened and Wexler emerged on his hands and knees. His eyes were wide with fear and, although he noticed Harker immediately, he let the door close behind him and huddled against its frame.

In the restaurant the bartender could be seen raising his arms above his head, before his upper torso was shredded by a hail of bullets and he dropped down out of sight. Simultaneously a man dressed in black approached Nicholas Wattling who, although slumped in his chair, had his hands also raised. Harker beckoned Wexler over. The good news was that Wattling hadn't yet been shot and instead it appeared the man clasping the Steyr AUG assault rifle to his chest was now engaging him in conversation.

Wexler slowly began to crawl over to the others. As the sounds of gunfire started up again on the hotel's first floor, flashes of light could be seen illuminating each of the rooms in succession.

Harker recognised the type of assault rifle being used – he had seen the same model in the hands of Legrundy's henchmen back in that decaying house – and so made an educated guess. 'Mithras,' he whispered to himself as Wexler finally reached them.

'Who the fuck are they?' Wexler hissed, sounding as if Harker should know.

'I think they're the same people you were working for at the dig site,' Harker whispered. 'The ones you thought wanted to kill you.'

There was no shock in Wexler's eyes. Clearly, he had been expecting them to find him eventually.

'We need to get back to the train,' Harker decided. And then he looked up towards the restaurant to see the gunman fire a single round into Wattling's chest. Clearly he had not got whatever answers he wanted.

'Jesus Christ,' he muttered as Wexler looked on in horror at the death of his friend. 'Stay focused, Michael – if you want to live. Keep low and keep quiet. Let's go.'

The gunmen appeared to be killing everyone they found, and as the three crawling figures reached the end of the veranda overlooking the front patio, they crouched together nervously.

Again, the muffled sounds of gunfire could be heard coming from the rear of the hotel, as the meticulous mop-up operation continued. The Mithras – if that was indeed who they were – obviously did not care to leave any loose ends.

When Harker peeked over the edge of the veranda and down to the hotel entrance, he saw the train was still at the platform.

The drop was about three metres, and although it didn't look like much, someone could quite easily crack an ankle on impact.

'We're going to drop down this gap and make our way to the train,' he whispered. From the expression on their faces, one would have thought he had just asked if they would give themselves up so he could slip away safely into the night.

'We have to do something,' Wexler muttered quietly.

It was an honourable thing to say but they had few options. Protest and harsh language were no substitute for deadly weapons.

'What *can* we do? We're not armed. We'll contact the police the moment we get ourselves down the mountain.'

Wexler offered an unhappy nod of the head but Doggie looked troubled by this plan. 'Do you know how to drive a train?'

It was a good point that Harker had not yet considered. 'I'll figure it out. Now let's go. I'll drop down first.'

Doggie still didn't look convinced but the sound of gunfire starting up again on the far side of the hotel overcame any concerns he had. So, with a nod from the Dean, Harker clambered over the railing and seeing the coast looked clear, he dropped to the ground with a thud. He was already gesturing to Wexler to take the plunge, when the sound of footsteps had him slinking backwards until he was flat against the wall. The patio in front of the main entrance was covered in broken glass where the door had been shot out, and Harker quickly nestled his chin below the collar of his jacket, not wanting his warm breath to give him away. Then he waited.

The sound of footsteps moving slowly closer could still be heard, then came a crunching of glass as the tips of a pair of black, rubber-soled army boots became visible in the doorway, along with the tip of an assault rifle at about waist height. A thick mist of warm breath was exhaled into the cold outside, and Harker now restrained his own breathing as much as he could, without risking the need to gasp suddenly.

The killer was less than a metre to his right, and Harker was already forming a plan in case the man took a single step forward, in which case his hiding place would be blown. As another misty breath emerged from the entrance, he came up with the only choice available to an unarmed man wearing a pair of trousers, a shirt and a puffer jacket. If the killer moved forward, Harker would grab the barrel of the gun and proceed to deliver a bone-crunching Glasgow kiss to the fellow's nose. If that head-butt connected, he would then pull the gun away, shoot the man and hold the others off, if needed, until Doggie and Wexler reached the train, before finally making a run for it himself, firing back as he went. It was a plan with a lot of drawbacks admittedly, but beggars can't be choosers, and he was preparing himself to go berserk – clear-minded but absolutely bloody berserk – when the gunfire ceased deep within the hotel. A single last breath was blown out into the cold air, then the boots disappeared and Harker could hear the sound of footsteps growing fainter and more muffled, until finally he could hear them no more.

He was already waving for Wexler to jump, and within seconds the man let himself drop without incident, before he also hugged the wall. Next came Doggie who also dropped without a problem. With a final peek around the corner towards the entrance, they crouched as low as they could and in a tight procession cut through the snow, taking the shortest possible route to the station platform.

They slowed down as they approached the train and the other two paused in the shadows, well out of range of the station lighting high above, as Harker crept forward to take a look. There was no sign of movement and the train's sliding doors were open wide, so he nipped inside and, still crouching below the window level, he waved the others over to join him. Once they were inside the first carriage, Harker pulled open the driver's cabin door and peered inside.

The sight was not a pleasant one, for he found the corpse of the driver still wearing his round hat, but with a deep knife wound across his neck and his shirt soaked in his blood.

Harker ignored this gruesome scene and instead focused on the train's controls, which fortunately looked simple enough. There was a basic stick throttle to go forwards and backwards and just two buttons: one red and one green. Harker chose green, and poised his finger over the green button, his other hand holding the throttle. He pushed firmly down on the green button and immediately a horn began wailing loudly while the train's exterior lights blinked rapidly.

Harker retracted his finger as if the button was red hot and ducked as the horn reached a climax, then faded out, leaving them in silence once more.

'*Shit!*' Harker cursed and he glanced back at Doggie, who was staring at him angrily. From the direction of the hotel the sound of footsteps could be heard, getting ever closer. Harker scanned the driver's dashboard, then he peeked outside and what he saw was, frankly, not a surprise.

Three of the killer ninjas now stood on the platform, aiming their assault rifles directly at the train. Harker ducked his head back down as a man with a French accent called out.

'Dr Wexler, we wish to speak with you, if that is not too inconvenient. I promise you no one will be harmed.'

The killer's words did nothing to reassure them. Harker thought that if they exited the train they – perhaps minus Wexler – would likely be shot there and then. If they stayed on it, the gunmen would board it and then they would definitely get shot for their defiance. So Harker did the only thing he could and that was to press the green button for a second time.

Once more the train's lights began to flash, and the horn wailed away, as Doggie shook his head at Harker in despair.

The killer called out to them again. 'You need the keys to make it start, idiot,' he shouted, and they heard what sounded like a set of keys rattling. 'You foolish professor, you stupid roast beef,' he taunted, and his words gave Harker pause for thought. Not about the roast beef, of course, since that was a standard French insult, but that he had mentioned 'professor'. It meant they knew who was hiding on board with Wexler, and that it was Harker.

If this were true then these killers were definitely the Mithras, for who else would be after him? And, more importantly, they were unlikely to shoot him on sight, as they had done unhesitatingly with the other hotel guests. It also meant they may not know Doggie was with them.

'Come on now, boys,' the killer shouted impatiently. 'If you make us come in there, I promise to blow off your kneecaps for causing the extra effort.'

It wasn't much of an option and Harker pointed at Doggie and gestured his hand down towards the floor, signalling him to lay low as the other two exited. It was a gamble but maybe they would not bother to check the train after the two of them surrendered. He then looked at Wexler and, with a nod, slowly stood up to see a number of assault rifles pointing at him.

'OK, Dr Wexler and I are coming out.'

The pleased look on the lead ninja's face seemed to confirm they didn't know about Doggie. And now Wexler also rose to his feet, and the pair of them began to slowly make their way towards the still open carriage doors. As Harker reached the exit he heard a faint buzzing noise and looked across at the gunmen, who were scanning all around to find the source as the noise grew louder. Then suddenly, like a car radio turned up to max at the flick of a wrist, the buzzing turned into a tremendous roar overhead, whereupon the sound of a shot rang out. The gunman on the far right's head literally exploded into a puff of red mist and he dropped to the floor, at which point the other two made a run for the hotel. Overhead, the underbelly of a Hughes 500C helicopter screamed by, sending a down draft through the open train doors. It spun back around and in one smooth move landed directly on the large viewing platform on the other side of the train.

'Move!' Harker shouted, dragging Doggie to his feet.

'Who are they?' Doggie yelled above the roar of the engine.

'I've no idea but they're not shooting at us, so move your arse, Thomas.'

The three men leapt onto the platform and ran around the front of the train, as bullets began flying from the direction of the hotel. As they reached the helicopter, with the train providing a wall of cover, the pilot's window slid down to reveal Xavier Botha.

'Can't leave you alone for a second, Harker, you idiot. Now get in the front before we're shot,' he yelled, only just audible over the whine of the rotors. 'You two, get in the side.'

Harker jumped into the passenger seat. At the same time one of Botha's men pulled Doggie and Wexler inside the cramped rear, before he reloaded his Barrett M82 sniper rifle with another 0.50-calibre round, and began looking for a target through a small hole in the window.

Harker was feeling nothing but absolute relief as, in silence, Botha barely lifted them off the ground before tipping the Hughes 500C forwards and skimmed off to the right, followed by a hard ascent over the same tall rocky outcrop from behind which he had emerged. He then dropped down the other side of it and headed deeper into the mountainous valleys.

Botha pointed to a pair of headphones hanging on a clip. Harker slipped them on and Botha's voice filled his ears.

'You really are a pain in the arse, Alex,' the Templar began as they continued to descend in altitude.

Harker ignored this friendly welcome and instead glanced back at Doggie, who was looking thoroughly relieved.

'How did you know where I was?'

Botha looked unusually serious and he began to grind his teeth, his habit when something truly got under his skin. 'It's a long story. And I'll give you the full picture when we land, but you should know the Templars now have a mole within their ranks. Someone's been working with the Mithras.'

The admission shocked Harker. He knew the Templars were an extremely tight-knit organisation, because most of them had grown up within the fold, and to think there was a breach somewhere was a difficult pill to swallow. 'Who?'

'I'll tell you soon,' Botha replied with a deep grimace, looking more disappointed than angry. 'But you're not going to believe it.'

Chapter 19

'David,' a voice called out, causing Carter to jerk his head up from the row of books he was buried in, slamming it against the metal shelf above with a painful bang.

'Ow,' he moaned and rubbed his scalp furiously.

'Sorry, David, I didn't mean to startle you.'

Carter readjusted his steel-rimmed glasses and, still wincing, turned to see Sebastian Brulet standing close behind him, wearing a black pinstripe suit and with his long, white hair neatly tied in a ponytail.

'Not a problem, Sebastian,' Carter lied, giving his head a final comforting rub as he made his way over to the Grand Master. 'I wasn't expecting a visit. Everything all right?'

Even with the pair of aviator sunglasses covering his eyes, it was apparent from Brulet's expression that everything was most definitively not all right.

Carter began to feel concerned. 'Alex?'

'No, Alex is fine,' Brulet replied, whereupon Carter crooked his head curiously.

'Doggie?'

'No, they're both fine. I wondered if we could have a word, though.' Brulet was now gazing around the numerous rows of shelves running the length of this secret Templar vault located deep beneath the foundations on the island of Mont-St-Michel, off the coast of northern

France. 'I hope we've not had you confined too much down here. It can get somewhat suffocating at times.'

When David Carter had been offered the position of overseer of the Templars' most prized possessions he had been ecstatic. With well over two thousand years' worth of historical antiquities and documents, collected by generations of successive Templars, the vault was like nothing else on earth. There was no public or private collection anywhere in the world that matched it – and it even made the secret Vatican archives look like a public library, as far as Carter was concerned. He relished every moment spent in this place, the 'holy of holies' as he liked to call it. His days were consumed with unearthing and cataloguing every meaningful item that the Templars had ever collected, and while others might be gallivanting around topside in their adventures, that bothered him not one iota. For the real mysteries were right here, all around him, and never a week passed when he did not come across something remarkable, and usually of significance, whose existence even the world's leading scholars didn't know about.

'I'm in seventh heaven, Sebastian,' Carter replied with a contented smile. He patted his protruding stomach. 'I've even lost weight, although I think a lack of alcohol could account for that.'

'Splendid, David. Good to hear.' Brulet smiled and tapped his thigh. 'So could I bend your ear, then?'

'Of course. What can I do?'

'Come walk with me.'

Brulet rarely visited the vault these days, and as the two walked back towards the entrance, Carter began to feel anxious. Not because of this unscheduled visit but rather because of the two broad-shouldered, six-foot security personnel now standing by his work desk.

'I wanted to know if you've spoken with anyone since I called to tell you Alex was on his way back from Gibraltar?'

Carter's nose began to wrinkle and he shook his head. 'Apart from the conversation we're having now, no.'

Brulet merely nodded, and coming to a stop by Carter's desk he reached over and tapped the smartphone lying on it. 'No one at all, using this phone?'

The question, while not exactly accusatory, for some reason had the hairs standing up on the back of Carter's neck.

'No, Sebastian, I've not called anyone. But I did go up to the coffee shop a few hours ago to get myself a drink.'

'Mmm.' Brulet stopped tapping the phone and placed his hands on his hips. 'That's curious.'

Squinting at the Grand Master through his thick lenses, Carter was now feeling a bit uncomfortable, and was about to ask what exactly was being implied when the main lift down to the vaults beeped and its doors slid open.

John Schroder stepped out and made his way briskly over to join them, wearing a charcoal work suit and red tie and clutching a thin brown folder. With a stern glance in Carter's direction, he dropped the folder onto the desk.

'I have the information you wanted,' he began, his eyes never leaving Carter's. 'And it's just as we thought.'

At the best of times David Carter was not a man who enjoyed confrontation, and as both Brulet and Schroder stared at him, he began to feel like a cornered rat.

'Look, I don't know what all this is about, but you have my word I've not made a single call since we last spoke. Besides, the reception is bloody awful down here.'

Brulet remained expressionless as he picked the file up off the desk, flipped open the front cover and began to read. Schroder continued meanwhile to glare judgementally at Carter.

'Does the name Herbert Pelosi ring any bells?' Brulet asked.

Carter thought about this for a moment, then shook his head. 'Doesn't sound familiar, but why?'

Brulet licked his finger and with it pulled a single sheet of paper from the folder, then dropped the folder back onto the desk. 'Because John here was able to get a copy of your phone records, and it shows you've made three calls to him during the past twelve hours.'

Schroder shot Carter a smirk. 'One of benefits of working for GCHQ is the access to information – in this case yours.'

Carter's neck was beginning to twitch visibly and, although he looked the image of a guilty man, he shook his head fervently. 'How could I? I don't even know this man. Now, come on, what's all this about?'

'It's about betrayal, David,' Schroder snapped, pointing a finger directly into Carter's face. 'You've been working for the Mithras, haven't you?'

Carter at first looked stunned, then his cheeks began to flush as the nervousness turned to outrage. 'How dare you accuse me! I would never throw my lot in with that bunch of degenerates,' he yelled. Then, looking over at Brulet, he added, 'I don't even know any of them.'

The three men stood in silence for few moments, and then Brulet waved the sheet of paper in his hand. 'Herbert Pelosi is a contract killer regularly working for the Mithras, and he has been hot on our heels ever since we took Avi Legrundy into custody.'

Carter was having none of it. 'Then perhaps you should ask *her* about him, Sebastian.'

'We would have,' Brulet answered, pulling a phone from his pocket and holding it out for Carter to see, 'but she's been murdered.'

The screen displayed an image of Avi Legrundy on her knees and bent forwards in a hunched position. Her shirt had been removed, and from her back two white lungs were protruding from her skin and hanging down like fleshy wing flaps. All the skin had been removed between her neck and shoulder blades and three of her ribs, on each side of the spine, had been violently cracked, and then pulled backwards so they stuck upright like thorny spikes.

'The Vikings called this a "blood eagle", I understand, and I should tell you we believe Ms Legrundy was most likely alive throughout that torture.'

Blood drained from Carter's cheeks and he raised his hands to his mouth, looking as though he might vomit.

Brulet continued, 'We're not sure of its significance or why Pelosi killed rather than rescued her, but there can be no doubt that he – and the Mithras – want to get hold of that inscribed coin Alex discovered, and will do whatever it takes to secure it.'

As Carter composed himself, Brulet slipped the phone back in his pocket and returned his attention to the sheet of paper. 'And looking at your phone records, it appears you've been contacting this sick individual, Pelosi – one can only assume to aid in his quest.'

Carter was now breathing heavily, his eyes darting back and forth. But suddenly he grew calm, as if a realisation had popped into his head. 'How do you know it's this Mithras assassin's mobile number?'

'What?' Schroder asked, still looking ready to punch Carter there and then.

Carter stood up straight and drew his shoulders back. 'I said, how do you know that number I supposedly called was Pelosi's? You would have needed to know his number in the first place.'

There was instantly a lost look in Schroder's eyes, and Brulet now turned his attention to the MI6 agent. 'That's a very good point, John. How did you know?'

All eyes were now on Schroder, including the two security men right behind him, whose hands hovered inside their suit jackets.

'I checked it and the number was registered to one Herbert Pelosi.'

'It seems rather a foolish move for a contract killer to place his working phone under his actual name, doesn't it, John?' Brulet questioned, taking a step back from Schroder and moving closer to Carter. 'And, come to think of it, how did you know Herbert Pelosi was involved with Mithras in the first place?'

A vacant look spread across Schroder's face, but he was already shaking his head defiantly. 'I ran his name through the GCHQ database, and it turns out we have quite a dossier on him.'

Brulet slowly removed his glasses to reveal those cross-shaped pupils of his as he let out a sigh. 'As good as MI6 may be, you know as well as I do that the Mithras people don't even appear on their radar, as neither do we. The fact that both our groups have been around for so long – centuries before modern intelligence services were even imagined – has thankfully allowed us to unnoticed and remain in the shadows, as it were.'

Schroder said nothing to this as Brulet continued. 'Dear God, John, how long have we known each other, trusted each other, been each other's confidants? I never in a million years would have believed that you, of all people, would be the one to betray us.'

Schroder still said nothing – and thereby said it all.

'How long?' Brulet persisted, sounding bitterly disappointed.

Schroder relaxed his body and then he expelled a deep breath. 'From the beginning, Sebastian. From the very beginning.'

Brulet looked sad and shocked as the MI6 agent continued.

'I was born into the Mithras – like my father, and his before him. At a time when the Templars were waging an all-out war with each other… you remember?'

Brulet gave a slow nod of his head. 'I remember.'

'Well, I was tasked with infiltrating MI6, purely to become an asset, which I did. Then, later on, when you believed the Mithras had been defeated, I wormed my way into your ranks. A ploy which, judging by the look on your face, was a complete success. And as the years have passed, I have kept them updated on the Templars' actions – mainly so they could keep out of your way, I should add. But that all changed a few months back when Father John Davies decided to rekindle our association through his attempts to induct Alex Harker into the Order.' Schroder shook his head contemptuously. 'Through one idiotic act the Mithras were dragged back out of the shadows, as you put it, and placed centre stage once again. And with their anonymity in shreds, they are coming back fighting, Sebastian. They've amassed a lot of power and wealth, and you should know that this is just the beginning. They will stop at nothing in bringing you down and resetting the balance as they view it. You see, the discovery of that pyramid in Gibraltar was a complete fluke. But what they now hope to gain from it is nothing short of miraculous.'

Schroder smiled in admiration and clasped his hands together. 'You see, the stories are all true. That corpse you took from Legrundy is a genuine bona fide extraterrestrial, and the coin Harker has in his possession is the key to a world of wonders.'

Brulet and Carter stood rigid in stunned silence as Schroder seemed to find renewed energy from what he was saying, his gesticulations becoming more animated. 'They arrived long before humanity got its act together and their civilisation ruled here for thousands of years. But then something happened: a worldwide calamity that sent the planet back to square one. We haven't been able to figure out how or why, but we do know the new arrivals helped mankind rebuild, planting the seeds of knowledge that would grow into the modern world. They were the gods regularly described to us in ancient texts, giant beings with technology that we can only imagine, and then... poof, they retreated into the shadows until they might be needed again.'

Schroder's story was now sounding as outlandish as a sci-fi B-movie plot. But Brulet remained silent because, regardless of what he thought, it was clear that Schroder spoke with absolute conviction.

'The coin Alex found? He was almost right. It's not an invitation exactly, but the means of finding the location where these beings still wait to this day, and many within the Mithras believe that place – that Ark of Knowledge – holds technology that has not only the power to change the world but grants absolute power to those who possess it. And therefore they will stop at nothing to find it.'

This all sounded preposterous, and the only thing that had Brulet withholding judgement was the strange humanoid corpse they had in their possession. 'Where did the body come from and why did Legrundy have it, if she was so out of favour with the Mithras?'

Schroder gave a small shake of his head and rolled his eyes. 'Two of the archaeologists working at the site – Audrey Banford and her sidekick Miguel – claimed they had found the location of this Ark of Knowledge, or whatever you want to call it, and then they simply disappeared without another word. A week later a boat was found adrift in the Bay of Bengal, with the dead body of Miguel and no sign of Banford. But what they did find on board was the corpse you now have, then still alive and caged. From what I hear, it was half dead already, and when the Mithras got wind of it they ordered it to be retrieved immediately. Unfortunately for us, Legrundy got there first.'

'I thought Legrundy was one of the Mithras,' Carter said.

'She was, but after that stupid induction stunt carried out at Father John Davies's instruction, she wanted to barter *it* for the safety of their little bunch of merry idiots.' Schroder let out a grunt. 'As you know, Alex got to her first and now here we are.'

'But why the need to barter? And for what?'

'What do you think? For their lives. A peace offering, if you will. After screwing up royally and letting the cat out of the bag that the Mithras were still around and as strong as ever, they were put on a kill list… They deserved it too.'

This casual mention of murder had Brulet unable to hide his revulsion as he realised his trusted friend was nothing like the man he had believed him to be. He was just as immoral as the Mithras and had the complete lack of empathy that the cult considered a positive trait. 'Is John Davies still alive?' he asked.

Schroder shook his head. 'Not any more. Their loss of the creature's body to the Templars was the final straw. I don't know the details but I guarantee you won't be seeing him again.'

He threw up his arms like a man with nothing to lose. 'And there you have it, a fantastical tale that happens to be true, and I can see in your face that you don't know what to believe. The great Sebastian Brulet, for once in his life, completely at a loss.'

Schroder appeared to be enjoying the stunned reaction he was receiving, and as he let out a single joyous bellow of laughter, Brulet's mouth clamped shut and his usual calm composure returned to him.

'Not so much confused, John. Just a bit disappointed at realising you're not the good and honourable man I always believed you to be.'

Schroder's hands now dropped to his side and he snarled at the Grand Master. 'Disappointed! Let me tell you what real disappointment is,' he cried out. 'Real disappointment is my having so many opportunities over the years to slit your throat before you even knew what was happening, but having to restrain myself for the greater good. The greater good of the Mithras.' He was now swaying from side to side and his jaw muscles tightened. 'Real bitterness is spending years having to serve the Templars – the ones who caused the Mithras such devastation.'

'The Mithras were – and are – murderers, liars and psychopaths, with little care for anyone but themselves and their own interests, John.'

Schroder puckered his lips and spat on to the floor. 'Such a veritable knight in shining white armour you are, Sebastian. So decent and good and kind. Please… it's enough to make me puke. Empires aren't built on your beloved morals. No, they're built on oppression, brutality, and the sweat and blood of the people they dominate.'

'And all empires fall eventually, John, but ideology – belief in whatever god – remains untouched and continues in the minds of people forever.'

Schroder was now looking pretty full of himself, and clearly glad to be able to finally express himself after so many years. 'And when Dr Cordon gets you the results of the DNA taken from the corpse, and you realise that everything I'm saying is true – that the gods are truly nothing but evolved beings who used technology to planet-hop and shape our world as they wished it – what then of your Christian God and all the Papal bullshit you've shaped your whole life around? When you come to realise that ultimately we're all just animals with base instincts, and that violence and power are the only things that matter… what then?'

Brulet gazed down at the floor and thought about that for a moment, before looking back up again with a smile. 'Then I believe I'll have a drink in your honour, and thank the heavens that your primitive, primordial and twisted sensibilities have been cast out by the majority of humans existing on this planet. I will then have another drink and thank God that you are locked up behind bars or in a mental facility, incarcerated for the rest of your life where you will never cause anyone harm again.'

Schroder took in this veiled threat with a smile and did not struggle as the two security guards grasped him by both arms and began to drag him back towards the lift. Then suddenly he screamed out loudly, 'You've not heard the last of me, Sebastian. I'll be back.'

'How very clichéd of you, John. Have a safe trip… and be sure to write.'

The lift doors clunked shut, leaving Brulet and Carter alone amongst the rows of shelving, and a few seconds passed before either one of them spoke.

'Bloody hell,' Carter said loudly, resting his fists on the desk top. 'Do you think all that stuff about aliens is true?'

Brulet gave a gentle shrug. 'To be honest, David, I don't know what to believe. But I'm sure Dr Cordon will find out soon enough.'

The Grand Master's answer was delivered in such a placatory manner that it had Carter staring at him wide-eyed. 'How can you be so calm about all this, Sebastian? John Schroder is a Mithras spy and there's potential proof of extraterrestrial life on our planet!'

'That's exactly why. Until we have such proof there's not much to discuss, so let's keep our heads down and deal with other things first.'

'Such as?'

'Such as – are there any other spies within the Templars? If Schroder managed to pull the wool over all our eyes, then anything is possible.'

Brulet placed a hand on Carter's shoulder and tapped it lightly. 'And I must apologise to you for the deception, but I was worried Schroder might take off if I hadn't suggested confronting you with his false phone records.'

Carter grinned. 'Glad to be of help,' he said proudly as Brulet began making his way towards the lift. 'So long as you know *I'm* on the side of the Templars.'

Brulet paused, turned back and wagged a finger. 'My dear David, I would never believe otherwise.'

As Brulet was about to step into the lift, Carter called after him with a final query. 'There's one thing that's been bugging me, Sebastian. How did you know the name Herbert Pelosi in the first place?'

The Grand Master turned back to face Carter. 'Ah, now that's the real question, isn't it?'

Chapter 20

'I just can't believe that John Schroder was a Mithras spy,' Harker gasped, and Doggie seemed equally flabbergasted. 'He's been with the Templars for so many years, and I've known him myself for at least two!'

Botha gave a solemn nod, looking thoroughly demoralised. 'It gets worse. Sebastian confronted him about an hour ago, and Schroder took off – managed to get away. God knows where.' Botha looked like a man about to go on the warpath. 'I'm glad I wasn't there to see it as I'd have shot him in a heartbeat. But trying to put a positive spin on it, at least we know how Legrundy came to be in possession of the creature, and what the Mithras are looking for. Not sure it helps us much, though.'

Gathered on the available seating in a small hotel room not far from Zermatt, the three men stared at each other thoughtfully, while the fourth simply looked confused.

'Who is John Schroder?' Wexler asked, and received a stern look from Botha.

'I would have thought you'd know, Doctor, seeing as you worked for them.'

Wexler looked offended by the mere association and began to deny it vehemently. 'I have absolutely nothing to do with those murdering psychopaths,' he declared. 'I hadn't even heard of the Mithras people before you

213

lot turned up. I assumed they were a privately funded company which had secured a unique archaeological site.'

'Well, that part is true,' Harker conceded. 'They are privately funded.'

This did little to pacify Wexler. 'Might I remind you that I've just seen a good friend of mine murdered in cold blood, and if Mr Botha had not rescued us, I would most likely be in the same condition.'

After Botha's miraculous appearance and their escape by helicopter, they had been flown to a field on the outskirts of the small town of Tasch, about five miles from Zermatt. Botha's colleague had then taken off again, leaving them to make the short walk to the Hotel Elite. In their puffer jackets they looked like tourists and had not garnered much attention, although the receptionist had raised an eyebrow at four men taking a room containing only one bed.

'How the hell did you find us anyway?' Harker asked, until now so thankful for Botha's shock appearance that this had not crossed his mind.

'The same way I found out that Schroder was a spy,' Botha replied. 'We were intending to move Avi Legrundy to a more secure location, so I went ahead to make sure it was suitable. It was, but when I got back I found we'd been hit.'

Botha's grimace gave the impression that he felt partially responsible. 'Legrundy was dead – and you don't want to know how, believe me.'

'I do,' Doggie interrupted, oblivious to the painful story Botha was telling.

Botha pulled a mobile from his pocket and tapped its surface before passing it over. 'It's not a pretty sight,' he warned. 'Anyway, almost all my men were dead, along with one of our associates, and that was the grisly scene we found.'

Doggie recoiled at the gruesome image of Legrundy and quickly passed the phone to Harker.

'Oh my god, nobody deserves to die like that. Not even Legrundy,' Harker exclaimed wincing and, soon having his fill of the gory pictures, he thrust the mobile back into Botha's hands. 'You said *almost* everyone was killed?'

'Brian made it,' Botha explained, clearly taking some solace in that fact. 'Someone knocked him out, stole his clothes, and gave him a nasty concussion, but at least he survived. Thank God for small mercies.'

Brian Holden was a good man, and Harker knew it. He had been on Harker's protection detail from the beginning and was there when they apprehended Legrundy. His survival was the sole bright light in an otherwise horrible incident.

'The first thing I did was check the hidden surveillance cameras, which the killer clearly hadn't discovered, and I was able to watch the whole sickening event play out.' Botha swallowed in distaste. 'The woman was alive throughout... Anyway, straight afterwards the killer made a phone call and I could hear him asking for—'

'John Schroder,' Harker supplied with a sigh.

'The one and only. After informing Sebastian, I had a friend of mine run a facial scan on the killer's image and it came up with a name: Herbert Pelosi.'

'Who?' Harker had never heard the name before.

'He was originally in the military – special operations – but he received a dishonourable discharge.'

'For what reason?' Harker questioned.

'Some nasty shit during his final tour of Iraq back in '04, including civilian killings, rape parties and even a few child murders.'

'Jesus,' Harker winced, as Doggie and Wexler looked on in disgust. 'And they only discharged him?'

'Fog of war and all that… Like I said, some nasty shit and a dangerous man. Though you wouldn't realise it to look at him. Short, thin, little bastard with a pointy nose and small eyes.' Botha looked just as repelled as everyone else. 'He then disappeared into the private sector, for mercenary work, and apparently ended up with the Mithras. Not surprising really, since they're a bunch of savages.'

The four men went quiet for a moment, as if all engaged in dark thoughts. Noticing the mood, Botha moved onto a more positive topic.

'When Brulet realised the Mithras knew where you were heading, he asked me to come and check in on your pathetic arses. And when I visited Dr Wexler's house, I was informed by a very attractive lady in red – who was exceedingly drunk, by the way – that you'd taken a trip up the mountain and, voilà, it was there I found you.'

'That was Estelle, my sister. She's the only person I told where we were going.'

'Sister?' Botha looked momentarily surprised and then he began to grin. 'Well, Dr Wexler, you might want to check the family tree and see if you're adopted, because there's no way that woman shares your genes.'

Wexler gave an aggrieved smile even as Harker asked Botha another question. 'How on earth did you get hold of a helicopter on such short notice?'

The man's smile widened and he looked particularly pleased with himself. 'It's a trade secret, Alex, but you already know how I like to plan for all eventualities.'

That much was true, Harker realised. The Templar was probably already on the phone to his contacts before Brulet had even finished assigning him the task. 'Well, we're all glad you did,' he confirmed and the other two nodded sincerely.

'So,' Botha began, clearly happy to receive this acknowledgement. 'I would say let's go home now, but given your story about... what was it, an Ark of Knowledge and... oh yes, the end of the world, then I suppose that's a bust.'

'You don't believe it?' Harker asked, though not in the least surprised.

'Let's just say that, either way, you can count me in, and not just because you have a habit of getting into the shit, Alex, but because I want Pelosi, and I know he wants you bad.' Botha put his feet up on the coffee table and placed both hands behind his head, as if he owned the room. 'Now, why not tell me how I can help you, and why he has such a crush on you, the doctor and the good dean here?'

'You can start by getting your feet off the table,' Harker replied, knocking Botha's boots to the floor with a forceful shove. 'And now you can take a look at this.'

He pulled out the gold coin and placed it carefully on the table between them. 'I got it at the dig site in Gibraltar.'

'Underneath Gibraltar would be more accurate,' Doggie interjected with raised eyebrows.

'Yes, OK, whatever. The point is that *we*,' he said, gesturing at Wexler, 'think this coin was created to allow survivors of a cataclysm eleven and a half thousand years ago to find their way to the Ark of Knowledge. I think that this ancient civilisation used pyramids like the one at Gibraltar as meeting stations where survivors could go to receive directions to the Ark, where they would be given the knowledge needed to begin reseeding a new civilisation.'

'First, that's a lot of "thinks", and second, why have people traipse all the way to one place only to find they have to make another journey somewhere else? It doesn't make sense,' Botha said, but Harker was already shaking his head.

'Just think about it, Xavier. The world is devastated by flooding, a meteor hits or God knows what, with all the consequences of such destruction, but one group of people with technology and the knowledge to rebuild a new world managed to survive. It would take hundreds of years, if not thousands, for whoever survived to begin life again, and I'm talking of just rebuilding and repopulating communities. And presumably they would have considered it was an act of god or something. It's easily conceivable that any surviving communities would become highly introverted and keep to themselves for a long time. If the world got wiped out today and only a few people survived, do you think their first mission would be to go out and explore the world? No, of course not. Instead they would focus on building up their populations again and a society. Also, if the archaeological records are correct, then human beings were still only hunter-gatherers before the flood. So they are hardly going to make some massive technological jump straight after an apocalyptic event such as the one described in so many religious documents from around the world. Of course not.'

Botha still looked dubious, but Harker could tell he appreciated the logic behind the theory, as did Doggie. 'Now, let's say, for argument's sake, you have a small band of survivors who belonged to a pre-flood civilisation which possessed knowledge of agriculture, animal husbandry, seafaring, architecture, and everything else modern civilisation is based upon. I mean, there are Egyptian hieroglyphs depicting what look like giant light bulbs linked to boxes, and there's the Iraq battery that appears to be thousands of years old.'

Botha's eyes were beginning to glaze over, and Harker realised he was sounding a bit out there, so he quickly reined it in. 'The main point here is that, supposing this surviving group had such knowledge, on a devastated Earth with only pockets of human survivors spread all across the world – how would you go about attempting to start over?'

Given this was largely Wexler's theory, the man himself was staying remarkably quiet, but that did not deter Harker.

'You would have to wait for maybe hundreds or even a few thousand years to elapse before you even attempted to bring that knowledge back into the world. And how would you do it? Well, there's only two ways. One, you go out with all the knowledge you'll need, searching for survivors who have, over time, developed into communities. Or – and this is the most sensible way – you somehow entice them to come to you.'

Judging by their engaged expressions Doggie and Botha were beginning to open up to at least the possibility of his theory, and Harker pushed ahead quickly for fear of losing momentum.

'Now, the last thing you would want is to leave sign-posts pointing to your exact location, because who wants thousands of hunter-gatherers turning up suddenly on the doorstep, armed with spears and arrows and wanting to take what you have? That would be bloody suicide. So what would you do? You would build meeting places, perhaps pyramids if that was what you already knew, and have some of your own people wait there to see who turned up. If the new arrivals prove aggressive, violent, untrustworthy, then you send them packing. But if they seem reasonable, peaceful and trusting, then you give them the necessary directions.'

Harker now pointed to the gold coin lying on the table. 'Directions to show where they could gain the knowledge to rebuild a modern civilisation anew. And a shining pyramid standing alone in a wasteland is definitely going to catch the eye of anyone who sees it. Plus look at the location of Gibraltar. We know that hunter-gatherers used boats, and Gibraltar is the only way into the Mediterranean. If you were sailing through that narrow strait, how could you not spot it, and in turn want to take a closer look?'

Harker's theory was now gaining support from Doggie, who was nodding his head at intervals. However, Botha still seemed hesitant.

'OK, Alex, there's a lot of good points in there, and some of what you're saying actually makes sense, but' – Botha began to grin childishly – 'you think these knowledgeable types from a past civilisation, who wanted to help rebuild the world after an apocalypse, were aliens?'

Harker had been expecting this question since he began and he held both hands up in surrender. 'OK, now

I think we can all agree that the whole "alien" concept is making us feel uncomfortable' – he looked over at Wexler, who was shaking his head – 'apart from Michael, of course.' He turned back to the other two. 'I agree, I get it, so why don't we call this group an advanced human civilisation?'

This proposal received supportive nods from both Doggie and Botha, but Wexler pushed a finger in the air as if a light bulb had gone on inside his head, and his eyes widened enthusiastically, raising his eyebrows even higher. 'Or an *advanced being* civilisation?'

'No, Michael, we're not going to call it that,' Harker stated bluntly, and without giving the man time to respond, returned his attention to the gold coin.

'If an advanced human civilisation did actually exist, and in part survived a galactic catastrophe then the directions inscribed on this gold coin could reveal the location of this Ark of Knowledge. And seeing how seriously the Mithras are obviously taking it, then we would be fools not to act accordingly.'

Botha and Doggie seemed unopposed to his idea, so to tip the scales in favour of his argument, he decided to place a cherry on top of it – even if it was a rotten one. 'And anyway, if the world really is going to end in the next week or so, then I say why not give it a shot?'

'Not exactly an encouraging pep talk, Alex,' Botha remarked, but Harker could already tell that the Templar was on board. Doggie, however, seemed rather more cautious about the prospect.

'I don't know, Alex,' said the dean. 'If the world really is coming to an end, then I can think of a few other things I would rather be doing than going off on this wild goose chase of yours.'

This reaction was not that surprising to Harker. Over the past twenty-four hours they had been shot at, survived a gun-toting car chase, been shot at again, then rescued by helicopter, and the dean had even wet himself. Hardly an overwhelming temptation for anyone now asked to get back into the ring again.

'If I'm wrong, then just think how good it will feel for you to tell me over and over again how foolish I've been,' Harker suggested. 'For a week at least, anyway.'

Doggie let out a sigh and turned to Botha, who was already nodding his head. 'OK, Alex Harker... what's your plan?'

Harker returned his attention to the gold coin. He pointed to the side facing upwards and ran a finger around its central depiction of the Eye of Horus. 'This side is intended to show who the knowledge and the coin belong to – like the Queen on our own currency. It's an obvious way of letting whoever holds it know where it comes from.' He flipped it over. 'And this side contains an emblem and inscription describing the Ark of Knowledge – which is the same as that tattoo we found inked on the humanoid.'

'Advanced being,' Wexler corrected, and Harker waved his hand dismissively in the doctor's direction.

'Whatever. But what's been bugging me are these.' He now ran a finger around the coin's rim and indicated the smaller markings appearing at intervals along its circumference. 'Now my knowledge of cuneiform script is pretty basic, I'll admit, but I recognise these markings. They're numbers.'

Wexler leant over to scrutinise the edges. 'I missed that,' he confessed almost apologetically, as Harker began counting them.

There were fourteen in all and he pulled out his smartphone and began to jot them down on his notepad app before handing it over to Wexler. 'Is that correct?' he asked as the doctor began to check them against the engravings on the coin itself.

'Almost, but these two numbers are wrong,' Wexler stated and plucking the smartphone from Harker's fingers and tapping in the corrections. 'Now it's correct.'

'So, what are they?' Doggie asked as everyone now focused in on the doctor.

Wexler sat back and mulled over the numbers, and after a few minutes of muttering and numerous glances between the three other men, he finally began to shake his head. 'I'm not really sure. They could be a system of dating or even an identification number for each individual coin.'

'That's impossible,' Harker replied, and he took back the smartphone and began to stare at the screen. 'Fourteen numbers? That's in the billions and there'd be no need for so many. And a fourteen-numbered date? I can't see that working.'

Wexler thought about it for a moment longer before he placed the coin back on the table, looking defeated. 'I could spend years studying this and still get no closer to the meaning, I'm afraid.' Harker could feel his heart sink as Wexler now got to his feet. 'If you would like me to take this coin and continue analysing it, I would be happy to do so.'

'Thank you for the offer, Michael, which is much appreciated, but I'm not quite ready to give up on figuring it out just yet.'

Wexler did not look disappointed by this rejection, but leant closer and placed his hand on Harker's shoulder. 'You should spend the coming week with your family, Alex, rather than poring over this fascinating but, in the end, useless coin. And now, forgive me, gentlemen, but I would like to get back to join my own family for the short time we have left.'

Harker couldn't blame him. In fact, eyeing his friends' faces, he wondered if they would rather be with their loved ones too. 'Of course, Michael. Where will you go?'

'Well, I would normally go home, but since there's a hit squad after me, I think I'll take a taxi to that fallout shelter poor Nicholas mentioned. I called my sister during the helicopter flight, so they should all be there already, safe and sound.'

'Very well, Michael.' Harker shook the doctor's hand. 'Good luck.'

There was a heavy sadness in the air as Wexler shook Botha's and Doggie's hands too, thanking them for their help. It was a horrible, isolating feeling to know that in such a short time the entire globe might be shaken to its core, only to herald another eleven thousand years of galactic amnesia.

Harker now turned his own mind to Chloe and the wedding that would never be, as Wexler made his way to the door and offered a final wave.

'Who knows, my friends, maybe we'll see each other again, on the other side.'

With that, he was gone, and Harker was left wondering if the man had meant in the hereafter, or after surviving the apocalypse to come. Either way it was wholly depressing.

'Well, I have to say, boys, that all in all this has been a remarkably shitty day.' Botha groaned and placed his feet back up on the table. 'I don't know if this whole apocalypse business is real, but if it is, then all I can say is… damn.'

At the coffee table, Harker began to idly rotate the gold coin between his fingers. *So close and yet so far*, he thought as Doggie headed for the minibar and a whisky miniature with his name on it, while Botha picked up his mobile and began dialling a number.

'I'm going to call the jet and speak to the pilot,' he said, putting the phone to his ear. 'I'll give him our coordinates and see if he can find a private airstrip here on our side, so we can avoid having to go back through Zermatt.'

A single word hit Harker like a brick to the head and he looked up at the Templar with wide eyes. 'What did you say?'

'I said I'm going to call the pilot, see where he can pick us up from.'

'No, after that.'

'What… give him our coordinates?'

Harker's eyes now gleamed with excitement, and Botha cottoned on to what he was thinking immediately.

'Give me a break. That's too simple.'

Harker ignored him and pulled out his phone, brought up Google Earth and began to type in the numbers from the coin. 'They're coordinates,' he said triumphantly as Doggie came to join him at the table with an open miniature bottle.

'They can't be, Alex. The first systems of longitude and latitude weren't invented until the second century BC,' Doggie insisted. 'I may not know my astronomy, but my history is pretty tight.'

'I'm not suggesting it was not our invention, Doggie,' Harker said, gesturing to the gold coin he had placed back on the table, 'but what if it was theirs too?'

'Codswallop, Alex,' Doggie replied, taking a swig from the bottle.

Harker watched as the digital representation of Earth began to rotate and then, as it zoomed in on an empty part of the Andaman Sea, his heart once more began to sink. But after thinking about it for a moment he realised his miscalculation.

'Longitude is measured from north to south, right? With the zero line passing right through Greenwich.'

'Ah, the days of empire,' Doggie joked, polishing off the little bottle in a second swig.

'Yes, but what if I use Gibraltar as the zero line?' Harker continued as he began to prod at the screen.

His mouth dropped open. 'Port Blair in the Andaman and Nicobar Islands.'

'Is that supposed to mean something?' Doggie said, scratching the back of his neck.

Botha now looked riveted. 'The Bay of Bengal,' he said sharply and Harker was already nodding in agreement. 'Didn't Schroder say they found the boat with the humanoid floating adrift in the Bay of Bengal?'

'Yes, he did,' said Harker with a smile, already pondering travel plans. 'It's a long trip, way off the coast of India. Probably twenty hours' flight time, with possibly three or four stops. We'll be better off taking commercial flights rather than the jet.'

Harker was beaming as Doggie looked up from the new miniature whisky he was trying to open.

'Did you say India?'

'That's exactly what he said,' Harker replied, grabbing the bottle from Doggie's hands, unscrewing the cap and downing the contents in one go.

'And what are you hoping to find, Alex? Surely you don't believe there's some alien technology that can prevent an asteroid impact?'

'It's certainly better than moping around here, watching the clock tick down.'

Doggie stared at him in disbelief, then he placed both palms over his face and took a long moment to rub at his eyes. 'Very well, then,' he said. 'Count me in.' The dean then stood up, hands on hips, and looked off into the distance theatrically. 'Well, gentlemen, it appears the game is afoot.'

Harker let out a chuckle, but Botha remained unimpressed. 'Yeah, take it easy, Sherlock.'

Doggie maintained his pose for a few more seconds. 'Sorry,' he said with an embarrassed smile, 'but I've always wanted a chance to say that.'

Chapter 21

John Schroder glanced up at the bronze statue of Justitia and then flipped a coin into the water below it, which landed with a splash before sinking to the bottom. The Justice Fountain with its sculpted goddess holding a sword and scales had been watching over the city of Frankfurt for a very long time, in front of the town hall which dominated one side of the square. Crowds of people moved past him, all going about their busy lives. He gave a quick nod to Justitia before heading away towards a row of payphones. There he inserted a few coins, dialled a number and waited for a reply.

'Thank you for calling the psychic hotline,' a woman's voice announced in a high-pitched German accent. 'There is no one to take your call at the moment, but if you would like to leave a message, then one of our talented clairvoyants will call you back.' The line then fell silent, followed by a beep.

'This is John Schroder and I need to speak with Mr Berger, immediately.'

He hung up then rested against the side wall. Please make it quick, he thought, and in less than thirty seconds the phone began to ring.

'Hello,' Schroder replied and the same high-pitched female voice came on the line.

'I'm just putting you through, Mr Schroder.'

There was a series of clicks and then the familiar voice of Milat Berger who, as usual, sounded like he hadn't a care in the world. 'John, it's a surprise to hear from you so soon. Is there a problem?'

Schroder cupped his hand around the receiver as a red-haired woman with a nose ring began to use the payphone next to him. 'I've got a problem all right,' he hissed. 'The Templars know about me.'

There was a short pause on the line, and when he next spoke Berger's pleasant tone had evaporated. 'How?'

'That idiot Pelosi named me after his love-in with Legrundy. Why didn't you tell me he was going after her? I could have been of help.'

'Sorry, John, but I never put all my eggs in one basket at any one time. I'm sure you can appreciate that.'

Schroder gritted his teeth, feeling especially annoyed because this suggested he did not have the other man's complete confidence. 'Well, it's lucky for both of us that I managed to escape before I ended up God knows where. I did have to kill two of the Templars – but no love lost there. Look, I need to meet with you, and the entire Council, as soon as possible.'

'The entire Council! Why on earth would I arrange that?'

Schroder's grip on the phone tightened. Berger knew damn well that, with his cover blown, there was only one place for him to go and that was back to the Mithras. 'I have new information on Alex Harker, and the elders are going to want to hear about it directly, because it's likely to blow a lid off all your plans.'

Berger began to chuckle. 'He's a slippery one, that professor. We just had a team corner him and Michael Wexler, and yet they still managed to slip past them.'

This was news to Schroder, who felt his anger rising. 'Do you plan to continue keeping me in the dark about everything? I thought we had an agreement.'

'We do, John, but you can't expect me to tell you everything. Besides, it was a very last-minute incident. Now, why don't you tell me what information you have, and I will pass it on.'

'No,' Schroder growled, fed up with being held at arm's length. 'I want to come in from the cold, and I want to see the Council in person.'

A long pause ensued before Berger came back on the line, his voice sounding chipper once more. 'Very well, you can plead your case directly. I assume you have a new mobile?'

'Yes, I do.'

'Good, then text the number over to me and I will get back to you with the address and a time. Fortunately we are convening tomorrow night to discuss current events. So hole up somewhere safe in the meantime, and make sure you attend wearing a dinner jacket, as it's a formal occasion. I'll see you there.'

Schroder emitted a small sigh, and his grip on the phone loosened. 'Thank you, Milat. I'll see you then.'

As the line went dead, Schroder hung up the payphone and stood for a while observing the people around him. There was a mother and her child playing pat-a-cake over by the fountain, next to an old man feeding a biscuit to his white Scottish Terrier. On the far side of the square a couple were kissing intently even as group of teenage boys walked past them, wrapping their arms around their own bodies as if pretending to be in the sweet embrace they were witnessing. Just ordinary people going about their lives and wholly unaware that in less than a week the world as they knew it would be over. And in a twist of galactic fate, those few that managed to survive would emerge as simple hunter-gatherers – to begin the cosmic cycle all over again.

Schroder closed his eyes and listened to the crowds all around him, letting the sensation wash over him like rain during a storm. It is strange, he thought, how all the things that seem important in one's everyday life – career, family, ego – just melt into unimportance when you realise your life, along with everyone else's, is coming to a close.

Chapter 22

The cooling breeze blowing across Harker's face was invigorating as he and Doggie bounced about in the back seat of the three-wheeled taxi rickshaw, which buzzed along Vip Road towards the centre of Port Blair. Their driver, a young local boy named Papa, had met them at Veer Savarkar International Airport – or Port Blair Airport, as it was better known to tourists – and after Doggie had propelled himself forward as the group's negotiator, they had settled on a fare and headed into town. Of course, in most negotiations the usual result was to bargain the price down, whereas Doggie had somehow managed to increase it. A remarkable achievement for a man who was so adept at securing large sums of money from the patrons of Cambridge University.

Botha was following behind in a second rickshaw, and as they made their way down the busy street, Harker was feeling relieved just to have arrived. The entire journey had taken them over thirty hours, starting with a comfortable flight from Zermatt to Milan, then on to Abu Dhabi for a connecting flight to Kolkata in India, before a final leg to the Andaman Islands and Port Blair. Their red-eye-inducing journey had comprised over six thousand miles, nine plastic-tray meals, six in-flight movies, five trips to the toilet, two blazing rows with airport check-in staff, and one very serious argument between the three of them that had almost ended in blows.

The quarrel could have been about any number of concerns they each had, the main one being that, apart from following the coordinates inscribed on the coin, they really had no idea where to head upon reaching Port Blair. But instead it had come down to the most insignificant of issues: who would get the last beef Wellington and Yorkshire puddings when the airline ran out. Maybe it had been due to their overall lack of sleep, or the child whose parents could not have cared less that their little treasure kept running up and down the aisle screaming, but in the end a squabble over a stupid meal had been the straw that broke the camel's back. Harker had resolved it by swapping his own beef Wellington for a dodgy-looking vegetarian meal served with rice, whereupon both Doggie and Botha had shaken hands and made up. It was a ridiculous thing to have happened, but their nerves had been frayed to breaking point.

Now, as Harker sucked in another breath of fresh air, he was simply relieved that his air-conditioning induced dry throat was starting to pass. 'We need to take the next right turn,' he called out to Papa in front, after noting the directions on his smartphone. 'And then stay on it for a few miles.'

Papa glanced back and gave an understanding nod before making the turn.

'We should get there in twenty minutes,' Harker said loudly over the whirring of the engine, but Doggie seemed far more interested in the road ahead and the number of pedestrians crossing it.

'I've not yet seen one traffic light,' the dean said cheerfully. 'Can you imagine that in the UK? There would be pile-ups every minute of the day!'

'The people here clearly just have good road sense,' Harker replied, as a small red scooter with nearly flat tyres whizzed past them carrying three teenagers. 'Maybe not all of them, but there's a freedom about it all, and I bet you don't get nearly as much road rage.'

Doggie was already nodding. 'It's a beautiful place – bit undeveloped, but beautiful. I just hope we get to find what we're looking for.'

He was right about the island's beauty. The white sand beaches they had seen while flying in radiated purity, and the waters shimmered in a wonderful green-blue colour that put the English Channel to shame. The built-up areas looked a bit run-down by Western standards, with most buildings in dire need of a fresh coat of paint, but out in the rural areas the view was transformed. Lush vegetation lined the coastline, and from the beaches other islands in the archipelago could be seen, giving it the feel of a desert island paradise. And this was the reason tourists made such an effort to get here, keen to discover somewhere off the beaten track that European package holiday-makers would never experience.

During their long flight over Harker had been developing serious feelings of apprehension and anxiety, and it wasn't just their in-flight meals that had been responsible. The idea of ancient aliens, not to mention magic-like technology that could prevent an impending cataclysm caused by a meteor strike, stirred up ideas that tore at his insides like butterflies, only with steel claws. This was not territory he felt at all comfortable with, and it seemed part of what one could only describe as conspiracy culture. But still he couldn't simply dismiss the being they had found in Legrundy's charge. It was such a strange-looking creature and those elliptical eyes were the most haunting feature of all, but not because they appeared in ancient Egyptian culture or matched images of the fabled Sumerian gods called the Annunaki. It was that they looked so… well, alien, and unlike anything of Earth's human history. Of course, Neanderthals, Cro-Magnon and all the other species of the Homo sapiens archaeological record were distinct from modern humans, but that strange fellow was truly bizarre. And, more importantly, where could such a group of creatures hide and thrive – and to what ends? Was it in fact just one of many extraterrestrials who travelled back and forth from some distant planet, like unearthly anthropologists, documenting and intervening in human history and thus shaping our very existence? Determining our history by means of manipulation, whether good or bad?

As the rickshaw taxi headed ever further from the bustle of Port Blair, Harker began to feel a renewed sense of purpose. It was possible this whole endeavour could lead nowhere further than disappointment, but as the palm trees grew denser and the traffic faded away, he began wondering what they would find when they got to the location on the western shore that the coordinates pointed to.

Twenty minutes later they were walking on Wandoor Beach on the western shoreline of Andaman, which turned out to be even more utopian than it had looked from the air, and the expanse of blue ocean that lay beyond was heavenly. One could not think of a better place to be shipwrecked in the days of eighteenth-century buccaneers, which seemed at complete odds with the reality of the penal colony the British Empire had established here. The history of these islands was long, but as Harker now wandered across the sand with his jacket folded across one arm, it was not the historical aspects of the place he was preoccupied with.

'There's nothing here,' Botha called out from the edge of the trees, where he was taking refuge from the heat. 'Nothing here but beach and ocean.'

Doggie had also taken up a temporary position in the shade of a palm tree, and was busy fanning himself with a copy of *Air Weekly* which he had appropriated on the flight over.

'Xavier's right, Alex. There's nothing here but sea and sand. Are you sure you've got the correct coordinates?'

Harker had already checked the coordinates on his phone map multiple times, and there could be no doubt that their location was dead on target. Either whatever had been here eleven thousand years ago was long gone, or his theory about those numbers on the coin was mistaken.

'We gave it a shot, Alex,' Botha yelled, while Harker continued to stare at his phone as if it was about to magically reveal something. 'Why don't we head back to Port Blair and find a hotel to crash in,' Botha continued, glancing over at Papa and the other driver, who were patiently waiting back on the road. 'I don't think I can take another thirty hours of travelling without at least one good night's sleep. Besides, maybe it's time we all contacted our families.'

His friends' voices seemed nothing more than background noise to Harker as he pulled out the gold coin again and began tracing those numbers with his fingers. It was a desperate attempt, but he truly felt as if he'd overlooked something. It was like a stick constantly poking him, like an unconscious note he had made without even realising it. And as he scrutinised each cuneiform number in turn, it suddenly hit him.

'He got it wrong,' Harker muttered to himself and then he yelled it out. 'He got it wrong!'

'Who got what wrong?' Botha shouted back, then hurried across the sand towards him. He was followed by Doggie, holding *Air Weekly* over his head as protection from the sun.

'We screwed up the numbers. That's not a five and a two,' Harker said excitedly, 'it's a one and a three. The coordinates are about twenty miles that way,' he added, pointing towards the blue of the ocean.

Botha looked remarkably unimpressed and his eyelids were beginning to droop. 'OK, so instead of being on a beach, it's in the Bay of Bengal. What a revelation.'

Doggie was also looking doubtful, but Harker grinned from ear to ear. 'No, gentlemen. It's a place that hasn't been touched by outsiders for maybe as long as sixty thousand years. A place where the very few who dared to enter it have ended up dead. It's therefore perfect, just perfect.'

Botha and Doggie glanced at each other uncertainly as Harker stared out across the ocean.

'Alex, if you're thinking of Skull Island from the King Kong movies, then you're in for a big disappointment,' Botha said. 'Because that was only a film, you know. Just fiction.'

Harker was still looking extremely excited as he slapped both hands on Botha's shoulders. 'I know it is, but I bet you money that Skull Island was based on this place... Xavier, we'll need a boat – a fast one.' Harker was now looking mightily proud of himself. 'Can you hire one?'

Without hesitation Botha offered a nod. 'OK, when –
and to where?'

'We'll go tonight once it gets dark, and as to the
where…' Harker turned his gaze back to the ocean. 'Let's
just say that tonight we're going back in time.'

Chapter 23

There was an uncomfortable chill in the air as the silver Mercedes limousine slowly made its way up the narrow, looping road to Neuschwanstein Castle, and each of the flaming torches lining it flickered as the car passed by. The castle was considered one of the most beautiful buildings in the world, perched high in the Bavarian Alps above the small tourist town of Hohenschwangau, less than a mile away, and offering views of numerous lakes in the green plateau below. Built in the late nineteenth century at the behest of the Bavarian King Ludwig II on a site chosen especially for its idyllic views extending for miles around, this turreted mountain retreat rose upwards like a beacon of fairy tale perfection, with a forest of towering trees surrounding its white-brick base. Even Walt Disney was supposed to have taken inspiration from it when building his world-famous Magic Kingdom, and in modern times the castle had seen over sixty million tourists passing through its gates since opening to the public.

On this particular evening though, there was no sign of inquisitive sightseers with their cameras at the ready, and as the Mercedes approached the main entrance, a woman wearing a black tuxedo waved it to a halt. She took note of the registration number, checked her list, then signalled it onwards through an arch leading into the main courtyard. With a squeak the limousine's tyres made a sharp turn and came to a stop, as a man dressed in red livery embellished with gold braid strode over to the passenger door and opened it with a genteel bow.

John Schroder descended from the vehicle and glanced carefully around the inner courtyard as the servant gently closed the door behind him.

'Mr Schroder,' the man began politely, in English but with a thick German accent. 'Welcome to Neuschwanstein. If you would be so good as to follow me, they are already gathering in the Throne Room.'

Schroder merely smiled and followed his chaperone towards a large oak door at the top of a flight of stone steps.

'Didn't they film *Where Eagles Dare* here?' Schroder asked, but this was met with a look of disapproval from the fancily dressed servant.

'No, that was Hohenwerfen castle, over in Austria, but it is a common mistake. Neuschwanstein is altogether far more exquisite.'

As Schroder was led up the steps and then inside, his first impression was not one of bedazzlement and wonder, for the gift shop and cafeteria were simply testament to living in modern times. But, as his guide led him to the upper floors, he quickly changed his thinking.

Most of the art, he was told, had been inspired by Wagner's operas, and the Lower Hall was indeed glorious – with its walls showing scenes from the Norse Sigurd saga.

'The floor we're on now and the fourth floor above us were used specifically by the king himself,' the servant continued. 'On the right there are the royal apartments, but tonight our guests are in the most splendid room of the castle.'

It was clear the fellow knew his history.

'Do such events happen often?' Schroder asked, whereupon the servant shook his head abruptly.

'I was brought in just for tonight, sir, but I was led to believe this is the first private function the castle has had in years, and I have no doubt you will have a most enjoyable time.'

The response was telling and as the man gave a small grin Schroder realised that even the guide was a Mithras operative, if only for this one night. The Cult of Mithras had a penchant for anonymity and privacy and it made sense that not even function staff would be anything but trusted colleagues. It was this guarded mindset that had allowed the ancient organisation to survive for so long, hidden in the shadows of world history. No chance was taken, no precaution left unexploited, and as he followed the servant Schroder couldn't help but admire that fact.

They passed a final mural set into the marble and proceeded to a central stone archway containing two glass-paned doors, with large rose insignias wrought in metal within each pane.

The servant pushed open a door leading into a short connecting anteroom, where he placed his hand on the door handle and paused ostentatiously, before announcing. 'Sir, may I welcome you to the Throne Room.'

Once the door opened Schroder found himself surrounded by an array of vivid colours. The door opened up into the middle of a huge room, where spread across the floor was laid a series of red carpets so that the white-tiled mosaic underneath could now only be seen at the outer edges. There was a two-tier array of pillars lining both side walls, whilst on the other side was a long veranda. The throne itself was now missing and all that was contained in the concave half sphere built in to the wall was a majestic image of Jesus Christ with his arms raised, protectively looking down at the exact spot where the king would have sat. In the very middle of the room was suspended a many-branched, two-tier chandelier with its candles lit, hanging just feet above the twenty or so assembled guests, all dressed in the finest evening wear.

To many it might have seemed the height of social distinction, but to Schroder it all reeked of over-extravagance, and he was struggling to disguise his distaste when someone tapped him on the shoulder.

Milat Berger stood smiling beside him, wearing a smartly tailored dress suit and pearl cufflinks that appeared to glow radiantly in the overhead lighting.

'Glad you made it, John,' he said. 'You look pretty good for a man on the run.'

Since being detected by Brulet, Schroder had been feeling sick to his stomach. It could be because he had betrayed his only real family, or that he knew only too well how good the Templars were at tracking people down. But as he now looked around at the glittering diamond bracelets and necklaces, the opulence of it all had him realising he had made the right choice.

'I'm tired of running, Milat.'

This comment had Berger looking confused. 'You've only been on the run for just over a day, John. Surely you MI6 boys are made of tougher stuff than that?'

'I mean running from myself,' Schroder replied, still feeling dazzled by the sight of so much wealth in one room. 'I'm tired of trying to convince myself that I don't want all of this.'

He waved towards the crowd of extravagantly dressed people, and Berger's smile now grew wider.

'You're with friends now, John, and you've made the right decision. Even though your cover has been blown with the Templars, I've no doubt you can still be of great service to the Mithras.'

It was now Schroder who smiled and after letting out a deep sigh, his shoulders began to loosen. 'I was worried that it might be a problem for you.'

'Not at all, John,' Berger replied. 'I believe you'll be of great help to us in taking apart the Templars and destroying them for good.'

Berger gripped his shoulder again softly, and he knew everything was going to be all right.

'Now I've a speech to give to my guests, so please excuse me,' Berger declared and took a couple of steps before turning around and raising a finger to his lips in a gesture of secrecy. 'And don't go too far, John. I have a surprise for everyone here that I think you'll appreciate.'

Schroder watched as the Mithras leader made his way through the adoring guests and headed up the steps to where the throne would have been. There he picked up a microphone and began to address the crowd.

'Ladies and gentlemen, may I have your attention.'

The conversations evaporated in an instant and all eyes now turned to Berger.

'It has been far too long since we all met together in one place, and indeed it is a sight to behold. For many years we have been saddled with the burden of anonymity and veiled ourselves within the shadows – forced there by our Templar oppressors.'

There came a few sympathetic groans from the crowd, and Schroder watched as Berger started shaking his head.

'My friends, we should not see what they have done to us as something to be reviled or resented, but in truth we should be thanking that pathetic collection of religious fools and zealots, because the hardships they have caused us have only succeeded in making us stronger. And that same project we set ourselves six months ago would not now be so near completion, if not for one of their own, Alex Harker, who by blood – his DNA – is one of ours… Mithras.'

There was a light patter of applause before Berger continued. 'Even as I speak, that same Templar stooge is leading one of our agents directly to our goal, and with that we will have the means to address the imbalance of power in this world which has foiled us for so long.'

Berger looked up through the nearest window towards the evening sky outside, and he shook his head. 'Who could have envisaged that we would discover proof of what we've held central to our beliefs for so many millennia. That the world's core religions are nothing more than puny constructs to keep the populace sedated. And, over time, that has led us' – Berger looked genuinely disgusted – 'to a world of individualism where the weak and useless are considered equal to the rest. The people of the Western world have now forgotten that it is our base, natural instinct that decides the status quo. And essentially that instinct is one of brutality, one of violence, one of suppression and of bending the will of those we consider weaker than ourselves.'

Curiously, the guests were not getting as worked up as Schroder would have expected. But as he watched, he caught glimpses of the severe expressions on many faces and he realised what the truth of it was. Each person present was a dedicated top-level member of the Mithras – their High Council – and every one of them was already totally invested in the ideology Berger was proclaiming. They had no need to express their agreement to what their elected leader was saying, because it was already a given. They believed wholeheartedly in the total oppression of anyone unworthy. As Berger launched into his next theme, it was obvious how sympathetic to it they were, and Schroder felt his first twinge of anxiety.

'You know, my friends, there are many in the world who view Adolf Hitler as a monster, the devil incarnate... but I think the man had the right idea. He understood that human beings are nothing more than animals, possessing the same urges, and that survival of the fittest is the only true, fair path to enlightenment and equality. The weak must die so that the strong survive. It is a concept so simple yet so brilliant, and it is with this in mind that I now come to our own project and my belief that it will grant us the fairer world that we seek. As you all know, when we discovered that pyramid in Gibraltar there were many who failed to recognise its importance. Even I myself was doubtful at first about—' Berger's nose wrinkled and his lip curled as if he had just detected some nauseating smell. 'About an ancient civilisation, pre-dating ours... alien in origin... the Ark of Knowledge... These are the fringe ideas that belonged not in our own minds but those of nerdy teenagers with tin-foil hats. The same kinds of fool whose brain cells are matched only by the number of dispensed tissues in their waste bins.'

These analogies drew a ripple of laughter from the crowd, even as Berger's expression now hardened and his tone lowered. 'Who would have thought that, after six months, those insane ideas could have borne fruit and that such a fantastical tale could actually be true? All those years and money spent on groups like SETI and the construction of gigantic telescopes, all searching for extraterrestrial life out there in the cosmos, when all they had to do was explore the very planet we live on for the evidence they so desperately sought.'

The group had fallen silent once more and Berger shook his head and let the mic hang limply from his hand, like a bar singer who had drunk too much, before jerking it back towards his lips.

'We all saw the images of that creature that our late friend, Avi Legrundy, had in her possession, and it was enough, in my mind, to justify continuing expenditure on this project, even if she did manage to let it slip away. But what you do not know is that as of this moment, right now, one of the agents who followed our lost soul Alex Harker believes that Harker may have discovered the exact location of the Ark of Knowledge. If this is true, then we can only imagine the secrets contained within it. This discovery could lead to a revolution in world technology – a leap so massive that it would make the creation of the computer look like nothing more advanced than the invention of the wheel. Ladies and gentlemen, this same discovery would rejuvenate the Mithras's fortunes and, as everyone here knows, money equals power and with it comes the power to control. The kind of control that can enslave people's minds. We've seen how social media has managed to play into the basest of human instincts, that of tribalism. It has turned so many people against each other, so just imagine what the technology that awaits us could do. And the Mithras will be ready to capitalise on just that.'

Berger then began winding down his speech. 'Now, to celebrate, I have the surprise that you all requested. So, if everyone would make their way to the courtyard, we can begin.'

There was a look of excitement on the faces of the attendees as they waited for Berger to take the lead, then hurried to follow him.

'Come and see, John,' the Mithras leader beckoned, and along with the others Schroder made his way back through the castle and out into the forecourt he had initially arrived in. The limousine had disappeared and in its place at the centre of the courtyard there was a metal pole about six feet high, sticking straight up into the air from a wooden plinth. At its base kindling and straw was now being stuffed into gaps between the thick logs of wood surrounding it, by a couple of servants dressed in red livery, one of whom had escorted Schroder earlier. That on its own was no reason for alarm, but what did make an impression on Schroder was the figure bound to the central stake, wearing only a piece of linen cloth wrapped around his groin and a brown sack over his head.

As the crowd gathered round, Berger clicked his fingers and two men in burgundy – stretch skinny suits, approached from the courtyard's main entrance and stood on either side of the stake.

'Ladies and gentlemen, for your viewing pleasure and to kick off tonight's celebrations, I give you an act of repentance by someone who has caused us so much trouble lately in revealing our organisation to the Templars.' Berger stepped up onto a wooden stool next to the stake, then gripped the brown sack and ripped it off to reveal his special guest.

Father John Davies hung suspended from the pole with a look of dread across his face. His body was shaking visibly in the cold evening air, and a thick gag was tied around his mouth with dark spots where his saliva had soaked through.

'This is the man whose unwise actions drew us back out of the safety of the shadows through his foolish notions of kinship with his Templar nephew, Alex Harker.'

The Council all began to clap, clearly happy with this surprise, whereupon Berger picked up one of the flaming torches that lined the courtyard and moved over to hand it to Schroder. 'Would you do the honours, John?'

Without hesitation Schroder accepted the torch and slowly made his way over to the victim, where he held the flame just inches away from the straw, as Berger came and stood directly in front of the condemned man.

'To truly repent one must burn away one's sins, "Father" Davies,' he declared menacingly, then stood back and gave Schroder a nod. 'Prove to us you are truly Mithras, John Schroder, and thus be welcomed into our family.'

With no sign of emotion Schroder did as instructed and began to lower the torch, even as Father Davies began screaming, though the sounds were muffled by the gag. 'Sorry, Father, but we all have to die sometime.'

The first bullet hit the guard standing on the left, followed by a second into the chest of the one on the right, and both men dropped to the ground like sacks of potatoes. Floodlights now erupted into life from the top of the castle walls, so that all the members of the Council were lit up in a dazzling circle of light. From the main entrance a group of eight men armed with MP5 assault rifles appeared and swiftly surrounded the disorientated group of guests clad in their dinner jackets and ballgowns.

Berger had frozen in shock, and as both he and Schroder now watched, a man slowly made his way over to them and stopped a few feet short. Meanwhile, the gunmen began to restrain the Council members with cable ties, one by one.

'Good job, John,' Brulet said with a smile.

'Jesus, Sebastian, you cut it a bit close,' Schroder exclaimed before throwing the flaming torch off to one side. 'For a moment I really thought I was going to have to set this guy alight!'

Brulet smiled again and turned his attention to Berger as Schroder pulled a cable tie from his jacket pocket and wrenched the Mithras leader's arms behind his back, before tightening it securely around his wrists.

'Milat Berger, it's been a while since I saw you last. I never expected you to be the one to make it to the top of the Mithras dunghill.'

Berger was stricken speechless, his complexion turning white in stark contrast to his black tuxedo.

'We started searching for you months ago, the moment we discovered the Mithras was still alive and well,' Brulet explained flatly, and then he shook his head. 'I was interested to learn that the Mithras never really recovered from our last altercations with you. In fact, if what we've learnt is true, you're barely even a fraction of the size you once were... Brings to mind the emperor's new clothes.'

Berger seemed to be getting over his shock at what had happened and was now looking furious at how much the Grand Master appeared to have found out.

Brulet continued, with his eyebrows raised, 'I must say I was surprised that you let John here into your confidence so quickly. Shows you must be more desperate than I thought. Even as we speak, Interpol are picking up your associates all over Europe, which was the easy part given that most of them are criminal psychopaths with a long list of convictions.'

Brulet leant in closer and his eyes narrowed. 'Your discovery of the pyramid is fascinating, though, and the possibility of extraterrestrial life is mind-boggling, but I'm afraid we will have to take over from here. If the Ark of Knowledge is real, then it belongs in hands far more responsible than yours. And if there is any way to stop these terrible events happening, I pray to God that Harker finds it. I'm surprised you can be out here celebrating, Milat, when there's such a real chance the world is about to come to an end. I would have thought you'd be hiding away already in some underground bunker.'

Berger looked stunned and his nose wrinkled in puzzlement. 'End of the world? What are you talking about?'

Chapter 24

'I think I'm going to be sick,' Doggie moaned above the hum of the twin outboard motors as they glided across the choppy black waters of the Bay of Bengal.

'That's the fourth time you've said so,' Botha remarked, clearly becoming more frustrated with every complaint. 'If you want to throw up, then do it already!'

Doggie had been looking green from almost the outset of the hour-long journey, but had not so far managed to accomplish the deed. 'I wish I could, but I just can't,' he replied weakly and sucked in a deep lungful of salty sea air.

Botha now leant over close to his ear. 'Just imagine a piece of sloppy light-brown dogshit with crunchy peanuts in it being smeared across a slice of mouldy white bread. Now fold it over in your hands and take a long succulent bite.'

Doggie flung himself across to the side of the boat and began puking, throwing his shoulders forward violently with each heave.

'Christ, Xavier, that's disgusting,' Harker complained, clasping the boat's steering wheel more tightly as he tried to wipe the vile image from his mind.

'It worked, didn't it?' the Templar replied as Doggie returned to his seat, wiping his mouth.

'Don't forget to take another nice sloppy bite,' Botha added, and this time it was Harker who felt a rising in his throat, before he pulled back on the throttle and followed Doggie in blowing chunks into the water below. In hindsight he wished he had used the other side because as one of them retched, the other one witnessed it, and the sight set them off again in turn.

'That's it, boys. Get it out of your system and let me handle the driving for a bit.' Botha slapped them both on the back before taking hold of the wheel and powering up the engines. 'I tell you, I could really go for some chicken chow mein right about now.' He said it with an amused smile even as the sound of retching started up all over again.

To find a boat that could make the twenty-two mile trip had been easy, and Botha had sourced one within an hour. The hard part came when Harker had explained to them where they would be going. North Sentinel Island was far from a tourist destination, and on hearing the name, Doggie and Botha had looked very wary at the prospect. In all the world there were few places people genuinely feared to tread, but this island in the Bay of Bengal was one of them. Around the entire island a six-mile exclusion zone was enforced by patrol boats of the Indian army, although there were few laws prohibiting anyone setting foot there. These drastic measures were not due to radiation or a top-secret military base, but something just as dangerous to any visitor who dared set foot there. The island was home to one of the few uncontacted tribes in the world, the Sentinelese, who were practising hunter-gatherers still using technology that had not progressed since the Stone Age. Missionaries, anthropologists and shipwrecked sailors had all arrived on the island over the years, only to leave as corpses thrown back into the sea. Attempts had been made to establish contact, but only rarely did these visits not end in bloodshed under a hail of spears and arrows. The Sentinelese were thought to have arrived on the island as far back as sixty thousand years ago, and only a few pictures existed, taken from helicopters or passing boats, of these mysterious folk adorned with red warpaint, thought to number anywhere between fifty and five hundred. It was truly an island lost in time – a time when woolly mammoths, sabre-toothed tigers and Neanderthals still walked the earth.

Doggie and Botha had expressed grave concern right from Harker's first mention of the place, but had reluctantly agreed once it was clear he would not back down. Had the forbidding prospect of an apocalypse not been on the horizon, Doggie most certainly would have refused to go along, but ever since Gornergrat and Nicholas Wattling's revelations of impending doom, the dean had seemed ever more introverted, and who could blame him. It was hard enough for most people to come to terms with their own mortality, no matter how far off, let alone being told it would be occurring in less than a week.

'How are you doing, Tom?' Harker asked, as they retook their seats after recovering from their Botha-induced seasickness.

'A lot better, thank you,' Doggie replied. 'There's something about the constant swaying motion that really gets to me.'

'I don't mean that, Tom. I mean about all this ahead.' Harker was pointing towards the lone island, now less than a mile away, with its trees silhouetted against the night sky.

Doggie glanced towards their destination and managed a smile. 'It's difficult to put into words, Alex,' he began, and then after a few seconds of silence he gave it a go. 'You spend your entire life creating a place in the world for yourself: a house, a career, your circle of friends, and then someone pops up and says "Sorry to tell you but the world is going to end in just a few days. Good luck and ta-ta."'

As the boat rocked back and forth, his body swayed with it, as if he had no energy left to resist. 'I always thought I would have time to meet someone, settle down and, well, you know… have a life. But time seems to have passed me by.'

For the first time since they had met Wattling, the dean was revealing just how much the startling revelation had affected him. Harker gave him a friendly tap on the knee. 'It's never too late, Tom.'

'And some might just say, given the world is about to end, that it probably is,' Doggie replied. Then he chuckled. 'Unless the Sentinelese ladies prefer to keep older white men alive instead of spearing them to death at first sight!'

He looked out across the calm waters. 'Time passes so quickly, Alex, and you can never truly understand that until you get older. I think it's about all the possibilities open to you when you're young. Then, your life could be in a rut – or not where you want it to be – but you still feel like anything is possible, anything could happen, even if it doesn't. But as time passes, your options begin to narrow, like the roots of a tree all leading to one trunk, an amalgamation of all those years of making decisions that lead you onto a single path that you now just can't get off.'

Worried now that Doggie was descending into a gloom that would affect them all just when they needed to be on top of their game, Harker reached over and slapped him firmly across the face.

'Snap out of it, Tom,' Harker yelled as Doggie recoiled. 'You are the Dean of Archaeology at Cambridge University. You have hundreds of adoring colleagues and students who think you're awesome. You have great friends – including me, by the way – who love you, and more money in the bank than I will likely ever see.'

Doggie stared at him blankly as Harker continued.

'As for a love life, you need to get off your fat arse, take a chance and see what's out there. Until you're lying in a hospital bed with the priest reading you the last rites, you can create as many new paths as you want. And so far as the coming apocalypse goes, I have absolute faith that whatever we find on this island is going to sort the whole mess out.'

If Harker were being honest, he had no faith in that whatsoever, but he was too deep into making his point to stop now. 'I'm getting married in just over a week's time, and I intend to be there. So I'll make you a deal right here, right now. When we get through this whole thing, I promise that you can be my best man. But I want your solemn promise that from that moment on, you will make an effort to get out there and start looking for that special person. And' – Harker threw a finger up in the air – 'that you will make a bucket list and force yourself to do everything you've always thought about doing but never got round to, no matter how stupid or difficult.'

Harker thrust his arm out for a handshake, but Doggie was still looking unconvinced.

'Oh, come on, Tom, for Christ's sake, we're probably both going to get speared to death the moment this boat lands in a few minutes' time, so I say – what the hell!'

A smile began to creep across the dean's face and then he laughed out loud before grasping Harker's hand and giving it a firm shake. 'Deal.'

The two men released their grip and sat waiting with a renewed sense of energy, ready to take on whatever might be thrown at them next.

'Oh, and Alex…' As Harker turned to face him, Doggie slapped a palm hard across his face. 'Don't ever do that again.'

The dean kept on smiling, and Harker glanced over at Botha who was doing likewise, but then the Templar's expression began to harden and he pointed ahead of them.

The approaching shoreline was devoid of any lights, and with only a hundred metres to go, Harker began to feel that familiar nervousness in the pit of his stomach. Who knew what they would find here, or if there was indeed some alien technology hidden on the island that could really halt a meteor strike? The very idea seemed frankly ludicrous, but when all options have been exhausted, the final, most crazy one becomes increasingly attractive.

As Harker now pinned his hopes on the fantastical, Botha whispered across to them. 'OK, gentlemen, here we go.'

Chapter 25

The forest interior was far denser than expected and, as Harker swept away the vines and vegetation with his hands, the sound of this activity was amplified by their encroaching surroundings. Their boat had been left moored five metres off the beach, so as to make a quick retreat possible. With Harker at the front, Botha at the rear and Doggie in the middle, they had made slow progress forward for about forty-five minutes Botha had also surprised them by producing two Heckler & Koch USP handguns, which Harker had initially refused but was now glad he had accepted, given the eerie surroundings of the forest. Doggie, on the other hand, had preferred to remain unarmed, theorising that if they were to be attacked, the first ones on the Sentinelese kill list would be those holding weapons… if they even recognised the guns for what they were.

So they pressed ahead, with next to no conversation, for another twenty minutes before coming to a small rocky outcrop with a single stream running through it. Harker gingerly approached it, cupped his hand and drew some of the water to his lips.

'It's fresh,' he declared, and the others joined him to sample it. 'This could be somewhere they get their drinking water from, so if we want to meet them we should follow it to its source.'

Doggie gave a silent nod but Botha looked like he had something else on his mind. He leaned in and whispered to them both, 'I think we're being followed.'

Harker's immediate reaction was to look around, his eyes darting back and forth. Doggie did likewise till the Templar grabbed them both by the arm.

'Just relax. I keep hearing a rustling far behind us, but if the tribe want to show themselves, let them do it in their own time. We don't want to panic them.'

Botha then unclipped a small metal canteen from his belt, gave everyone a swig and refilled it from the running water. Then they continued onwards using the stream as a guide.

Harker now felt incredibly exposed, but he knew Botha was right. If they strode ahead boldly, they were only likely to scare their pursuers and inflame any situation that might arise. There was something else niggling at Harker – and had been since their decision to travel to this island. There were many reasons for strangers not to visit this place but near the top of the list was the risk of disease. Having been isolated for so long here, it was almost certain that they would not have immunity to any diseases, so potentially even a serious cold could cause devastation to their community. However, the overall stakes were just too high for this to be a priority. If this place was the location of an Ark of Knowledge, then they had to find it. As a precaution, he had insisted that Botha bring with him several packets of antibiotics, but he already knew it was an unworkable idea, since how would they be able to persuade the tribe to swallow them? Still, it seemed the right thing to do.

Botha now took the lead, with Doggie at the tail end, as they followed the stream through forest which quickly became dense once more, and they continued like that for over an hour. It was a suffocating environment and to say their trek was laborious would be an understatement of epic proportions. The walking itself was not the problem, because the stream over time had created a natural widening at its edges which gave room for a single person to move with ease but, with the similarity of the trees and foliage and the lack of any moonlight penetrating the canopy, it felt like one was constantly walking in a circle. Harker was beginning to worry that they had done exactly that when finally, after another forty-five minutes, they heard the sound of cascading water off in the distance.

Botha turned around with an eager expression, but as he looked further behind, it turned to one of worry. Harker instantly glanced back to see nothing but the dark, empty trail they had been following.

'Doggie!' he whispered loudly but the dean was nowhere to be seen, so Harker began investigating the deep undergrowth over to his right. 'He was just here,' he exclaimed, becoming increasingly agitated. 'Doggie!' he yelled, whereupon Botha slapped a hand across his mouth.

'Keep it down,' he hissed. 'Do you want everyone to know we're here?'

'They've got Tom, Xavier. They already know we're here!'

It was a fair point and Botha had begun to call out too when something caught Harker's eye, a movement in the bushes about six metres away. It was too dark to see anything more, so he instinctively raced over and swept the bushes aside.

There was nothing there, and as he strained to peer into the dark, he called back to Botha – only to be met with silence. Harker snapped his head around to see just a dark, empty trail ahead of him. He darted back to where he had been earlier, but there was nothing to hear or see except the sound of splashing water up ahead and the shadowy silhouettes of trees and bushes all around.

From somewhere off to his left came a rustling noise, and with his pulse now racing in fear, Harker took off at a run along the path towards the running water, without looking back. He could have pulled out his gun but chose not to, for at this point it would probably only make matters worse. After a full fifteen minutes he broke through the limit of the trees and into an open area, whereupon he dropped to his knees, struggling to catch his breath. His exhaustion caused him to feel light-headed and as he looked up towards the clearing in front of him, with the moon shining down upon it, he could just make out a small, shimmering waterfall that had been making all that noise. It wasn't a big drop, maybe only five metres, but the water landed on a large stone at the bottom with a slapping sound. Back at the boat they had agreed not to use their torches unless absolutely necessary for fear of scaring away – or attracting – the Sentinelese, until they knew where the latter were located and had formed a plan of introducing themselves. And, even though the trees shut out most of the moonlight, it had been easy enough to navigate. But as he looked over at the trees on the other side of the clearing, he spotted something that had him reaching for his torch.

The trees were moving!

Harker pulled out the torch instantly but before he could turn it on, something slammed hard into the back of his head and sent him flying forwards onto the ground. It was a hard blow and, as he turned his head to look, what he saw had his heartbeat surging.

A huge head with long tendrils dangling from the sides slowly bore down on him, grunting at first and then beginning to sniff at his head. The aroma was oddly smoky, like a lavender incense stick. And as the head pulled back the silhouette of a paw made up of clawed talons now appeared above him. The sight was terrifying but Harker had already figured out what it was. He very slowly slipped his hand deep into his pocket and proceeded with the initial plan he had decided upon back at Port Blair. Everything now hinged on it having the desired effect.

The gold coin glimmered in the moonlight as he held it up, and the creature paused for a moment before plucking it from his hand. It now stood back upright and began making a series of low melodic grunts.

From the fringe of the trees, a flickering of light caught his eye and Harker looked over to see a series of flaming torches illuminating the forty or so humans holding them. They were mainly naked except for loincloths, and as Harker looked back at the creature which had attacked him, the torchlight revealed what he had already suspected. The man was probably a little over six feet tall and the mask he wore was leather, as were the tendrils attached to it – black leather strips which stuck out at various points. On one hand he wore a cumbersome-looking glove made of numerous straps of animal skin bound together with bird claws holding them in place, and the only visible part of the fellow's face was the eyes, whose pupils appeared as black as the night.

He now passed the coin back to Harker, and with a final grunt, gestured with his gloved hand and began walking back towards the others.

Harker took this as a sign to follow. The tall man took a flaming torch from a small, black-skinned Sentinelese female, whereupon all the shadowy figures now extinguished their own torches in the earth and seemed to melt back into the trees, leaving just Harker and the masked man. After glancing back to ensure he was being followed, the man began to lead Harker into the forest.

Harker realised these must indeed be the Sentinelese people, the uncontacted tribe whose ancestors had first come to this island tens of thousands of years ago. But as awe-inspiring as it was to be in their company, Harker could only think of Doggie and Botha and wonder where they were.

He stayed silent as the pair of them proceeded because he knew his guide would not speak a word of English. No one in the world truly knew what language the Sentinelese spoke. There were educated guesses, based on dialects used in the surrounding areas, but no one really knew for certain.

They continued in silence for another ten minutes until the masked man came to a halt by a large boulder rising up from the ground. He turned round, lowered his torch towards the rock itself, and pointed.

Harker took a few steps forward and saw what he was pointing to. It was a small, round hole about the same size as the coin and so he reached over and placed the coin in that opening.

There followed a high-pitched whine and, without a sound, his guide took off into the forest, leaving Harker in sudden darkness as a rumbling could be heard from behind the rock and the soil beneath his feet began to vibrate. Then the middle section of the rock began to slide sideways and he was bathed in a white light.

Harker raised his hands to cover his eyes, but the intensity was so bright, so consuming that he had to turn away. Just as it became almost unbearable, it appeared to fade and he turned back and slowly lowered both hands.

A long set of black steps led down into the ground, and at their lowest point he could make out a lighted doorway. His initial reaction was to back away, but as he looked back out into the creepy forest he decided to move forwards instead and so began to make his way downwards. The floor below was glass-like and undeniably similar to the strange surfaces he had seen back in the pyramid in the Strait of Gibraltar.

He had made it halfway down when the rock doorway above began to slide shut, but he made no attempt to run back up to it. What would be the point? He was here for a reason and it would not be answered back in the forest covering North Sentinel island.

Harker continued down the steps until he reached the door, scanning its outer edges and the thin white neon lighting that surrounded them. This was all too surreal! Finally, with a deep breath to steady himself, he pushed against the door's cold, black, glassy surface and stepped inside.

Up until now Harker had not been sure what to expect. A silver UFO sitting grandly before him, a group of little, grey extraterrestrials perhaps... or even God himself seated on a white throne, with a long beard and a welcoming look on his face? But as Harker glanced around the small concrete space, he felt only bewilderment. The room was lit by a single overhead strip light and completely empty except for a man with white hair and a goatee standing in the middle of the room – and he sure as hell wasn't God.

Michael Wexler stared back at him and shook his head in disappointment. 'I hoped you wouldn't make it this far,' he began, keeping his arms crossed as Harker let the door slide from his fingers and close behind him.

'Michael!' he exclaimed, completely stunned. 'What is this?'

Wexler gave a smile and took a step forwards. '*This* is something that no one is ever supposed to see.'

The answer was baffling and Harker shook his head in confusion. 'Not supposed to see… what? A concrete basement underneath an island forest with an uncontacted tribe living above it?'

Wexler let out an amused laugh. 'You have a funny way of thinking, Alex. Has anyone ever told you that?'

'Many times, Michael,' Harker replied, his confusion now tipping into anger. 'But that's not what's on my mind at the moment. What is on my mind is where my friends are and what the hell is going on here.'

'Oh, your friends are fine. There's no need to worry about them, and they'll be joining us shortly.'

'OK, that's good to hear, but now how about you tell me what exactly we're doing down here?'

There was real strain evident in Harker's voice and Wexler looked concerned. 'You're here because you believe that shortly a cataclysm is about to take place that could wipe out humanity, and would doom those few who survive to begin rebuilding civilisation once again. You also believe that this disaster has happened many times before, in an endless cycle of galactic death and then rebirth.'

'The ninth planet,' Harker replied, and Wexler nodded his head slowly.

'You've also been led to believe that the advanced civilisation before us was alien in origin, and that their technology was stored away in the Ark of Knowledge, just waiting to be found so that it could be used to stop this terrible tragedy from happening.'

'No, that's what *you* think,' Harker said defensively. 'That's what *you* told me. I've never believed it.'

'So why then are you here?'

Harker was not a man of violence and he had always prided himself on that fact. He could defend himself with violence if needed – he wasn't a pacifist – but as he stared now at Wexler's smug, knowing face, he was incredibly tempted to deliver a blow that would knock the man out.

'I had no idea if any of it was actually true, but if the world is truly ending, then at the very worst it would be a wasted trip.'

'OK, I believe you,' Wexler said, 'but would you like to know what all this is really about?'

Harker bit his tongue but he nodded. 'Yes, Michael, I really would, please.'

Wexler continued smiling, and he even offered a courteous bow. 'Firstly you should know that everything I've told you about the ninth planet is true.'

Harker's heart immediately sank but he stood firm as Wexler continued to explain.

'But it won't be entering our solar system for quite a long time.'

'How long?'

'Not for another two thousand years. And secondly, those alien gods, the Annunaki, they're not aliens… they're us.'

'What?' Now Harker felt really confused.

'Have you heard of Homo floresiensis?' Wexler asked, and Harker offered a nod.

'It's a human subspecies of which they found miniature skeletons back in... 2004, if I remember correctly. They were only three feet tall and died out, what, about thirteen thousand years ago.'

'That's correct,' Wexler agreed, seemingly impressed with Harker's knowledge. 'Along with all the other subspecies, they help make up the evolving history of modern humans. And if you follow the DNA strand back far enough, we even find a common ancestor: a primate from which, over millions of years, we all evolved.'

Harker now had some idea of where Wexler was going with all this. 'Are you telling me these giants, or gods – the Annunaki – are a subspecies of modern human beings?'

'Yes, Alex, but rather than just having the intelligence we possess or only the strength of a Neanderthal, they had both – as well as their size, which overshadowed any humans that ever lived. Their civilisation was advanced – you yourself saw their pyramid constructed with materials that we have only begun to replicate ourselves in recent times – and don't forget this was over eleven thousand years ago. I'm not saying they were more advanced than we are, but nonetheless it was all very impressive, and their knowledge of the skies and of astronomy was second to none. When the catastrophe happened, sending their world back to basics and nearly wiping out the human race in the process, some of them survived and set about passing on what they had learnt to modern humans, who named them the Annunaki and treated them as gods. You have to remember that the generations who came *after* the Great Flood had no knowledge of this race of giants, and in view of their offerings of knowledge, what else could they have been but gods?

'But when our own civilisations began to grow, and under their guidance we became the dominant force around the world, this lost tribe – these Annunaki, the bringers of civilisation – retreated from our world. And by this time there were very few left anyway, as modern humans took over more space and power. We don't know exactly why their populations never grew again as ours did, but we do know why they retreated. Before the cataclysm that took place twelve thousand years ago, when they were the dominant civilisation, we do know they were very cruel and treated modern humans like cattle, as nothing more than a workforce.'

Harker thought back to that mural in the underwater pyramid and its depiction of the violence inflicted by the giant gods, and he could only imagine what it must have entailed. Modern humans must have seemed puny in comparison to them and thus easily taken advantage of.

'Who knows?' Wexler threw his hands up. 'Perhaps they believed the cataclysm was a punishment for their cruelty from the gods they themselves believed in. The truth is we will never know, but what they did afterwards, and their determination to help rebuild civilisation along with us… well, that can be in no doubt.'

Harker was struggling to take what he was being told at face value. If it were true, then it changed everything the scholars believed about ancient human history. To even consider that we were not the first civilisation to exist, but also were here only because a bunch of giant intelligent apes made it so – it was archaeological heresy and it would be professional suicide to even consider such a thing without proof. And yet here was Wexler attempting to do just that. Harker kept silent and attentive as the doctor continued.

'You know all those stories about Noah's ark that were replicated around the world?'

Harker managed a nod as Wexler spoke enthusiastically, like a teacher taking great pleasure in enlightening his student by passing on the knowledge he himself had learnt.

'As I told you back in Zermatt, truth gradually turns into legend, until one day it is seen as truth again. And if enough time passes, it falls back into legend – but a different legend entirely. Noah's ark wasn't a boat, Alex. It was just a symbol: a simple story to explain something that people were not ready to hear. The ark was a place where knowledge – not animals – was stored, to ensure civilisation could once more rise from the ashes when the right time came.'

Wexler then pressed his hand against a small panel in the concrete wall. There followed a rattling sound and Harker watched as several steel shutters began rolling upwards and disappeared inside the upper wall, to reveal a sight that he could never have imagined.

'Welcome to the Ark, Alex. I mean the real Ark,' Wexler said, as bright light flooded the room.

Harker walked forward to the large observation window that had been revealed, and gazed out onto a gigantic cavern stretching ahead for probably half a mile. There were tall three-storey buildings constructed of stone, marble and some materials that he had never seen before, which now shone in a multitude of colours. Between them lay wide cobblestone roads lined with glowing street lamps, and at the centre of it all a large pyramid towered, with a golden Eye of Horus at its highest point.

'What is this place?' Harker gasped.

Wexler clapped him on the shoulder and smiled. 'This is where the next civilisation will come to start all over again when the moment arrives and the cosmos sees fit to reset the clock. There are no electrical devices or design schematics for cars, but instead all the knowledge that survivors of such an event will need in order to begin again.'

Harker was mesmerised by the sight, realising that from where he stood only a fraction could be seen. But as he turned away, looking over at the proudly smiling Wexler, his head was now brimming with questions. 'Who are you, Michael?'

Wexler pulled up his sleeve to reveal a tattoo on his forearm. It was now so familiar to Harker that he barely gave it a second glance, for it was the outline of a bag with straps, the same as those already seen on the coin and the tattoo of the creature they had found.

'I am one of many, Alex. We are the Guardians of the Ark, and we have been watching over this place for a very long time.'

Even though this underground facility was truly incredible, and it demanded one's whole attention, there were so many unanswered questions that Harker really didn't know where to start.

'I am so confused, Michael,' he began, now just wanting to hear the truth after being fed so much crap over the past few days. 'Don't get me wrong, just seeing this place is mind-blowing, but how do the Mithras, myself and the strange being we found fit into all this? And why did you have me believe the end of the world was just around the corner? Have you got any idea how much worry you've caused us?'

Wexler looked apologetic and immediately set about explaining the bizarre set of events that had brought Harker to this island. 'We Guardians make up over one thousand people, Alex, and we devote ourselves to the upkeep of this place, as did our ancestors and the generations before us. Our bloodlines date back to the ancient Sumerians. When the Annunaki realised their very existence meant them being looked upon as gods, they decided that if humankind was to evolve socially, culturally and intellectually, they themselves had to disappear. Either that or people would forever rely on their "gods" to take care of them. Like a parent who must let their beloved child leave home when the time is right, to learn to fend for itself. With this path decided, the Annunaki retreated to this place to prepare for a day when they would be needed again, and some of our own ancestors chose to join them. You have to remember, Alex, that with their astronomical knowledge, and having witnessed and recorded the ninth planet first-hand along with the damage it did with each cycle around the sun, the Annunaki knew it would return at regular intervals and cause the same devastation as before. So they evolved into a quasi-monastic society that would keep the Ark prepared for when it happened again – a task passed down from one generation to the next.

'As the centuries passed, and human beings grew in power and number, eventually there was no further place for the Annunaki, and so we the Guardians acted as their conduits to the outside world. There were some Annunaki, from time to time, who could not stand this isolated existence and headed out again into the world.

And their lives became the stuff of legend and religious teaching, such as in the story of David and Goliath, or the giant cyclops in the *Odyssey*, or the hundreds of other stories from every continent that tell of giant men – good or bad – who roamed the Earth long ago.'

Wexler was obviously enjoying his grand revelation of this secret history, and the more Harker heard, the more fascinated he became. He wanted to learn everything he could.

'What you don't know,' Michael continued, 'is that the Annunaki, with their two hearts and their giant size, had a far longer lifespan than modern humans – on average double our own – which is how tales of the Annunaki kings surviving for so long came about. Back then over four generations of humans could come and go, and still the same giant gods would be alive. And so the accounts of their age were greatly exaggerated, as we find in the Sumerian texts recording kings living hundreds of thousands of years, which of course is impossible. But can you imagine knowing that your great-great-grandfather lived under the same god king as you did? It would seem magical, supernatural, and it's not surprising that such beliefs, however misguided, came to be recorded as fact.'

Wexler peered through the glass of the observation window and over towards the pyramid and all that lay around it, and he shook his head. 'Our symbiotic relationship lasted thus for close to six thousand years until finally, just over a century ago, the last of the Annunaki passed away. Since then we have been watching over the Ark ourselves, passing the task from one generation the next, and when the technology became available – only in the past ten years, really – we decide to recreate them from whatever tissue we still possessed. The creature that you found, that strange-looking being, was the first of many cloned from his forefathers. That is, until he died.'

At this point Harker realised why, back in Zermatt, Wexler had seemed so upset on learning of its death. For him it was a personal connection borne out of thousands of years and countless generations. Like he said, it was a symbiotic relationship that they wanted to renew – but why?

'For what purpose?' Harker asked, his voice tinged with sympathy.

'Because, Alex, we believe it is only right that they continue, doing what they have done for thousands of years. But there is a far more practical reason, which is simply that they live so much longer than us. Imagine how many generations of us humans would be needed to maintain the Ark for another two thousand years! And what if our descendants decided not to continue with duty, or some of us died unexpectedly and broke the chain? What then? But the Annunaki, living their monastic life here, would need only half the number of generations to reach the date of the next cataclysm, and during a time when not just their knowledge but their very size and strength would be so important as well. This way therefore offers the best chance of not only keeping the Ark a secret, but more importantly making sure it is still here when needed most.'

There were so many things Harker was struggling to get to grips with at this moment, but his mind kept circling back to the creature he had encountered, because there was something about it that did not fit into the narrative he was being told. 'If the Annunaki were so big, then how come the one you cloned was so small?'

Wexler gazed down at the floor morosely. 'Because he was just a child, Alex, no more than eight years old.'

Harker drew back in shock as if the very words were causing him physical damage. He could only imagine the terror and pain that the child had gone through at the hands of Legrundy. It had been heartbreaking even though he had not guessed how young the Annunaki had been. At five feet tall, he had assumed that whatever it was had been fully grown.

'I'm so sorry, Michael. I had no idea.'

Wexler appeared to accept the apology, even though Harker himself had done nothing wrong. But just being party to such a tragedy was enough.

'It wasn't your fault, Alex. And from what I heard you were there to comfort him near the end.'

How Wexler might know that was a question for another time, and the Guardian now moved on to answer the further questions he knew Harker must have but had not yet voiced.

'This all started by pure accident, and if it had not been for the ship that sank in the Gibraltar strait, and in doing so revealed the pyramid, then I doubt we would be having this conversation. But it did and here we are. The pyramid you explored was built many years after the cataclysm occurred, as a place to which survivors might be attracted over the millennia. Then the Annunaki *semis*, or steward, would determine if those who visited were suitable. If they seemed peaceful and decent, then they would be given a coin, and we, the Guardians, would trek here with them to the Ark. The Annunaki had already developed the concept of latitude and longitude and so, using maps, the Guardians would guide those considered worthy from pyramid meeting points all over the world. Once they arrived at the Ark, that coin was – for lack of a better word – used as a chit to be handed over, and then the teaching of agriculture, animal husbandry, stonemasonry and other essential crafts could begin. Then, in time, that knowledge would be taken back to their own communities. The trek itself was seen as a test of character, a challenge to overcome and thus prove one's determination. If, on the other hand, they were deemed unsuitable by the current steward, then they were turned away, by force if needed, and told never to darken the door of any of the pyramids again.'

'That's smart,' Harker said, acknowledging the simplicity of it all. 'You wouldn't want communities based on war and violence to thrive, so why allow them the means?'

'Exactly,' Wexler replied, glad to see that Harker was keeping up. 'But when enough time had passed and human empires began to emerge, there was little the Annunaki could do except be regarded as gods, or endorsers for the people in charge, and that is when they began to retreat. To retreat back to the Ark and prepare once again for the next cosmic throw of the dice. But then that pyramid in Gibraltar was discovered and – lo and behold – who swoops in but the Mithras. Well, that changed things in a very short period of time. For it would not have taken them long to figure out the coin's meaning, and with that information they would eventually have been standing where you are now, but with domination and greed as the only priorities on their minds. Just revealing the existence of the Ark would have meant ruin for what has constituted the final insurance policy for the continuation of humankind.'

'I'm amazed you even knew about the Mithras,' Harker said.

'We may stay hidden in the shadows, Alex,' Wexler replied sternly, 'but I can assure you that we are very aware indeed of the Mithras… as we are of the Knights Templar.'

This mention of the Templars had Harker looking twitchy, but Wexler quelled that with a knowing smile. 'Why do you think we chose to involve you in the first place?'

'You involved *me*?' Harker replied, highly doubtful about what he was hearing.

But it seemed Wexler was being deadly serious. 'Once we heard that the Mithras had discovered the pyramid, we decided to infiltrate the site and attempt to put them off the path. I was chosen along with Dr Khan to offer our services, and because of our experience as Guardians, it was easy to offer our combined knowledge. But the Mithras hired others and after one of them, archaeologist Audrey Banford, uncovered the true meaning of the coins, she quickly discovered this location and used one coin, as you did, to gain access to the Ark we are now standing in. Unfortunately she took it upon herself to abscond with the youngster – not difficult really, because being only eight years old he possessed the mind of a child. Our Sentinelese protectors managed to stop her, but not soon enough I'm afraid. And by the time we Guardians even realised what was happening, the boat had been found drifting by the Indian military. And then the Mithras managed to use their connections within the government, and took it from there. The only concession Audrey Banford allowed us was that she undertook the journey without alerting Barbara Holtz directly. For if she had done so, then none of us would be standing here today. And if Avi Legrundy had not compounded the error, the Mithras would have had the child in their grasp, thus adding another piece of the puzzle which could lead them to the Ark's location.'

Harker remained silent, his gaze drawn occasionally back to the spectacular sight of the cavern, but more than happy just to listen. But there was still something that he couldn't figure out, and it finally emerged.

'Why did the boy have the tattoos?' he asked.

Wexler was pleased to enlighten him. 'It is the age-old right of every Annunaki that those words are imprinted under their skin, using a unique device developed a very long time ago. It's a religious rite that we honoured in accordance with their ancient traditions. It is a way of symbolising that wherever they go, the Ark goes with them. And that,' Wexler added with a smile, 'is where you came in. We knew of your ongoing trouble with Legrundy. And how do you think Templar security were able to pinpoint her location in the first place? We knew you would take care of her in order to protect the child. For that is in the Templars' nature. When we learnt of Legrundy's death you were already on the way to see Barbara Holtz, and unfortunately you were caught up in what we saw as the only way to stop them finding the Ark's location. By that I mean we were the ones who blew it up, and I am sorry that you were almost killed. But no one was supposed to be there. Once we found out you'd acquired one of the coins, we knew it was just a matter of time before you discovered the Ark for yourself. So the Guardians then decided to use the Templars to do our dirty work for us, and take care of the Mithras yourselves – with a little guidance from us. I am sorry therefore to say that your involvement – along with that of the Templars –

was simply to serve one purpose, and that was to rid us of the Mithras. What you might not yet be aware of is that earlier today they were all apprehended by your Grand Master at a party held for the elite at Neuschwanstein Castle. They even got the leader, a man named Milat Berger – a rather vile individual, I might add – and I heard most of their unsavoury band of henchmen were arrested by Interpol. And with that their interest in the Ark is at an end. I must say that Sebastian Brulet played this one beautifully.'

The notion of the Templars being used as pawns was not an attractive thought, but given the significance of the Ark's true purpose, Harker felt no animosity. They were simply doing what they had to for the long-term benefit of mankind. He now turned away from Wexler and again stared out over this place that the guardians had so desperately and understandably sought to protect.

'You could have just asked,' he suggested, and Wexler joined him at the window.

'Easier said than done, Alex, but is it not enough that we decided to place our trust in you to do the right thing? I could claim to you it's because we value your integrity, or your morality, or your persistence in seeing things through to the end… Or perhaps, if I am being more honest, it is also simply because you are a Templar, and therefore know how to keep a secret.'

This final suggestion was unquestionably the real reason the Guardians had allowed Harker to make it this far, and he looked back and smiled. 'I can't tell anyone about this, can I?'

Wexler stroked his goatee and frowned. 'I think it's best for everyone on this planet if neither the Ark nor the Templars end up on the front pages of every major newspaper. Wouldn't you agree?'

This was one of the politest veiled threats that Harker had ever received, and he couldn't help but grin as he replied, 'Is that a warning?'

Wexler shook his head. 'Not a threat, Alex, just a request that benefits us mutually.'

Yeah, it was a threat all right, but Harker understood why, and besides, he agreed with it. In two thousand years, humankind would be colonising other planets and using technologies he could only dream of – unless they blew themselves up meanwhile. Either way, the Ark would still be there to kickstart civilisation, if required. Like Wexler had said, it was an insurance policy for the species.

'But I'll have to inform Sebastian, and Xavier and Tom are already here. It would be hard to pretend this whole web of conspiracy doesn't exist.'

Wexler looked unconcerned by that. 'I have full confidence that the Grand Master of the Knights Templar can be trusted, and I will leave you to straighten things out with Xavier Botha. I would also suggest to you that describing these events as a conspiracy is less than accurate. It is a shadow conspiracy and, as such, more easily covered over.'

It was the first time Harker had heard the term and his nose wrinkled in curiosity. 'And what's the difference?'

Wexler emitted a chuckle and then shrugged his shoulders. 'In the modern age a conspiracy is usually a shadowy plan that most people believe to be untrue but that everyone knows about. A shadow conspiracy, on the other hand, is a very real truth that no one knows even exists. And regarding Dean Lercher, well, he was proving a bit unruly when our Sentinelese brothers captured him.'

'Is he OK?' Harker asked, wondering what Wexler meant by 'unruly'.

'He's fine but unconscious. Our Sentinelese protectors are quiet adept at such things and you should know they have been here since the Ark was first built. Apart from vaccinations and the medicines we provide, the tribe's religion, founded around the Annunaki, has remained pure for tens of thousands of years and they trust the Guardians in all things. I very much hope you'll provide Dean Lercher with a story that does not include the Ark but rather focuses on this uncontacted tribe.'

Up above them a rumbling sound could now be heard, and Wexler raised his hands in a placating gesture. 'That will be Mr Botha. I thought it best he saw this place for himself, and thus douse any nagging curiosity he might have in the future. He'll see with his own eyes what you would be telling him anyway. Curiosity, after all, can be a potent allure.'

Indeed, curiosity was something Botha had in spades. He could be like a dog with a bone, and always needed to be right at the centre of any discovery.

'Sensible decision,' Harker observed, hearing the sound of footsteps getting closer.

'I thought so,' Wexler replied. He then took a deep breath and expelled it in relief, as if physically releasing all the pent-up concern and anxiety he had stored up during the previous months of toil and worry that had confronted the Guardians. 'With the Mithras out of the picture and the Ark remaining a secret, I am happy to say that between us we killed two birds with one stone.'

'Oh, I wouldn't say that,' a voice interrupted from the doorway.

Harker looked across to see someone he didn't recognise pointing the barrel of a Walther P99 at him.

Herbert Pelosi grimaced at the two men and then took a step inside, just as Xavier Botha was hauled in after him, bound by a rope. 'So finally I get to meet you, Alex Harker. My name is Herbert Pelosi and I have been very much looking forward to our meeting.' The assassin's face began to drop at the sight of the pyramid beyond the observation window. 'The Ark of Knowledge,' he muttered, momentarily transfixed by the view. Then he grinned. 'Well, then, let's get this party started.'

Chapter 26

'Magnificent,' Pelosi exclaimed, pushing Botha forcefully over towards Harker, with his gun still aimed at them all. 'I had my doubts but… just look at it.'

'Sorry, Alex,' Botha apologised through gritted teeth as Pelosi continued to gaze out at what he believed to be potential riches. 'There's a lot of dead Sentinelese up there now. The rest took off into the forest and there was nothing I could have done.' The Templar looked down at his rope bonds. 'They already had me tied up.'

'Where's Doggie?' Harker asked anxiously.

Botha was already shaking his head. 'He's still up there, but don't worry. He's sleeping like a baby.'

This reply was at least of some comfort, and Harker now turned his attention back to Pelosi, who was still taking in the awe-inspiring sight while keeping everyone in his peripheral vision.

'It's not what you think it is,' Harker said loudly, but Pelosi looked undeterred.

'It's exactly what I think it is – and it's beautiful.'

As Pelosi remained preoccupied by the prize he and the Mithras had been chasing, Wexler began slowly edging back towards the wall as he gently tugged at Botha's shirt. The Templar acknowledged the gesture and also took a careful step backwards.

'How did you get in here?' Wexler demanded, and without looking away from the viewing window, Pelosi pulled a familiar gold coin from his pocket and raised it up in the air. 'You're not the only ones with an invitation,' he snarled with a brief glance in their direction. 'Even took a spare from the pyramid to keep for a souvenir. But now I've seen this lot, I'm sure I can find something better.'

It was now that Wexler caught Harker's eye, and he gestured towards a small square button just above his hand.

Harker assumed from this that something was about to happen, but exactly what, he had no idea. So he followed the others and slowly took a step backwards, nearer to the wall.

'This place is going to deliver a new future for the Mithras,' Pelosi boasted, still entranced by the sight. 'But first it's time we separated the wheat from the chaff, I think.'

Before he could turn back to face them, Wexler hit the button and a security wall with a small window at its centre slammed down to separate the room in half. On Pelosi's side a billow of white gas instantly began filling that part of the room. At the same time a concealed door on Harker's side of the room flipped open and, with Wexler heading through first, Harker dragged Botha along and the two men joined the Guardian on a narrow metal walkway directly beyond the door and inside the cavern itself.

'What was that?' Harker yelled as he and Wexler loosened Botha's ropes.

'It's a decontamination process for anyone entering or leaving the Ark,' Wexler explained. Having untied the last of the knots, he then took off along the gangway, with the other two close behind. 'It's to make sure we keep this place as sterile as possible… you know, from germs and infections.'

'How about us?' Harker asked as they reached a bend in the gangway, where steps led down to the cavern floor below.

'We don't really have much choice, do we?' Wexler called back, picking up the pace. 'It only takes thirty seconds to cycle through the decontamination process, then that security door releases – so get a move on.'

The atmosphere inside the cavern was cool and after they had raced down the steps and on to the rock floor below, Harker stopped to gaze up at the enormous pyramid before him, which looked even bigger and more impressive from this new vantage point. The stone slabs used to construct it were gigantic and he marvelled at the craftmanship – till Wexler reached back and dragged him forcibly forwards.

'We don't have time to dawdle. Just get moving.'

Wexler sped ahead, taking the lead, as back at the observation booth the cloud of white gas seemed to be clearing. As Harker glanced that way, he caught sight of Pelosi, red-faced and furiously banging at the window.

'In here,' Wexler called out on reaching a rectangular opening in the pyramid's base. By the time the others had got there the Guardian was already inside and scuttling along a dark passage.

'This is amazing.' Botha paused briefly to scope out the stone buildings lining the cavern as far as the eye could see. 'What is it all for?'

Before Harker could reply, a small section of the entrance's stonework exploded in a plume of dust. He snapped his head around to see Pelosi standing up on the gangway, with his pistol trained on the both of them.

'Move,' Botha yelled, grabbing Harker's arm and yanking them both inside the huge passageway, just as a second bullet skimmed off the stonework behind them with a ping. They hurried further inside the base of the pyramid, and then Wexler popped his head out from around a corner and beckoned them urgently.

'If we head up to the top tier,' he explained, 'there are steps leading back down on the far side. And so long as he follows us, we can then double back and head for the observation room. Then we can lock him inside the cavern and he'll be trapped with nowhere to go.' It seemed a sound plan and, with a nod from both Harker and Botha, Wexler took off again, leading them deeper into the structure's base, until they reached a flight of oversized stone steps leading upwards. On the other side there was a gloomy passageway running in the opposite direction, and a few metres along it there was a huge gong made with some kind of thin, bronze-coloured metal. The section of wall here had been cut back creating an alcove, and the instrument dangled from two hooks, beside which hung a wooden rod on a brown leather strap. Wexler gestured for them to pause by the steps, then hurried over to it, unhooked the rod and proceeded to smash the gong twice in quick succession, before scuttling back to them.

'What are you doing?' Harker whispered to the Guardian.

Botha's expression suggested that he already knew. 'Deliberate misdirection, Alex. Without that rod in view, he'll assume we slammed into the gong whilst scrambling past it.'

Wexler nodded in agreement, then slapped the thick wooden rod against the palm of his hand. 'And now we at least have one weapon – which is better than nothing.'

Against a 9mm bullet it really wasn't much, but there came no complaint from Harker. They then charged up the steps in single file, one stairwell after another. In the walls deep slits had been cut to allow light in, and the higher they climbed, the more peculiar to Harker it all seemed. Every one of the stone walls was starkly bare, devoid of any decoration, like a newly built house with foundations, walls and a roof, but no plasterwork, paint or flooring. Of course, this was a massive pyramid, hidden deep in a cavern underneath one of the few uncharted places in the world, but that fact aside, Harker couldn't shake off the feeling that this place did not feel old at all.

After five minutes of climbing, they approached what appeared to be the final leg of their journey. On Wexler's lead, they came to an abrupt halt. The Guardian placed a cupped hand to his ear, and they remained totally silent as they now listened for any noise coming from below. Nothing.

Through short breathless gasps, Harker took the opportunity to question Wexler about what had been bothering him.

'Why are all the walls empty? Where's the writing, the hieroglyphics?'

Wexler himself was the most exhausted of all and he waved a finger and sucked in a few much needed breaths before replying. 'Everything had to be removed… Cuneiform and hieroglyphics were designed for their own time, but two thousand years from now, who knows what dialects and languages may exist? The Ark must be ready for the day that will come, not the days that have passed, if the assembled knowledge is to be understood and passed on.'

That seemed like a sensible precaution, Harker thought, even though it must have taken the Guardians forever to eradicate all the symbols and ancient words. But Wexler was right, how could anyone predict who would survive?

After a final puff, Wexler began climbing the steps again and was soon up and out on the top level of the pyramid.

The first thing that struck Harker was the sheer size of it all. It was absolutely huge and, at all four corners, other great staircases led downwards, and in each of the walls a few of the stone blocks had been removed to allow a bird's-eye view of the vast underground cavern from every angle, so that for the first time Harker was able to realise its full scale. Beyond the pyramid, a long, cavernous tunnel stretched back a long way. And judging by its cylindrical shape, he suspected a tremendous lava flow had created it at some point in the distant past. More incredible still were the towering stone buildings and the network of wide pathways and cobblestone roads which ran for the cavern's entire length, as far as the eye could see. Every five hundred metres there were holes in the ceiling, and through one of these water fell, presumably from some large stream up on the surface, into a stone-built fountain, covered in mosaics, which stood some fifteen metres high. There was little sign of vegetation anywhere nearby, but in the distance he could make out vast patches of green surrounding an expanse of blue which might have been a lake or underground reservoir. It was hard to believe he was looking here at the remnants of an entire people, the Annunaki – an extinct giant humanoid species that had existed in this place for thousands of years, simply waiting for the timetable of planetary cataclysm to occur once again.

Harker was still absorbing this spectacular sight and reflecting on its history when Botha called out to him. He turned to see the other two men now standing over in one corner, staring down at a large white marble table. As Harker approached, he could see a body lying on top of it, and one that was sadly familiar. The motionless corpse of the Annunaki child that had set off the whole affair.

'The Guardians took his body?' Harker asked, and Wexler nodded sombrely.

'Do you really think we'd allow him to be dissected for study? He will be buried here, where he belongs, after the rites have been read.'

The sight was even more tragic because Harker now knew that the five-foot Annunaki was only a child – created in a lab to be the first of a new generation who would oversee the future of civilisation during its darkest hours. If anyone had ever doubted the sheer brutality of the Mithras, then the sight of this curled-up, five-foot child was all the proof needed, and Harker felt disgusted.

Botha was still looking puzzled, but he stood there respectfully with his hands clasped, as Harker now turned back to the issue at hand.

'We need to get moving,' he said. 'I refuse to let any of us be killed by the last member of the Mithras still running free.' Without any need for discussion, they were already taking their first steps towards the opposite stairwell when a voice suddenly stopped them in their tracks.

'The last… what.' the voice hissed, and they spun around to see Pelosi standing at the top of the steps behind them. He wasn't even out of breath.

Botha couldn't help himself, grunting, 'You're a quiet one, I'll give you that.'

Pelosi appeared uninterested in the Templar's assessment of his stealth skills as he raised the gun and aimed it directly at Botha. 'Templars!' he yelled, then spat on the floor. 'Don't you people ever have anything nasty to say?'

Botha looked unbothered, standing there proudly like a man with nothing to lose and refusing to be afraid of the skinny little man in front of him, despite his weapon.

'Speaking of nasty, I saw your handiwork back at the cottage, Pelosi,' he said with a wince. 'A blood eagle, indeed! You're one sick bastard. I mean, Avi Legrundy seemed about as low as it gets on the scale of human garbage, but you... Well, you're on a different scale altogether.'

Pelosi looked like he couldn't care less. 'I just needed to know what she'd told you Templars regarding the Mithras, and I did feel convinced she was telling the truth after I'd pulled her left lung out of her body.'

Botha slowly took a step towards the Mithras assassin. 'Well, that'll do it. You truly are scum and a psychopath to boot, Herbert. A real piece of shit. What made you hate the world so much? Were you born with a baby dick?'

Pelosi ignored the obvious goading and was now smiling, obviously enjoying having the drop on the Templar. 'You should never insult a man with a loaded gun his hand, you know.'

With both hands behind his back, Botha was now gesturing with a finger in the direction of the staircase, suggesting the others made a dash for it whilst he did his best to distract the killer. 'Then I guess I'm lucky you're not a man, then... Especially if I'm right about the baby dick.'

The shot rang out loudly and then echoes could be heard reverberating around the cavern. Botha raised a hand to his chest and then withdrew it to find his fingers covered in blood. He looked over at Harker and managed to utter the single word, 'Sorry,' before he collapsed to the floor.

'No!' Harker shouted, reaching out to try and catch him. But Botha had already lost consciousness as Harker dropped to the ground and tried to stem the bleeding.

'Christ, Xavier,' he yelled at his friend. But Botha's eyelids had closed and his body had gone limp.

Pelosi now had his gun aimed at Harker. 'You've got bigger concerns than a dead Templar, my friend.'

Harker stood up next to Wexler, as Pelosi's face began to contort and twist.

'Now, what did you mean just now by the "last member of the Mithras still free"?'

Ordinarily Harker would have attempted to stall for more time, but with Botha lying dead on the ground before him, he was in no mood to mince his words.

'Your insane masters, they are all gone, and will soon be spending the rest of their lives locked up God knows where.'

Pelosi looked unconvinced, then he snarled, 'Bullshit!'

'Not bullshit, Pelosi. They're in proper deep shit, right now. The Templars raided that little shindig they were having at Neuschwanstein Castle and Berger and his cronies were stopped in their tracks. I've even heard that all your miserable associates were taken in by Interpol, and I'm sure that whatever charges they dig up will ensure a long stay behind bars.' He now glanced over at Wexler. 'That bunch of psychopaths must have left enough carnage in their wake to pin a life sentence on each of them. And if they're foolish enough to mention the Knights Templar, they're likely to be locked up in a padded cell for being delusional.'

At the mention of Neuschwanstein, the snarl on Pelosi's face began to fade, and he now began to look uncertain even as Harker taunted him further.

'Wow, Pelosi, did you choose the wrong side? Here you are, all alone, and let's be honest, knowing your screwed-up temperament, I doubt you have any friends or loved ones to console you at what must be a really difficult time.'

Harker knew he was further provoking the killer, but with Botha lying there on the floor, his shirt sodden red, he just couldn't stop himself. Mentally he was seeing red and he now laughed out loud. 'You can do what you want to us—'

'Speak for yourself!' Wexler interjected, as Harker's eyes blazed with anger.

'—but I'll die knowing that wherever you go, wherever you hide, whatever shithole you crawl into, the Templars will find you and make your life a total fucking misery. That you can count on.'

Pelosi stared at him thoughtfully for a moment, but then the snarl returned and he raised the barrel of his pistol to aim directly at Harker's head. 'Then I'll have to make sure I savour this moment for all eternity.'

Pelosi's trigger finger began to twitch, then his head jerked back suddenly and he slapped at his neck with his other hand, before gripping something between two fingers which he held up and stared at in confusion.

Clutched between his fingertips was a small black dart, and even as the killer's knees began to shake and his gun clattered to the stone floor, Harker felt something sting his own neck. He reached up at this painful annoyance, and also retrieved a small black dart. It was no more than a centimetre in length, and as he stared at it in surprise, his knees began to buckle.

He could see Pelosi had slumped to the ground twitching, his eyes beginning to flutter. Harker's legs then gave way and he joined Pelosi on the ground, lying on his side, as stiff as a board. Though his body was paralysed, he could move his eyes, and as his vision began to blur he saw Wexler drop to one knee. Meanwhile, from one of the stairwells, a shadow began to emerge.

With his mind beginning to numb and his vision distorted, Harker watched as something big – something massive – stepped into the room and made its way over to the marble table, where it paused before picking up the body of the Annunaki child.

There was the smell of rosemary and lavender in the air and now more shadows began to appear. They were equally as tall and now towered over Harker as his vision swirled into a vortex. He felt his body being lifted high into the air… and then it all went black.

Chapter 27

With head throbbing and hands trembling, Harker shuffled slowly across the stone floor, with every footstep
seeming to make a sound that rattled his eardrums like a
cannon going off nearby. He was perspiring heavily and,
as he wiped his face with his shirt cuff, the sensation of
sweaty armpits had his stomach churning, and he leant
against the metal railing and tried to stop himself throwing
up. His balance was shot to pieces and every joint in his
body screamed in a cacophony of aches and twinges.

How long have I been out? He tried to remember, but
all that came to him was darkness. He lowered his head
down onto the railing and stood there, lurching forwards
occasionally and praying for his faculties to return to him
with every new breath he sucked in.

Pull yourself together, Harker.

With shaky new resolve he dragged his feet up the steps
slowly and, when he finally reached it, he pressed his face
against the thick door and enjoyed its coldness against his
face. It felt as refreshing as cool water and he rolled his
head around so his brow could enjoy the sensation too,
then with a hand raised he thumped his fist against it.

There were a few moments of silence before he
heard the sound of footsteps approaching, whereupon he
stepped back and stood up straight as best he could.

Slowly the door swung open and an angry face greeted him. 'I thought I told you to stay in the car,' Doggie fumed. He then looked around to see if anyone else was watching. 'I said I'd come and get you.'

In his cream linen suit and white Panama hat, the dean clearly believed he was dressed to impress, although Harker reckoned most people would make a beeline for the other side of the street seeing someone wearing that outfit.

'I thought we agreed on the charcoal grey suit and blue cravat I rented for you?'

'I changed my mind,' Doggie replied, gently tugging Harker inside the church doorway. 'Anyway, someone has to bring a bit of genuine style to the event.'

'Christ, Tom, did they loan you a calypso band to go with that outfit?'

'I happen to think it looks rather dashing,' Doggie declared starchily, then he pulled out a white handkerchief with 'TL' embroidered on it and wiped Harker's brow. 'You can keep that one now, as I've got a whole box of them back at home.'

David Carter now appeared behind his shoulder, thankfully wearing an appropriate usher's outfit.

'Damn it, Tom, the best man's meant to get the groom to the wedding on time... not poison him in the process.' Carter raised a finger and wagged it at him. 'Bad Dog.'

'It's just a hangover. He'll be fine.'

Two weeks had passed since Harker had collapsed, after being poisoned – or drugged more like – in the bowels of the Ark, and now everything was just about back to normal. Or as normal as it could be, given that he was about to get married. He'd woken up in the hospital at Port Blair, alongside Doggie, and with no idea how the two of them had got there. There was no record either of who had admitted them, and none of the nurses could provide an answer. But after just a few hours they had been discharged with only the clothes on their backs and, thankfully, their passports.

Within hours they had caught the earliest flight for the long trip back to the UK. Chloe picked them up at the airport and drove them back to Cambridge, with no idea of what they had been through. So far as she knew, they had been visiting a colleague at the National Archaeology Museum in St-Germain-en-Laye, and that was the way Harker had wanted it. Chloe had enough going on with planning their wedding without knowing how close she had come to losing the groom. Perhaps he would give her the full account after things had settled down.

Despite Wexler's instruction, he had ended up telling Doggie everything, and they had spent more than a few evenings at the local pub discussing the whole concept of the Ark and the Guardians who maintained it. The discovery of a human subspecies, the Annunaki, had seemed the hottest topic, however. It was incredible to think that this subspecies had existed, and that their culture and knowledge had helped shape and bring about our own – it was archaeological gold, even if they could never share it with anyone else. Harker had remained tight-lipped about what he might have seen just before he passed out at the top of the pyramid, because he really could not be sure. It might have been the other Guardians coming to help or his drugged mind playing tricks on him, but... no, he couldn't be sure either way. Perhaps sometime in the future he would risk making a trip back to Sentinel Island in order to take another look. The gold coin he had found in his pocket when he woke up in the hospital – it had to be a standing invitation from Wexler… didn't it?

The whole concept of the Annunaki was something Doggie had much to say about, though, and he planned to have the university delve into every possible Sumerian artefact they could find, even suggesting that funding should be made available for future digs. But so far that had not curried much favour. The academic community already possessed an established historical foundation of human civilisation, and they appeared content for the Sumerian tales of the Annunaki to remain in the background. Only time and further discoveries might change that.

The good news was that the dean had kept his promise to get more involved in everyday life, and during the two weeks they had been back he had bought himself a gym membership, although he'd not attended yet, and tried his hand at scuba diving even if it was only in the deep end of the local swimming baths. He had even signed up to a dating service – but had as yet failed to find someone he liked. The saying about old dogs and new tricks came to mind, but at least he kept pushing himself out of his comfort zone, and that in itself was a triumph of sorts.

Harker had a meeting with Sebastian Brulet the day after he arrived home, and told him everything. Despite some concerns, the Grand Master had agreed to leave the fate of the Guardians and the Ark as Harker had found them – underground and undisturbed. If Harker was being honest with himself, he was simply relieved that the end of the world was not already upon them… not for another two thousand years at least.

The Guardians using the Templars to take down the Mithras was, however, a serious sore point. And the fact that some Templars had been killed in the process was a bitter pill to swallow for the Grand Master, for whom the life of every man and woman in the organisation was sacred. But given the entire Mithras hierarchy had been dismantled in the process, he eventually considered it a price he could live with. The wealthy elitists and most of their cohorts were now in prison awaiting trial for a vast array of crimes, the details of which had been supplied by Schroder – anonymously of course – which had paved the way for a full investigation of their activities. Better still, not one of them had mentioned the Knights Templar, so far as anyone knew, and who would have believed them if they had?

Pelosi, on the other hand, was a different kettle of fish altogether. Whereas Harker and Doggie had woken up in hospital beds, the Mithras assassin had turned up outside an Indian police station with a memory card containing the recording of his murder of Avi Legrundy taped to his chest. How the Guardians had gained a copy of that footage was still a mystery, but the important thing was that the killer was awaiting extradition to the UK – thanks again to a bit of tradecraft from Schroder – and as of that moment he was sitting in a dark prison cell in the city of Mumbai. The Templars would be keeping a very close eye on him indeed.

Finally, there was Xavier Botha, a great man, a Templar to the core, and without whose help Harker would never have made it through this whole Ark debacle. The man had saved his life on more than one occasion and, despite what happened to him, it could have gone down a hell of a lot worse, and as Doggie and Carter now moved to one side, Harker was finally greeted by somebody who was actually smiling.

'Bloody hell, what are you doing here?'

Xavier Botha propelled himself forward in the wheelchair as he expelled a deep grunt. 'You know I wouldn't have missed this, Alex. Had an ambulance bring me here directly... Sebastian arranged it and I should be out of this bloody chair in a few weeks.'

'Now that's some good news.'

Just a day after arriving back in the UK, Harker had received a mysterious phone call insisting he pay a visit to St Bartholomew's Hospital in London. The caller left only a room number, and when Harker had found Botha there – in an induced coma – but stable, he had been elated. Of course there was no record of how he got there, but unquestionably it had been the Guardians' doing. A few inches to the left and the bullet would have pierced Botha's heart instead of his lung, and by the time he turned up at St Bartholomew's someone had already removed it and sewn him up. Perhaps a parting gift from Wexler? Regardless, everyone was just happy to have him back in one piece, and as Harker stared down at the Templar he was amazed at how quickly the man was recovering.

'What the hell happened to you?' Botha asked, gesturing to Harker's sweaty forehead.

'Doggie arranged the stag do for last night,' Carter explained, looking a tad weary himself.

'Last night? Why? Everyone knows you should hold it a few weeks before the wedding.' Botha was now looking alarmed at Harker's dishevelled appearance.

'Pish-posh,' Doggie said. 'The stag night is always the one just before the wedding. It's tradition.'

'Maybe in the eighteenth century, Tom, but not these days,' Xavier replied. He then pointed dismissively at

Doggie's linen suit. 'He might look like the man from Del Monte, Alex, but this time you should have said no!'

They all burst into laughter except Doggie himself, but before he could raise any objection, a grey Bentley Continental pulled up next to the main path leading to the church.

'Oh God,' Doggie exclaimed, looking panicked. 'Whatever happened to the custom of turning up fashionably late?'

Harker found himself being hastily bundled inside, and Botha spun a 180-degree turn and pushed the door shut. The next thing Harker knew, they were wiping his brow, straightening his cravat, and all of them acting like a bunch of nursemaids.

'Places, gentlemen,' Doggie urged in a hushed tone, whereupon Botha and Carter headed off down the aisle to their respective places. The dean then made a final adjustment to Harker's sleeves before giving him a nod. 'You ready?'

Harker took a deep breath and composed himself as best he could, given his pounding headache. 'Not really.'

A wide, confident smile spread across Doggie's face. 'Perfect.'

Together they made their way down the aisle with the entire congregation watching. Seated in the back row, the brothers Sebastian and Tristan Brulet gave Harker a nod of approval, and he winked back as they continued their slow and measured progress, Doggie dictating the pace.

So far as Harker could see, everyone was smiling, and some of the women were even crying, but as he reached the front, there was one unhappy visage amidst the crowd. That of a person who would rather be anywhere else but here.

The long face of Frank Stanton, Chloe's father, stared at him with the enthusiasm of a dead horse when Harker offered the man a polite smile.

'That charm offensive of yours really did the job. Thanks, Tom,' Harker muttered from the corner of his mouth.

'Give it time. The fellow's a lot of fun once you actually get to know him,' Doggie replied, though Harker doubted this was true. With a smile to the priest, he kept his back resolutely to the door as the organ music began to play. He then heard the door open, followed by the sound of heels clacking on stone, and as they got nearer he glanced back to steal a look.

Chloe appeared more beautiful than he had ever seen her before, wearing a white tiara and long white flowing dress trailing behind her.

He turned back to face the priest and took a deep breath. 'OK,' he muttered to himself, 'let's do it.'

Chapter 28

The dank, dark jail cell was sweltering hot as Herbert Pelosi shifted about on a stained and grubby mattress in the depths of Mumbai Central Prison. With a rusting bucket filled with his own slop in the corner, stinking the place up, he lay wrapped in the dirty grey blanket provided for him. He had pulled it as tightly around his body as possible so as not to expose any of his skin to the roaming hordes of cockroaches that visited the moment the lights went out.

It had been only two weeks since his arrival here, still awaiting the court's decision, but every minute of every day and night had been spent focusing on one thing and one thing only: Alex Harker and the Knights Templar. He had promised himself during his first night in this shithole that, however long it took and at whatever cost, he would exact retribution on those that had brought such a miserable and undignified end to an otherwise stellar career. The Guardians and the Ark were of no real consequence, and in time he would pay them a visit, but that was far, far down on his list of priorities. Harker, though, was sitting at its top, his name in flaming letters and Pelosi didn't know *how* yet, but he would find a way to destroy everything the man loved and cared about before finally putting him down like a dog.

Pelosi was still fantasising about the terrible things he would do when from further along the cell block he heard slow footsteps getting louder and louder, and then coming to a stop right outside his cell door.

'Herbert Pelosi?' a deep voice enquired, and Pelosi unwrapped the blanket from around his head, sending cockroaches dropping to the floor.

'Yeah,' he said, looking up at the figure standing before him.

'*The* Herbert Pelosi?' the deep voice enquired again.

'I said yeah, what do you want?'

It was too dark to see the man's face because the light coming through the small window only reached the cell door, but he watched as the figure knelt down and pushed his hands through the bars with both palms facing upwards – they were covered in blood.

'It was quite the task to get in here.'

Pelosi leapt up off the mattress and stood in the centre of his cell, both fists raised as the bloody palms disappeared back into the darkness.

'Who are you? What do you want?' Pelosi growled.

'I have something I would like you to do for me and your talents are exactly what I require.'

Pelosi now looked puzzled and he gingerly moved closer to the door. 'Maybe, if you can get me out of here and the rewards are right. What do you want?'

'We'll get to that,' the voice replied, and with a jangling of keys the door unlocked and then swung open. 'Rewards can only be measured by the man who asks for them, so tell me, Herbert Pelosi, what does your heart desire most?'

Pelosi took another step closer until his face was within inches of the shadowy figure and he began to grin. 'Oh, I have something in mind. Something beautiful.'